A DEATH IN SUMMER

Benjamin Black

ISIS
LARGE PRINT
Oxford

First published in Great Britain 2011
by
Mantle
an imprint of Pan Macmillan

Published in Large Print 2011 by ISIS Publishing Ltd.,
7 Centremead, Osney Mead, Oxford OX2 0ES
by arrangement with
Pan Macmillan
a division of Macmillan Publishers Limited

British Library Cataloguing in Publication Data
Black, Benjamin, 1945–
    A death in summer.
    1. Quirke, Garret (Fictitious character) - - Fiction.
    2. Pathologists - - Ireland - - Dublin - - Fiction.
    3. Detective and mystery stories.
    4. Large type books.
    I. Title
    823.9'2–dc22

ISBN 978-0-7531-8920-7 (hb)
ISBN 978-0-7531-8921-4 (pb)

Printed and bound in Great Britain by
T. J. International Ltd., Padstow, Cornwall

CHAPTER
ONE

When word got about that Richard Jewell had been found with the greater part of his head blown off and clutching a shotgun in his bloodless hands, few outside the family circle and few inside it, either, considered his demise a cause for sorrow. Jewell, known to the jauntier among his detractors as Diamond Dick, had been a wealthy man. The bulk of his money he had inherited from his father, the notorious Francis T. — Francie — Jewell, sometime lord mayor and proprietor of a highly successful newspaper chain that included the scurrilous and much-feared *Daily Clarion*, the city's top-selling paper. The older Jewell had been something of an uncut stone, given to violent vendettas and a loathing of trade unions, but his son, though no less unscrupulous and vengeful, had sought to polish the family name to a high lustre by means of well-publicised acts of philanthropy. Richard Jewell was known for his sponsorship of orphanages and schools for the handicapped, while the recently opened Jewell Wing of the Hospital of the Holy Family was in the vanguard of the fight against tuberculosis. These and other initiatives should have made Dick Jewell a hero in a city beset by poverty and chronic ill-health, but now that he was dead there were many among the citizenry who declared themselves ready to dance on his grave.

His corpse was discovered that Sunday afternoon in his office above the stables at Brooklands, the place in County Kildare jointly owned by him and his wife. Maguire, the yard manager, had come up by the outside stairs to give him a report of a stallion that was lame and unlikely to run the following Thursday in an evening fixture at Leopards-town. The door to the office was ajar but Maguire had known better than to walk in without knocking. Right away, though, he had the feeling that something was seriously amiss. When asked later to describe this feeling about it he could not; only the hair, he said, had stood up on the back of his neck, and he distinctly remembered hearing Blue Lightning sending up a whinny in the quiet below in the yard; Blue Lightning was Dick Jewell's darling, a three-year-old with the highest potential.

The shotgun blast had lifted Jewell out of his chair and flung him backwards at a crooked angle across the desk, where he lay with a bit of jawbone and a few teeth and a bloodied stump of spine, all that was left of what had been his head, dangling down on the far side. On the big picture window in front of the desk there was a great splatter of blood and brains, like a giant peony blossom, with a gaping hole in the middle of it giving a view of rolling grasslands stretching off to the horizon. Maguire at first could hardly take in what had happened. It looked as if the man had shot himself, but Diamond Dick Jewell was the last person Maguire or anyone else would have expected to blow his own head off.

Rumours and speculation started up at once. It added to the shock of the event that it had taken place on a drowsy Sunday afternoon in summer, while the beeches along the drive at Brooklands sweltered in the sun and the mingled smell of hay and horses lay heavy on the summer air. Not that many were privy to the details of what had happened. Who knew better than the Jewells how to hush up a scandal? And a suicide, in those days, in this place, was a very grave scandal indeed.

In the *Clarion* offices on Eden Quay the atmosphere was a combination of pandemonium and wondering disbelief. The staff, from copy-boys to editorial, felt as if they were moving under water, or through a medium heavier and more hindering than water, and yet at the same time everything seemed to be racing along like a river in spate and carrying all before it. The editor, Harry Clancy, had come in from Portmarnock, where a caddy had been sent on a bicycle to intercept him at the twelfth hole, and he was still in golfing gear, the studs in his shoes rattling out a tattoo on the lino as he marched back and forth in front of his desk dictating a eulogy, which his secretary, the no longer young, and faintly moustached, Miss Somers, was taking down in longhand on a pad of copy-paper.

". . . should have been struck down in the prime of life," Clancy was intoning, "by a cerebral haemorrhage —"
He broke off and looked at Miss Somers, who had

3

stopped writing and sat motionless with her pencil suspended over the sheaf of paper on her knee. "What's the matter?"

Miss Somers seemed not to have heard him, and began writing again. "... *in the prime of life* ..." she murmured, scoring the words laboriously into the cheap grey paper.

"What am I supposed to say?" Clancy demanded. "That the boss blew his brains out?"

"... *by a cer-e-bral haem-orrh-age* ..."

"All right, all right, cut that." Clancy had been pleased with himself for having hit on such an acceptable-sounding cause of death. It *had* been a kind of haemorrhage, had it not? There was bound to have been plenty of blood, anyway, seeing it was a shotgun Jewell had used on himself. The *Clarion* would not say it was suicide, nor would any of its rivals: suicides never got reported in the press; it was an unspoken convention, to spare the feelings of the relatives and make sure the insurance companies would not seize on it as an excuse to renege on paying out to the family. All the same, Clancy thought, better not to print an outright lie. It would get around soon enough that the boss had topped himself — Jesus, there was an apt phrase! — no matter what convenient lies were told. "Just say *at the tragically early age of forty-five and at the pinnacle of his professional career* and leave it at that."

He thrust his hands into his pockets and crossed clatteringly to the window and stood looking down at the river. Did no one ever clean this glass? — he was

4

hardly able to see out. Everything was shimmering in the heat out there and he could almost taste the cindery dust in the air, and the river had a bilious stink that no thickness of grimed glass could shut out. "Read it over to me so far," he growled. He had been on fine form on the course today, with three bogeys and a birdie at the ninth.

His secretary risked a sideways glance at him. That pink pullover might be all right on the golf course, she thought, but here in the office it made him look like a superannuated nancy-boy. He was a stout man with a head of auburn curls, greying now, and a cross-hatching of livid veins over his cheekbones that was the legacy of a lifetime's hard drinking. He should beware a brain haemorrhage himself, Miss Somers considered. He was the fourth editor she had worked for in the forty years of her employment at the *Clarion*, not counting Eddie Randall who had broken down after a fortnight in the job and been sacked. She remembered old man Jewell, the well-named Francie; over a hot port in Mooney's one Christmas he had made an indecent proposal to her that she had pretended not to understand. All the same, he was a real man, not like the fellows going about now, calling themselves journalists — whatever happened to *reporters?* — and spending half the working week playing golf and the other half in the pub.

Clancy was off again, pacing and prating. ". . . scion of a great Dublin family and a —" He stopped again, checked as Miss Somers delicately but unignorably cleared her throat. "What is it now?"

"Pardon me, Mr Clancy — but what was that word?"

"What?" He was baffled.

"Do you mean *scion*?" Miss Somers asked. "I believe that's how it's pronounced, not *skion*."

She would not raise her eyes to his, and he stood in the middle of the floor breathing hard and gazing at the white parting down the centre of her silver hair with an expression of angry helplessness. Bloody impossible dried-up old maid! "Oh, do forgive my ignorance, please," he said with weary sarcasm. "— *scion* of a great Dublin family . . ." And a ruthless bastard, he was thinking, who would tear out your heart as quick as look at you. He waved a hand impatiently and went and sat down behind his desk. "We'll finish it later," he said. "There's plenty of time. Ask the switch to get me Hackett over at Pearse Street, will you?"

But Inspector Hackett, of course, was out at Brooklands. Like Clancy, he was not in a good mood. He had just finished his Sunday dinner — a nice leg of lamb — and was getting ready to go down to Wicklow for a bit of fishing when the phone rang. A phone call on a Sunday afternoon had to be either from his sister-in-law, threatening a visit with her brood, or from the station. Today, somehow, just by listening to the bell shrilling, he had known which one it was, and that the matter was going to be a weighty one. The new fellow, Jenkins, had picked him up in a squad car; he had heard the yowling of the siren from three streets away. His wife had made him a sandwich from the leftover lamb — May's main task in life nowadays seemed to be to keep him fed — and the warmish wad of bread and meat wrapped in greaseproof paper and making his jacket pocket sag was an annoyance to him. He would have thrown it out of the window of the squad car when they got into the country except that he would have felt disloyal.

Jenkins was in a state of high excitement. This was the first serious job he had taken part in since he had been assigned to work with Detective Inspector Hackett, and serious it certainly promised to be. Although initial reports from Brooklands had suggested that Richard Jewell had killed himself, Hackett was sceptical, and suspected foul play. Jenkins did not understand how the inspector was managing to be so calm — even with all his years of service he could not have dealt with more than a handful of murder cases, and certainly not with one as sensational as this, if murder it was. All he seemed concerned about, however, was the fact that his fishing trip had had to be cancelled. When he had come out of the house, his missus had been hovering behind him in the shadow of the doorway, he had been scowling, and the first thing he had done when he got in the car was demand why the hell the siren had been going, since it was Sunday and there was hardly a vehicle on the streets, and after that he had not spoken a dozen words until they got to Kildare town. There they had to ask the way to Brooklands, which made him all the more annoyed — "Would you not have thought of looking at the bloody map before you set out?" And then, when they reached Brooklands at last, there was the worst humiliation of all. A corpse was one thing, but a corpse with nothing where its head should be except part of the jaw and that gristly bit of spine sticking out at the back was altogether another. "Get out!" the inspector had shouted at him when he saw him turn green. "Get out before you puke on the evidence!" And poor Jenkins had stumbled down the wooden stairway outside and coughed up the remains of his dinner in a corner of the cobbled yard.

It felt strange to Hackett to be standing here, on a fine country estate, with the birds singing all about and a slab of sunlight falling at his heels from the open doorway of Jewell's office, and at the same time to have the old familiar smell of violent death in his nostrils. Not that he had smelt it so very often, but once caught it was never to be forgotten, that mingled faint stink of blood and excrement and something else, something thin and sharp and insidious, the smell of terror itself, perhaps, or of despair — or was he being fanciful? Could despair and terror really leave a trace? He heard Jenkins down in the yard, dry-retching now. He could not find it in his heart to blame the poor chap for his weakness: Jewell was a frightful sight, sprawled across the desk as crooked as a corkscrew with his brains spattered all over the window behind him. The shotgun was a beauty, he noticed, a Purdey, if he was not mistaken.

Jenkins came clumping up the wooden stairs and stopped just inside the door. "Sorry, Inspector."

Hackett did not turn. He was standing at the desk with his hands in his trouser pockets and his hat pushed to the back of his head. There was a shine,

Jenkins noted, on the elbows and the backside of his blue suit. He peered past his boss's shoulder at the thing that had been thrown over the desk like a side of beef. He was disappointed: he had been hoping for a murder, but the corpse was holding the gun in its own hands.

They heard a car drawing up in the yard. Jenkins glanced back down the stairs. "Forensics," he said.

The inspector made a chopping gesture with the side of his hand, still not turning. "Tell them to wait a minute. Tell them" — he laughed shortly — "tell them I'm cogitating."

Jenkins went down the wooden steps, and there was the sound of voices in the yard, and then he came back. Hackett would have liked to be alone. He always had a peculiar sense of peace in the presence of the dead; it was the same feeling, he realised with a start, that he had now when May went up to bed early and left him in his armchair by the hearth, with a glass of something in his hand, studying the faces in the fire. This was not a good sign, this hankering after solitude. It was the other, sweeter, smells, of horses and hay and the like, that were making him think in this way — of the past, of his childhood, of death and of the ones of his who had died down the years.

"Who was it found him?" he asked. "The groom, was it?"

"Yard manager," Jenkins behind him said. "Name of Maguire."

"Maguire. Aye." Scenes such as this of bloody mischief were a stopped moment of time, a slice taken out of the ordinary flow of things and held suspended, like a specimen pressed between the glass slides under a microscope. "Did he hear the gunshot?"

"He says not."

"Where is he now?"

"In the house. Mrs Jewell brought him in, he was that shocked."

"She's here, the missus? — the widow?" Jewell's wife was foreign, he recalled. Spanish, was it? No, French. "Did she hear the gun?"

"I haven't talked to her."

Hackett took a step forward and touched the dead man's wrist. Cold. Could have been lying here for hours, no one the wiser. "Tell those forensics lads to come up." Jenkins went to the door. "And where's Harrison, is he on the way?" Harrison was the state pathologist.

"Sick, apparently."

"Or out on that boat of his, more likely."

"He had a heart attack, it seems."

"Did he?"

"Last week."

"Christ."

"They're sending Doctor Quirke."

"Are they, now."

Maguire was a big man with a big square head and square rope-veined hands that even yet were noticeably trembling. He sat at the kitchen table in a patch of yellow sunlight with a mug of tea before him, staring at nothing. He was ashen, and his lower lip, too, was unsteady. Hackett stood and gazed at him, frowning. The ones that look the toughest, he was thinking, are always the hardest hit. There was a vase of pink tulips on the table. Off in the fields somewhere a tractor was buzzing; hay-making, on a Sunday afternoon, to get the best of the weather. Rain was forecast for later in the week. A big wireless set standing on a shelf beside the sink was muttering to itself in an undertone.

Hackett had met Richard Jewell only once, at a fundraiser for Garda widows. Jewell had had a bland sheen to him, like all rich men, and only the eyes were real, set like rivets into a smiling mask. Good-looking, though, in a wolfish way, with too many big white teeth and a nose like the head of a stone axe. As he moved among the crowd, glad-handing the commissioner and the mayor and making the women weak at the knees, he seemed to be holding himself aloft, turning himself this way and that, as if he were indeed a precious gem to be admired and envied. Diamond Dick. It was hard not to be impressed. Why would such a man think of shooting himself?

"Will you take some tea, Inspector?" Mrs Jewell enquired. Tall, slender, with intense dark eyes, she stood by the sink with a cigarette in her fingers, cool and preternaturally calm, in a dress of dove-grey silk and narrow patent-leather shoes with stiletto heels. Her very black hair was tied back, and she wore no jewellery. Some tall, stately bird, a heron, say, would have looked less incongruous than she did in the midst of these homely surroundings.

"No, thank you, ma'am," Hackett said. Jenkins made a sound and Hackett half turned in his direction, lifting a hand. "This, by the way, is Detective Sergeant Jenkins." Whenever he said the young man's name he had to bite his lip in order not to grin. Jenkins: for some reason it made him think of a picture he had seen somewhere when he was a child, of a donkey wearing a hat with holes in it for the big furry ears to stick up through. And indeed Jenkins's own ears were remarkably large, and were even pointed a little at the tops. He had a long, very pale face and an Adam's apple that seemed to be attached to the end of an elastic string. Though eager and always obliging, he was a hapless specimen. Many are the things, Hackett told himself, that are sent to try us.

"Tell me, ma'am," he said carefully, "were you here when — when it happened?"

Mrs Jewell arched an eyebrow. "When *did* it happen?"

"We won't know for sure till the pathologist arrives, but my fellows think maybe four or five hours ago."

"Then no. I got here at" — she glanced at a clock on the wall above the stove — "three, half past three, something like that."

Hackett nodded. He liked her accent. She did not sound French, more like that Swedish woman in the pictures, what was she called? "Can you think of a reason why your husband . . .?"

She almost laughed. "No, of course not."

He nodded again, frowning at his hat, the brim of which he was holding lightly between the tips of the

12

fingers and thumbs of both hands; it irked him that in front of this woman he felt like an applicant for something or other, all meekness and humble deference. It struck him suddenly as odd that everyone was standing, except Maguire, sunk there in shock at the table. What was the matter with the fellow, had he lost his nerve altogether?

He turned his attention to the woman again. "Forgive me for saying so, Mrs Jewell, but you don't seem very surprised."

She widened her eyes — how extraordinary they were, black and glittering, the lids tapered at the corners like a cat's. "But certainly I am," she said. "I am" — she groped for the word — "I am baffled."

This seemed to allow of no further advance, and he turned to the yard manager again. "You say you didn't hear the gun?"

At first Maguire did not realise it was him who was being addressed, and Hackett had to put the question again, more loudly. The big man stirred as if he had been prodded from behind. "No," he said, frowning at the floor. "I was probably out on the gallops."

Hackett looked to Mrs Jewell. "The gallops, where the horses are exercised," she said.

She had finished her cigarette and was casting about for somewhere to deposit the butt, with an air of slightly amused vague helplessness; it was as if she had never been in a kitchen before, not even this one, and was both taken with and puzzled by the quaintness of all these strange implements and appliances. Jenkins spotted an ashtray on the table and came forward quickly and brought it to her, and was rewarded by an unexpectedly warm, even radiant, smile, and for the first time Hackett saw what a beautiful woman she was — too thin, and too chilly in her manner, but lovely all the same. He was surprised at himself: he had never been much of a connoisseur of women's looks.

"Did you go up to the office?" he asked her.

"Yes, of course," she said. He was silent, turning the hat brim slowly in his fingers. She smiled with one side of her mouth. "I was in France for all of the war, Inspector," she said. "It is not the first dead body I have seen."

Ingrid Bergman — that was it, that was who she sounded like. She was watching him, and under her scrutiny he lowered his eyes. Was that what her husband was to her now, a dead body? What a queer person she is, he thought, even for a Frenchwoman.

Suddenly Maguire spoke, surprising himself as much as them, it appeared. "He got me to clean the gun," he said. The three of them looked at him. "He gave it to me yesterday and asked me to clean it." He returned their looks, each one's in turn. "I never thought," he said in a tone of wonderment. "I never thought."

There was nothing to be said to this and the others went back to being as they had been, as if he had not spoken.

"Who else was in the house?" Hackett asked of Mrs Jewell.

"No one, I think," she said. "Sarah — Mr Maguire's wife and our housekeeper here — was at Mass and then to visit her mother. Mr Maguire himself, as he says, was out on the gallops. And I was still on my way here, in the Land Rover."

"There's no other staff? Yard hands, stable girls" — he did not know the technical titles — "anyone like that?"

"Of course," Mrs Jewell said. "But it is Sunday."

"Ah, right, so it is." That tractor, the needling sound of it, distant though it was, was giving him a pain in the head. "Perhaps your husband was counting on that, on the place being deserted?"

She shrugged. "Perhaps. Who can say, now?" She clasped her hands lightly together at her breast. "You should understand, Inspector . . ." She faltered. "Forgive me, I —?"

"Hackett."

"Yes, yes, sorry, Inspector Hackett. You must understand, my husband and I, we live . . . separately."

"You were separated?"

"No, no." She smiled. "Even still, sometimes, my English . . . I mean, we have our own lives. It is — it was — that kind of marriage." She smiled again. "I think perhaps I have shocked you, a little, yes?"

"No, ma'am, not at all. I'm just trying to understand the circumstances. Your husband was a very prominent person. There'll be a lot of stuff about this in the papers, a lot of speculation. It's all very . . . delicate, shall we say?"

"You mean, there will be a scandal."

"I mean, people will want to know. People will want reasons."

"*People?*" she said scathingly, showing for the first time a spark of passion, a spark, and no more. "—What business is it of *people*? My husband is dead, my daughter's father. That is a scandal, yes, but for me and for my family and for no one else."

"Yes," Hackett said mildly, nodding. "That's true. But curiosity is a great itch, Mrs Jewell. I'd recommend you keep the phone off the hook for a day or two. Have you friends you could stay with, that would put you up?"

She leaned her head far back and looked at him down the length of her narrow fine-boned nose. "Do I seem to you, Inspector," she asked icily, "the kind of person who would go into hiding? I know about *people*, about their *itch*. I know about interrogations. I am not afraid."

There was a brief silence.

"I'm sure you're not, Mrs Jewell," Hackett said. "I'm sure you're not."

Jenkins in the background was gazing at the woman with admiring fascination. Maguire, still lost in himself, heaved a great sigh. Mrs Jewell's anger, if it was that, subsided, and she turned her face away. In profile she had the look of a figure on a pharaoh's tomb. Then they heard the sound of another car squeaking its way on to the cobbles of the yard.

"That'll be Quirke," Inspector Hackett said.

The late afternoon had turned tawny and Hackett was pacing in a paddock behind the stables. The parched grass crackled under his feet and spurts of amber dust

16

flew up. The country was in need of rain, all right, though it was only the start of June. He saw Doctor Quirke approaching from the direction of the house and stopped and waited for him. Teetering along on those absurdly dainty feet of his, the big man seemed not so much to walk as to stumble forward heavily, limping slightly; it was as if he had tripped over something a long way back and were still trying to regain his balance. He wore as usual a dark double-breasted suit and a black slouch hat. Hackett believed that if they should chance upon each other in the middle of the Sahara desert Quirke would be in the same get-up, the jacket buttoned across and the hat pulled down over one eye and the narrow tie knotted askew.

"Doctor Quirke," the detective said, by way of greeting, "did it ever strike you we're in the wrong line of work? We only seem to meet up when someone is dead."

"Like undertakers," Quirke said. He lifted his hat and ran a hand over his damp and gleaming brow. "This heat."

"Are you complaining, after the winter we had?"

They turned together and looked back at the house and the straggle of stables. "Handsome spot," Hackett said. "And to think it's only Diamond Dick's little place in the country." The house was big enough to be a mansion, with fine Georgian windows and a sweep of granite steps leading up to a front door flanked by two stout pillars painted white. Ivy and Virginia creeper clung to the walls, and the four lofty chimneys of honey-coloured brick had at least a dozen pots apiece. "Did you encounter the widow?"

Quirke was still squinting in the direction of the house. "Yes," he said. "I met her before, can't remember where — some function or other."

"Aye, the Jewells were a great couple for the functions."

They were each aware of a constraint between them, small but almost palpable. Death had that effect: it was embarrassing, like a bad odour. They spoke of Harrison and his heart attack. Quirke said he had not minded being called out on a Sunday, and Hackett thought, Yes, single men don't care about their Sundays. Though he had heard Quirke was going out with some woman now — an actress, was it? He considered it best not to enquire: Quirke's private life was a tangled business at the best of times. If there was such a thing as a private life, the detective thought, in this country.

They set off ambling across the dry grass towards the house. "Did you have a look at His Nibs?" the inspector asked.

Quirke nodded. "Some mess."

"Indeed." There was a pause. "And what did you think?"

"Well," Quirke said drily, "there's hardly any doubt as to the cause of death."

They left the paddock, and Hackett shut and barred the gate behind them. An unseen horse in one of the stables spluttered through its lips noisily and gave a kick to something wooden. Other animals stirred too, then settled down again. A sense of unease lay upon the

Sunday quiet — or was it only imagined? But violent death is a definite presence; Hackett had felt the swish of its dark mantle before.

"There'll be some hullabaloo," he said. He chuckled. "What will the *Clarion* have to say, I wonder?"

"It will print the truth fearlessly, as always."

This time they both laughed.

"And what will that be?" Hackett asked.

"Hmm?"

"The truth."

"Ah, that's a question."

They came to the house and stopped to admire its noble frontage. "Is there an heir, I wonder?" Hackett mused.

"The widow will inherit, surely?"

"She hardly looks to me like one who'd be prepared to run a newspaper business."

"Oh, I don't know. She's French, after all. They're different."

"What age is the daughter?"

"I don't know — a child. Must be eight or nine, I suppose."

Jenkins came round the corner of the stables, whey-faced and shaky-looking still. "Are those fellows done yet?" Hackett asked him. Forensics teams always irritated him, he was not sure why.

"They're finishing up, Inspector."

"They never finish, those boys."

But when the three had climbed the outside stairs to the office the head chemist and his assistant were packing their things into their square black leather bags and preparing to leave. Morton was the older one's name, a heavy-set fellow with dewlaps and a mournful eye. "Jesus Christ," he said disgustedly, "— shotguns!"

"Well," Hackett observed mildly, "they're quick, that's for sure."

Morton's assistant had a bad stammer and rarely spoke. Hackett had a moment's trouble remembering his name. Phelps, that was it. Morton and Phelps: sounded like a comedy duo on the wireless. Poor Jenkins was looking everywhere except at what was left of Diamond Dick Jewell.

"You'll have a report for me by the morning, yes?" Hackett said to Morton, who rolled a moist eye and said nothing. The policeman was not to be put off. "On my desk, by nine?"

"It'll be ready when it's ready," Morton muttered, taking up his bag.

Phelps grinned and bit his lip. The two departed, tramping heavily down the stairs.

"What sort of an outfit is it we're running at all," Hackett asked, of no one in particular, "with the likes of those two clowns for experts?" He put a hand to his jacket pocket and felt the lumpy sandwich there, warmish still and soft.

Quirke was standing in the middle of the floor with his hands in his pockets and his head inclined to one side, gazing thoughtfully at the body on the desk. "No note," he said. Hackett turned to him. "No suicide note, or did you find one?" Hackett made no answer, and they continued to regard each other for a long moment. "Not what you'd expect," Quirke said then, "of the likes of Richard Jewell."

Jenkins, his head cocked attentively, was watching them with lively attention.

Hackett sighed and shut his eyes and pressed bunched fingers and a thumb to the bridge of his nose, which was as shapeless as a potato and had something of the same greyish hue. "Are you saying," he said, looking at Quirke again, "that what we have here may not be a suicide?"

Quirke met his gaze. "Just what is it you're driving at, Inspector?" he asked, putting on a clipped accent. They grinned at each other, somewhat bleakly. As youngsters they had both been keen attenders of the picture-palaces of the day.

"Come on," Hackett said, "let's go and have another word with the grieving widow."

In fact, Quirke remembered perfectly well where he had met Françoise d'Aubigny, which was how the independent-minded Mrs Richard Jewell had introduced herself to him, and he could not think why he had pretended otherwise to the inspector. It was at a Bastille Day cocktail party in the French Embassy the previous summer. There had been a diplomatic flurry early on when someone had declined to shake hands with the ambassador, an old Pétainist with exquisite manners, a majestic mane of silver hair and a sinister tic in his left cheek. Quirke came upon the woman standing alone at a window overlooking the garden. She was pale and tense, and he did not know what had drawn him to her other than her classical if slightly severe beauty. She was wearing a gown of diaphanous white stuff, high-waisted in what he believed was called the empire style, and her hair too was piled high and bound with a scarlet ribbon; bathed in the gold light from the garden, she might have been a portrait by Jacques Louis David. She was clutching a champagne flute in the intertwined fingers of both hands and almost upset it when he spoke, startling her. He was momentarily taken aback by the look she gave him, at once hunted and haunted, or so it seemed to him. She quickly recovered herself, however, and accepted a cigarette.

What had they talked about? He could not remember. The weather, probably, and France, no doubt, given the day it was and where they were. She mentioned her husband but did not say who he was, only confided, smiling, that he was here and was not pleased with her, for it was she who had refused to take the ambassador's expensively manicured hand. "My brother was in the Resistance," she said, and gave a small shrug. "He died." Other people had come to the window then and Quirke had drifted away.

Later, when Isabel Galloway, who was at the party, told him who the Frenchwoman was he was surprised and even somewhat disconcerted: he would not have picked Richard Jewell as the kind of man that the kind of woman he guessed Françoise d'Aubigny to be would marry. Isabel had been suspicious, of course, and had wanted to know what the two of them had been hugger-muggering about, as she said, there at the window, looking like Danielle Darrieux and Gérard Philipe, or somesuch. Isabel considered jealousy, quickly sparked and forcefully expressed, as love's necessary tribute. She and Quirke had been together only for — what? — half a year? In that time there had been bumpy passages: Isabel was an actress, and wore her theatricality offstage as well as on —

Hackett was speaking to him.

"Sorry?"

They were at the front door, waiting for their knock to be answered. Jenkins had been sent back to Jewell's office, to keep the corpse company, as Hackett had said, winking at Quirke.

"I said, what will we say to her? The wife, I mean."

Quirke considered. "It's not my place to say anything to her. You're the detective."

"I tried already, and got nowhere."

The door was opened by Sarah Maguire, the house-keeper. She was a wan creature with mousy hair, and had a flinching manner, as if she were constantly in expectation of being hit. Her pale eyes were red-rimmed from weeping. She stood back for them to enter and led them off wordlessly along the broad hall, over the gleaming parquet. The place smelt of flowers and furniture polish and money.

Mrs Jewell, Françoise d'Aubigny — what *would* he call her? Quirke wondered — was in the drawing room. At first when the two men entered they felt as if they had walked into a mass of hanging gauze, so dense was the light flowing in at four great windows, two each in adjacent walls. The windows were open wide at the top half, and the long trails of muslin curtain hanging before them were bellying languorously in the breeze. Mrs Jewell was standing to one side, holding something in her left hand, some kind of glass ball, and turning back to look at them over her shoulder. How slender she was, how narrow her face with its high cheekbones and high, pale forehead. She was far more beautiful than Quirke recalled. She gave him a quizzical look, half smiling. Did she remember him from that one brief encounter a year ago? Surely not.

"This is Doctor Quirke," Hackett said. "He's here instead of Doctor Harrison, the state pathologist, who's not well."

She extended a cool hand for Quirke to shake. "We meet again," she said. Surprise made him miss a beat, and he could think of nothing to say and instead attempted an unaccustomed bow, bobbing his head awkwardly. "You've been to see my husband?" she asked. She might have been speaking of a social visit. Her glossy black eyes took him in calmly, with the hint of a smile, ironic, a little mocking, even.

"Yes," Quirke said, "I'm afraid so. I'm very sorry, Madame" — he faltered — "Mrs Jewell."

"You are kind," the woman said, withdrawing her hand.

Quirke now was startled to notice, from the corner of his eye, that there was another person present, a woman, in her mid-twenties, reclining on a sofa in front of one of the windows, with her head back and her long legs extended sideways and crossed at the ankles. She wore jodhpurs and gleaming black riding boots and a moss-green shirt; a kerchief, knotted loosely at her throat, was the same shade of old-gold as the upholstery of the sofa where she sat. She was regarding Quirke and the policeman with an expression of the scantest interest. A misted cut-glass tumbler of what must be gin and tonic, with ice cubes and a wedge of lime, was balanced beside her on the arm of the sofa. *Not a hundred yards from this room and these svelte, poised women*, Quirke was thinking, *Richard Jewell is sprawled across a desk with his head blown off.*

"This is my husband's sister, Denise," Mrs Jewell said. "We call her Dannie."

Quirke went forward, offering his hand, with Hackett hard behind him. They were like a pair of clumsy courtiers, Quirke thought, stumbling on each other's heels in the presence of the queen and the crown princess. Dannie Jewell was as slim as her brother's wife, but fair where she was dark. She had short reddish-blonde hair and a face, broad at the brow and tapered at the chin, that showed a strong, even a jarring, resemblance, Quirke noted, to what he remembered of the man lying dead in his office across the cobbled yard. She hardly lifted her head from the sofa-back as she took Quirke's hand and then the inspector's, unsmiling. She said something but so softly it was inaudible, which made both men lean forward intently. Dannie Jewell cleared her throat. "I'm his half-sister," she said, in a tone almost of defiance. "We had different mothers."

The two men turned as one from the young woman and looked to Françoise d'Aubigny. "My father-in-law," she said, "was married twice, but both wives died. So sad."

This seemed to require a response that neither man could find the words to form, and in the awkward silence it was left to Françoise d'Aubigny to speak again. "I seem," she said, "to have been offering tea to people for hours. Doctor Quirke, what will you take?" She lifted her glass from where it had been standing on a low table. "Dannie and I, as you see, felt in need of something stronger than tea. Shall I ask Sarah to bring you something — a whiskey, perhaps?" She turned to Hackett, the corner of her lip twitching. "Although I suppose you are 'on duty', Inspector."

"That's right, ma'am," Hackett stolidly said.

Quirke too declined her offer, and she lifted a hand to her forehead in a gesture that even Isabel Galloway would have thought a trifle overdone. "How strange all this is," she said, "and yet familiar, like something one might read in the newspaper."

"Was it yourself that called the guards?" Hackett asked. "They told me it was a woman but that she wouldn't give her name."

For a moment Mrs Jewell seemed confused, then nodded. "Yes, yes, I placed the call," she said. She glanced from the detective to Quirke and back again. "It seems so long ago."

There was silence in the room, save for the faint sibilant sounds the billowing curtains made. Then Dannie Jewell stood up from the sofa. "I'll have to go," she said. "Françoise, will you be all right?"

Hackett turned to her. "Maybe you'd hang on a minute, Miss Jewell," he said, smiling his most avuncular smile.

The young woman frowned. "Why?"

"Ah, it's just I'm trying to get an idea of the — of the sequence of events, you know, and I'm interested to talk to anyone that was here earlier today."

"I wasn't here," she said, almost indignantly. "I mean, not when it — not when —"

"But you're in your riding gear, I see," he said. He was still smiling.

Now it was her turn to look confused. "Yes, I was riding. I keep a horse here. We went out early —"

" 'We'?"

"I — I mean Toby and I. My horse."

"So you didn't hear the gunshot?"

"How could I? I was out on the Curragh, miles away."

Quirke saw that what Mrs Jewell was holding in her left hand was a snow-globe, with a tiny stylised French town in it, complete with houses and streets and a château flying a tricolour from its narrow turret. "I feel," she said, addressing Hackett, "that we are being — how do you say? — cross-examined." She gave an apologetic little laugh. "But I'm sure I am mistaken."

Dannie Jewell lifted her glass from the arm of the sofa and took a long drink from it, thirstily, like a child. She held the glass in both hands, and Quirke thought again of Françoise d'Aubigny standing at the window in the embassy that day, with the champagne glass, and of the look she had given him, the odd desperateness of

27

it. Who were these two women, really, he wondered, and what was going on here?

Hackett had lifted both his hands and showed the palms placatingly to Mrs Jewell. "I'm only asking a few questions, ma'am," he said easily, "that's all I'm doing."

"I should have thought," Mrs Jewell said, with a sharper glint to her look now, "there can be no doubt as to what has happened."

"Well," Hackett answered, all ease and smiling, "that's the question, you see — what *did* happen?"

There was another silence. Mrs Jewell looked at Quirke, as if for enlightenment, then turned back to Hackett. "I don't understand, Inspector." She was holding her gin glass in one hand and the snow-globe in the other; she might have been an allegorical figure in a tableau, illustrating some principle of balance or justice.

Dannie Jewell sat down again abruptly on the sofa. With her head bowed she groped beside her blindly to set the tumbler down where it had been before and then covered her face with her hands and let fall a single muffled sob. The other three looked at her. Mrs Jewell frowned. "This has been a terrible day," she said, in a tone of mild amazement, as if only now registering the full weight of all that had happened.

Hackett took a step nearer to her, and stopped. "I don't know, ma'am," he said, "whether it will make it better or worse for you if I say that we think your husband did not kill himself."

The young woman on the sofa lifted her face from her hands and threw herself back almost with violence against the cushions and turned up her eyes to the ceiling, in seeming anger, now, or exasperation.

Françoise d'Aubigny frowned, leaning forward and putting her head a little to one side as if she were hard of hearing. Again she turned to Quirke to help her, but he said nothing. "But then," Mrs Jewell began to ask in a baffled voice, "— but then *who* . . . ?"

CHAPTER
TWO

There were times, brief but awkward, when Quirke could not recall his assistant's first name since he always thought of him simply as Sinclair. They had been working together for nearly five years at the Hospital of the Holy Family and yet knew almost nothing of each other's lives outside the pathology department. This did not trouble either of them unduly: they were both jealous of their privacy. Now and then, of an evening, if they happened to find themselves leaving at the same time, they would cross the road together to Lynch's opposite the hospital gates and share a drink, only one, never more than that, and even then their conversation rarely strayed beyond the topics of their profession. Quirke was not even sure where the young man lived, or if he had a girlfriend, or family. The time to have asked would have been at the start, when Sinclair first came to work with him, but he had not thought to do so, and now it was too late, for they would both be embarrassed if he did. He was sure Sinclair would not welcome what he would probably regard as prying on his boss's part. They were content, it seemed, to keep the relation between them as it was, not unfriendly but not friendly, either, and strictly if tacitly demarcated. Quirke had no idea of what Sinclair thought of him, though he knew Sinclair wanted his job, and recognised an irritation in the young man, an impatience for Quirke to be gone and himself to be in charge of the department, even though Sinclair knew as well as Quirke did that such a development was not in view, not in the foreseeable future.

An indication that Sinclair was living a solitary life was the fact that he never seemed to mind being called in to work outside regular hours. That Sunday evening he brought with him a faint suggestion of the beach — the smell of suntan oil, and salt water. He had been at Killiney all afternoon, and had barely arrived home, he said, when Quirke had telephoned.

"Killiney," Quirke said, "I haven't been out there in years. How was it?"

"Stony," Sinclair said.

He was putting on a white coat over his corduroy trousers and cricket shirt — cricket? did Sinclair play cricket? — and was whistling softly to himself. The skin of his face was swarthy and somewhat pitted, and he had a mop of gleaming black curls. His lips were very red, remarkably so, for a man. He would be, Quirke supposed, attractive to women, in an alarming sort of way, with that mouth slashed like a wound across the bottom of his dark and slightly cruel-seeming face.

"I was in Kildare," Quirke said. Sinclair appeared not to be listening. He had not even glanced through the long window that gave on to the dissecting room and the corpse laid out there under a white nylon sheet. Quirke had not yet said who it was they were going to work on, and was rather enjoying the prospect of what would surely be the young man's shocked surprise when he heard that it was the famous Diamond Dick Jewell. "Inspector Hackett asked me to come out, since Harrison is down."

"Oh, yes?"

"Brooklands."

"Right." Sinclair had gone to the big steel sink in the corner and with the sleeves of his white coat pushed back was scrubbing his hands and his forearms, on which whorls of wiry black hair thickly flourished.

"Richard Jewell's place, you know?"

Sinclair turned off the tap. He was listening now. "Who was dead out there?" he asked.

Quirke pretended to be busy, scribbling in a file on his desk. He looked up. "Eh?"

Sinclair had gone to the window and was peering at the body on the slab. "At Brooklands — who was dead?"

"Diamond Dick himself, as it happens."

Sinclair did not respond except to go very still. "Richard Jewell is dead?" he said quietly.

"That's him in there. Shotgun blast."

Very slowly, like a man moving in his sleep, Sinclair reached under his white coat and brought out a packet of Gold Flake and a Zippo lighter. He was still staring at the corpse resting at the centre of that deep box of harsh white fluorescent light beyond the window. He lit the cigarette and blew a ghostly trumpet of smoke that flattened itself against the plate-glass pane and slowly dispersed. "You all right?" Quirke asked, peering at him. He could not see Sinclair's face except as a faint reflection in the window where he was standing. His sudden stillness and slowness were at once more and less of a response than Quirke had anticipated. He went and stood beside the young man. Now both of them were gazing at what was left of Richard Jewell. At last Sinclair stirred, and cleared his throat.

"I know his sister," he said.

It was Quirke's turn to stare. "Jewell's sister? — what's her name, Dannie?"

"Dannie, yes." Still Sinclair had not looked at him. "Dannie Jewell. I know her."

"I'm sorry," Quirke said. He had lit a cigarette of his own. "I would have . . ." What would he have done? "Do you know her well?" He tried to put no special emphasis on that word *well*, but for all his effort it still came out sounding coy and insinuating.

Sinclair gave a brief laugh. "How well is well?" he asked.

Quirke walked back and sat behind his desk. Sinclair turned, and stood in that way that he did, leaning a shoulder against the glass behind him, his ankles crossed and one arm folded on his chest and the cigarette held at a sharp angle and fizzling a thin and rapidly wavering stream of smoke straight upwards. "What happened?"

"I told you," Quirke said, "— shotgun blast."

"Suicide?"

"That's what it was meant to look like. A pretty pathetic effort. Blow your own head off, you don't end up cradling the weapon in your hands."

Sinclair was watching him. It came to Quirke, with a sudden small shock, that his assistant despised him for his unsought and, even in his own judgement, unwarranted reputation as an amateur sleuth. Quirke had got involved, more or less by accident — mainly through his daughter, in fact — in two or three cases that had also brought in Inspector Hackett. In the two latest of these affairs Quirke's name had got into the papers, and on each occasion he had suffered a brief notoriety. That was in the past, now, but Sinclair, he could see, had not forgotten. Did the young man think him a publicity-seeker? It was all nonsense — he had been hardly more than a close bystander during certain occasions of menace and violence, although in one instance he had been badly beaten up, and still had the trace of a limp. There had been nothing he could do to avoid involvement, however accidental, or incidental. But his assistant, he understood now, did not believe that for a moment. Well, he thought, maybe this time he will find out himself what it is to be suddenly brought smack up against humankind's propensity for wickedness; maybe he too will be taken back along the dark and tortuous route by which that cadaver had arrived in this place, under this pitiless light.

"So he was murdered?" Sinclair said. He sounded sceptical.

"That's what it looks like. Unless he did do it himself and someone found him and for some reason put the gun in his hands. Forensics are checking for prints but Morton is pretty sure there weren't any except Jewell's. Anyway, it's not easy to shoot yourself with a shotgun."

"What does Hackett think?"

"Oh, God knows — you know Hackett."

Sinclair came to the desk and stubbed out his half-smoked cigarette. His face was a blank mask. "And Dannie?" he asked. "Was she there?"

"She was out riding, came back and heard the news."

"Did you see her? How was she?"

"Composed to begin with, then not so much. She and Jewell's missus put on a show together for Hackett and me."

"A show?"

"Gin and tonic and smart repartee. I don't know why they thought they had to seem not to care — one of them had lost a husband, the other one a brother, no matter how much of a bastard he may have been."

Sinclair had gone to the steel cabinet by the wall and found a pair of rubber gloves and was pulling them on. "You want me to get started?"

"I'm coming."

They went together into the dissecting room. There was the usual low hum from the big neon lamps in the ceiling. Sinclair drew back the nylon sheet and gave a low whistle.

"The blast left most of his head on the window in front of him," Quirke said.

Sinclair nodded. "Close range — that's a powder-burn on his throat, isn't it?" He drew the sheet all the way off the corpse. They saw that Richard Jewell had been circumcised. They made no comment. "Did Dannie see him like this?" Sinclair asked.

"I don't think so. His wife would have kept her away. A cool customer, Madame Jewell."

"I never met her."

"French. And tough."

Sinclair was still gazing at the place where Jewell's head had been. "Poor Dannie," he said. "As if she doesn't have enough troubles."

Quirke waited, and after a moment said, "Troubles?" Sinclair shook his head: he was not ready to speak of Dannie Jewell. Quirke took a scalpel from a steel tray of instruments. "Well," he said, "let's open him up."

When the post-mortem was done Quirke ordered a taxi into town and offered Sinclair a lift, and to his surprise Sinclair accepted. They sat at opposite sides of the back seat, turned away from each other and looking out of their windows, saying nothing. It was nine o'clock and the sky was a luminous shade of deep violet around its edges, though at the zenith it was still light. They went to the Horseshoe Bar in the Shelbourne Hotel. It had not been intended that they would go for a drink but here they were, perched side by side on stools at the black bar, uneasy in each other's unaccustomed company. Sinclair drank beer, and Quirke took a cautious glass of wine: he was supposed to be off all alcohol, having spent some weeks the previous winter drying out in St John's. The experience had been sobering in more ways than one. He did not want ever to have to go back into that place.

Sinclair began to speak of Dannie Jewell. He had met her in college, and they still played tennis together out at Belfield. "She's a good sport," he said. Quirke did not know how to reply to this. What, he wondered, would constitute being a good sport in a woman, and in this woman in particular? He tried to imagine Sinclair on the tennis court, diving and slashing, or crouching menacingly at the net, his hairy forearms bared and those shiny curls plastered to his sweating brow. He wanted to hear more of Sinclair's relations with Dannie Jewell, and at the same time he did not. Of the things in life that Quirke disliked, or feared, or both, the one that ranked highest was change. He and Sinclair had a perfectly good working arrangement; if they were to start trading confidences now, where were they to stop?

"Did you meet her brother?" he asked.

Sinclair had a cat-like way of licking his upper lip after each sip of beer, moving the sharp red tip of his tongue slowly from the left corner to the right; Quirke found this faintly repellent and yet every time he could not but watch, fascinated.

"I met him once or twice, yes," Sinclair said. "He seemed all right to me. Not a man to make an enemy of."

"I imagine he had quite a few of them — enemies, I mean."

They were alone in the bar, this quiet Sunday evening. The barman, hardly more than a big overgrown boy, with a shock of red hair, was wiping the counter with a damp cloth, round and round, marking out grey circles on the black marble that faded as quickly as they were made.

Sinclair was frowning. "Dannie said something about him, last time I saw her," he said. "Something about some business deal that went wrong."

Quirke felt a stirring at the very back of his mind, a tickle of interest, of curiosity, that same curiosity that had got him into trouble so many times in his life. "Oh?" was all he said, but he feared that even that was too much. He had the foreboding sense that he must not get involved in the mystery of Richard Jewell's death; he did not know why, but he felt it.

"I don't remember the details of the row, if Dannie told me. All very hush-hush, nothing about it in the papers, not even in the ones Jewell didn't own. Carlton Sumner was involved somehow."

Quirke knew who Carlton Sumner was — who did not? The only man in the city whose reputation for ruthlessness and skulduggery could rival that of Richard Jewell, Sumner was the son of a Canadian timber baron who had sent him to Dublin to study at University College — the Sumners were Catholic — but he had got a girl pregnant and had been forced to marry her, since her father was in the government and had threatened disgrace and deportation. Quirke, who was at college at the same time, remembered Sumner and his girl, though he had been a year or two ahead of them. They were a golden couple about the place, shining all the more brightly against the drabness of the times. After they were married and the child arrived they had dropped out of circulation; then a few years later Sumner, with the backing of his father's fortune, had suddenly emerged as a fully-fledged tycoon. His speciality was buying up venerable and respectably down-at-heel businesses — Benson's the gents' outfitters, the Darleys' café chain — and sacking the boards and half the staff and turning them into gleaming new money-spinners. The rivalry between him and Richard Jewell was an ample source of gossip and vicarious delight in the city. And now Diamond Dick was dead.

"What do you think the disagreement was about?" Quirke asked. "A takeover bid, maybe?"

"I don't know — something like that, I suppose. There was a meeting at Sumner's place in Wicklow and Richard Jewell stormed out in the middle of it."

"That sounds serious."

Sinclair was frowning into the dregs of his beer. He seemed distracted, and Quirke wondered if he knew more about that angrily terminated meeting in Roundwood than he was prepared to admit. But why would he hold something back? Quirke sighed. That niggle at the far end of his mind was growing more insistent by the minute. The itch to find things out would only be eased by being scratched, yet there was a part of him that would rather put up with the irritation than take on the burden of knowing other people's sordid secrets. From personal experience he knew about secrets, and just how sordid they could be. "You said the girl, Dannie, has troubles?"

Sinclair stirred himself out of his thoughts. "She had a breakdown. I don't know the details."

"When was this?"

"A few months ago. They put her in a place in London, some kind of nursing home. She was there for a long time — weeks. I didn't know about it until she came back."

"She hadn't told you where she was going?"

Sinclair gave him a sideways look. "You don't know Dannie," he said. "Even when she was well she did things like that, going off without a word to anyone. Last year she went to Marrakesh and no one knew where she was until she came back with a suntan and the look of someone who had been doing things she shouldn't. She has her own money, inherited from her father. It's probably not good for her."

"But she's better now, yes?" Quirke asked. "I mean in her mind."

"Yes," Sinclair said, but his look was troubled. "Yes, she's better."

"But you're wondering how she'll react to her brother's death."

"How did she seem today, when you saw her?"

"I told you, she and Jewell's wife put on a show of being cool, though in the end she couldn't hide the fact of how upset she was. Maybe you should call her, go to see her. Where does she live?"

"She has a flat in Pembroke Street," Sinclair said, in a distracted voice. Quirke waited. "She's a funny person," Sinclair went on, "— secretive, you know? She won't talk about things, especially not herself. But there are demons there." He laughed. "You should see her on the tennis court."

Quirke had finished his wine and was wondering if he might risk another glass. The taste of it, at once acid and fruitily ripe, had made him feel slightly sick at first, but the alcohol had pierced straight, like a gleaming steel needle, to some vital place deep inside him, a place that now was clamouring for more.

"What happened when she had the breakdown?" he asked.

"She crashed her brother's car on the Naas dual carriageway. I wouldn't be surprised if she did it deliberately."

"Was she injured?"

"No. She ran the car into a tree and walked away without a scratch. She joked about it — *Trust me,* she said, *smashed up the bloody car and still couldn't manage to do myself in.*"

"You think that's what she was trying to do — to kill herself?"

"I don't know. As I say, she has her demons."

Quirke fell silent, then signalled to the barman to bring the same again; one more glass would be safe enough, he was sure of it. Sinclair, it was clear, cared more deeply about Dannie Jewell than he was prepared to admit — about, or for? Quirke felt a protective pang for the young man, and was surprised, and then was more surprised still to hear himself inviting Sinclair to join him and his daughter for dinner on Tuesday night. "You've met Phoebe, haven't you?"

"No, I haven't," Sinclair said. He was looking uneasy. "Tuesday," he said, playing for time, "I'm not sure about Tuesday . . ."

"Eight o'clock, at Jammet's," Quirke said. "My treat." Their drinks arrived, Quirke lifted his. "Well, cheers."

Sinclair smiled queasily; he had the slightly dazed look of a man who has been manoeuvred into something without realising until too late what was being done. Quirke wondered what Phoebe would make of him. He drank his wine; it was remarkable how the taste was softening with each new sip he took.

In the papers next day the reports of Richard Jewell's death were unexpectedly muted. The *Clarion* ran the story on its front page, of course, but confined it to a single column down the right-hand side. The leader page was cleared, however, and given over entirely to accounts of the late proprietor's life and achievements, along with Clancy's editorial that Miss Somers had quietly knocked into more or less literate shape. The *Times* put the story into three paragraphs at the bottom of page one, with an obituary inside that was out of date on a number of points. The *Independent*, the *Clarion's* main rival, which might have been expected to splash the story, instead ran a restrained double-column item on page three, under a photograph of a distinctly furtive-looking Richard Jewell receiving the seal of a papal knighthood from the Pope in Rome three years previously. All the press, it seemed, was holding back out of nervous uncertainty. In none of the reports was the cause of death specified, although the *Clarion* spoke of a "fatal collapse".

Quirke read this and snorted. He was sitting up in bed in Isabel Galloway's little house in Portobello, with a cigarette burning in an ashtray on the sheet beside him and a large grey mug of tea, which he had not yet touched, steaming on the bedside table. Morning sunlight streamed in at the low window and, outside, the bluish air over the canal was hazed already with the day's heat. Isabel, in her silk tea-gown, was seated at the dressing-table in front of the mirror, pinning up her hair. "What's that?" she asked.

Quirke looked up from the page. "Diamond Dick," he said. "The papers don't know what to make of it."

He was admiring the cello-shaped line of the woman's back and the twin curves of her neat bum set just so on the red plush stool. She felt his eye on her and glanced at him sideways past the angle of her lifted arm. "And you?" she asked, with a faint smirk. "— Do you know what to make of it?" He could not understand how she could hold three hairpins in her mouth and still manage to speak. The silk sleeve of her gown had fallen back to reveal a mauve shadow in the hollow of her armpit. The harsh sunlight picked out the tiny wrinkles fanning out from the corner of her eye and the faint soft down on her cheek.

"Somebody shot him, that's for sure," he said.

"His wife?"

He put his head back and stared. "Why do you say that?"

"Well" — she extracted one of the pins from her mouth and fastened a wave into place — "isn't it always the wife? Goodness knows, wives usually have good cause to murder their ghastly husbands."

Quirke saw again Françoise d'Aubigny standing between the two tall windows with the softly billowing curtains and turning towards him, holding the snow-globe in her left hand. "I don't think Mrs Jewell is the type," he said.

Catching something in his tone she glanced at him again. "What type is she?"

"Very French, very self-possessed. A bit on the cold side." Was she cold, really? He did not think so.

"And to cap it all, smashing-looking."

"Yes, she's good-looking —"

"Hmm," she said to her reflection in the glass. "I don't like the sound of this at all."

"— a bit like you, in fact."

"*Alors, M'sieur, vous êtes très galant.*"

Quirke folded the newspaper and put it aside and got out of bed. He was in his underpants, and a man's old string vest, which Isabel had found for him at the bottom of a drawer, and which might or might not have been his originally, a point it was better not to dwell on. She asked if he wanted breakfast but he said he would get something at the hospital. "I wish you'd eat properly," she said. "And besides, you need to go on a diet."

He glanced down at his gut. She was right: he was getting fat. Again he had that image of Richard Jewell's widow turning to look over her shoulder at him in gauzy sunlight.

"Can we have lunch?" Isabel asked.

"Not today, sorry."

"Just as well, I suppose — I have rehearsals in the afternoon."

She was doing something by Shaw at the Gate. She began to complain about the director. Quirke, however, had given up listening.

On the way to work he stopped in at Pearse Street and called on Inspector Hackett. The detective came down from his office and they walked out into the sunlight together. As usual Hackett's old soft hat was set far back on his head, and the elbows and knees of his blue suit gleamed in the sun's glare, and when he put his hands in his trouser pockets his braces came into view, broad, old-fashioned, their leather button-straps clutching on to the waistband of his trousers like two pairs of splayed fingers. The inspector suggested they should take a stroll by the river, seeing the day was so fine. The stalled traffic made Westmoreland Street look like a pen crowded with jostling sleek dark animals all bellowing and braying and sending up ill-smelling clouds of smoke and dust. It was half past ten by the Ballast Office clock, and Quirke said he should really be getting to work, but the policeman waved a dismissive hand and said surely the dead could wait, and chuckled. On Aston Quay a red-haired young tinker galloped past bareback on a piebald horse, disdainful of the clamouring cars and buses that had to scramble to get out of his way. A street photographer in a mackintosh and a leather trilby was snapping shots among the passing crowd. Seagulls swooped, shrieking.

"Isn't that river a living disgrace?" Hackett said. "— The stink of it would poison a pup."

They crossed over and walked along by the low embankment wall. "You saw the papers?" Quirke said.

"I did — I saw the *Clarion*, anyway. Weren't they awful cautious?"

"Did they speak to you?"

"They did. They sent along a young fellow by the name of Minor, who I think you know."

"Jimmy Minor? Is he with the *Clarion* now?" Minor, a sometime friend of his daughter's, used to be on the *Evening Mail*. Mention of him caused Quirke a vague twinge of unease; he did not like Minor, and worried at his daughter's friendship with him. He had not noticed Minor's byline on the *Clarion* report. "Pushy as ever, I suppose?"

"Oh, aye, a bit of a terrier, all right."

"How much did he know?"

Hackett squinted at the sky. "Not much, only what he put in the paper."

"A 'fatal collapse'?" Quirke said with sarcasm.

"Well, it's the case, isn't it, more or less, when you think about it?"

"What about the inquest?"

"Oh, they'll fudge it, I suppose, as usual." They paused just before the Ha'penny Bridge and rested with their backs to the wall and their elbows propped on the parapet behind them. "I'll be interested to see," the inspector said musingly, "which will be the preferred official line, a suicide, or something else."

"What about your report? — what will *your* line be?"

The inspector did not answer, only looked down at the toes of his boots and shook his head and smiled. After a moment they turned from the wall and set off over the hump of the little bridge. Before them, a ragged paper-boy on the corner of Liffey Street called out raucously, "*Paper man's tragic death — read all about it!*"

"Isn't it a queer thing," Hackett said, "the way suicide is counted a crime? It never made much sense to me. I suppose it's the priests, thinking about the immortal soul and how it's not your own but God's. Yet I don't see where the mortal body comes into the equation — surely that's not worth much and should be left to you to dispose of as you please. There's the sin of despair, of course, but couldn't it also be looked at that a chap was in so much of a hurry to get to Heaven he might very well put an end to himself and have done with the delay?" He stopped on the pavement and turned to Quirke. "What do you think, Doctor? You're an educated man — what's your opinion in the matter?"

Quirke knew of old the policeman's habit of circling round a subject in elaborate arabesques. "I think you're right, Inspector. I think it doesn't make much sense."

"Do you mean the act itself, now, or the way it's looked on?"

"Oh, I can see it making sense to put an end to everything."

Hackett was gazing at him quizzically, his big shapeless head on one side, the little eyes bright and sharp as a blackbird's. "Do you mind if I ask, but did you ever contemplate it yourself?"

Quirke looked away quickly from that searching gaze. "Doesn't everyone, at some time or other?" he said quietly.

"Do you think so?" Hackett said, in a tone of large surprise. "God, I can't say I've ever looked, myself, into that particular hole in the ground. I think I wouldn't trust myself not to go toppling in head first. And then what would the missus do, not to mention my two lads over in America? They'd be heartbroken. At least" — he grinned, his thin froggy mouth turning up at either corner — "I hope they would be."

Quirke knew that he was being mildly mocked: Hackett often used him as a sort of straight-man. They walked on.

"But then," Quirke said, "Richard Jewell didn't kill himself, did he?"

"Are you sure of that?" Again the policeman struck a note of surprise, but whether it was real or feigned Quirke could not tell.

"You saw the gun, the way he was holding it."

"Do you not think someone might have found him and picked up the gun and put it into his hands?"

"I thought of that — but why? Why would anyone do that?"

"Oh, I don't know. To make everything neat and tidy, maybe?" He gave a little laugh. "People do the queerest things when they come upon a dead body all of a sudden — have you not found that yourself, in the course of your work?"

On O'Connell Bridge the photographer in his greasy leather hat was taking a picture of a woman in a white dress and sandals who was holding by the hand a small boy wearing a toy cowboy gun strapped to his hip; the mother was smiling self-consciously while the boy frowned. Quirke watched them covertly; orphaned early, he had never known his mother, was not even sure who she had been.

"Anyway," Inspector Hackett was saying, "it makes no odds to me what they say about it in the papers, or what they speculate might have happened. I have my job to do, same as ever." He chuckled again. "Like I say, Doctor Quirke, aren't we a queer pair? Connoisseurs of death, that's us, you in your way, me in mine." He pushed his hat farther to the back on his skull. "Will we chance a cup of tea in Bewley's, do you think?"

"I have to get to the hospital."

"Oh, aye, you're a busy man — I forgot."

Quirke could not understand why, but the dinner with Sinclair and Phoebe was not a success. Sinclair was at his stoniest and hardly spoke a word, while Phoebe throughout looked as if she were trying not to laugh, though not because she was amused. The food was good, as it always was at Jammet's, and they drank two bottles of a fine Chablis, *premier cru* — or Quirke drank, while Phoebe took no more than a glass and Sinclair sipped and sniffed at his as if he thought the chalice might be poisoned — but it seemed that nothing could lift the pall that had settled over the table as soon as they sat down. Then Sinclair left early, mumbling something about having to meet someone in a pub, and Quirke sat nursing his wine glass in a fist and gazing off bleakly at the opposite wall.

"Thank you for dinner," Phoebe said. "It was lovely." Quirke said nothing, only shifted morosely, making the little gilt chair creak under him in protest. "I liked your Doctor Sinclair," his daughter went on determinedly. "Is he Jewish?"

Quirke was surprised. "How did you know?"

"I've no idea. It just came to me that he was. Funny, I never think of there being Irish Jews."

"He's from Cork," Quirke said.

"Is he, now. Sinclair — is that a Jewish name?"

"Don't know. Changed from something else, probably."

She gazed at him with a hapless smile. "Oh, Quirke," she said, "don't sulk. It makes you look like a moose with a toothache." She never called him anything but Quirke.

He paid the bill and they left. Outside, a soft grey radiance lingered in the air. Phoebe had recently moved from the flat in Haddington Road that she had not liked and was now living in one room in Baggot Street. Quirke had urged her to find something better, and had offered to pay half the rent, or even all of it, but she had insisted, gently but with a warning firmness, that the little room suited her perfectly. The canal near her place was lovely, it was a ten-minute walk to work, and she could get all her provisions at the Q & L — what more did she need? He hated to think of her, he said, cooped up in so small a place, with nothing to cook on but a Baby Belling and having to share the bathroom with two other tenants. But she had only looked at him, smiling with her lips compressed in the stubborn way that she did, and he had given up. Once he had suggested that she might come and live with him, but they both knew that was impossible, and she was glad that the subject had been dropped. She was a solitary, as he was, and they would both have to accept it was so.

They walked up Kildare Street, past the National Library and the Dáil. A bat, a quick speck of darkness, flittered above them in the violet air. "You should phone him," Quirke said. "You should phone Sinclair."

She linked her arm in his. "What are you trying to do?" she said, laughing. "You'd make a terrible match-maker."

"I'm just saying you should —"

"Besides, if anyone is to do the phoning it will be him. Girls can't call fellows — don't you know that?"

Despite himself he smiled; he liked to be made fun of by her. "I'm sorry he was so quiet," he said. "He's had a shock. He knows Richard Jewell's sister."

"The man who killed himself?"

He turned his head and looked at her. "How do you know?"

"How do I know what?"

"That he killed himself."

"Didn't he? It's what everyone is saying."

He sighed and shook his head. "This city," he said.

They came to the top of the street and turned left.

"It could hardly be kept a secret," Phoebe said, "given who he was."

"Yes. Word gets around, but word is almost always wrong."

The last of the light was fading and the great masses of trees crowding behind the railings of St Stephen's Green seemed to radiate darkness, as if night had its source in them.

"Is he going out with her — the sister?" Phoebe asked.

"Sinclair? Going out with Dannie Jewell? I don't think so. She has problems. *She* tried to kill herself."

"Oh. Then it runs in the family."

He hesitated, then said, "Richard Jewell didn't kill himself."

"He didn't?"

"No. Someone did it for him."

"Not the sister!"

"I hardly think so."

"Then who?"

"That's the question."

She stopped, and made him stop with her. "You're not getting involved in this, are you, Quirke?" she said, peering hard at him. "Tell me you're not."

He would not meet her eye. "*Involved* is not the way I'd put it. I had to go down and look at the body — the state pathologist is ill, and it was a Sunday, so they called on me."

"'They'?"

"Yes, you've guessed it."

"Inspector Hackett? Oh, Quirke. You can't resist it, can you? You should have been a detective — you'd probably have made a better one than he is. So: tell me."

He gave her an outline of what had happened, and by the time he was finished they had arrived at her door. Darkness had fallen without their noticing it, yet even still a faint mauve glimmer lingered in the air. She invited him in, and he sat in the only chair while she made coffee on the little stove that stood on a Formica-topped cupboard in one corner, beside the sink. Most of her things, which were not many, were still in cardboard boxes stacked on the floor at the foot of the narrow bed. The only light was from an unshaded sixty-watt bulb dangling from the centre of the ceiling, like something that had been hanged. "Yes, I know," Phoebe said, glancing up at it. "— I'm going to buy a floor lamp." She brought him his demitasse of coffee. "Don't look so disapproving. The next time you come here you won't recognise the place. I have plans."

She sat on the floor beside his chair, her legs folded under her and her own cup cradled in her lap. She was wearing her black dress with the white lace collar and her hair was pinned back severely behind her ears. Quirke felt he should tell her she was making herself look more and more like a nun, but he had not the heart: he had hurt her enough, in the past; he could keep his mouth shut now.

"So, obviously," she said, "you think Richard Jewell's death had something to do with the fight he had with Carlton Sumner."

"Did I say that?" He did not think he had; he realised he was a little drunk.

She smiled. "You don't have to say it. I can guess."

"Yes, you're getting good at this death business."

Now they both frowned, and looked aside. People that Phoebe had known, one of them a friend, had died violently; it was her grim joke that she would be called the Black Widow except that she had never been married. Quirke drank off the last bitter mouthful of coffee and rose and carried the cup to the sink. He rinsed it and set it upside-down on the draining-board.

"Something felt wrong in that house," he said, drying his hands on a tea-towel. "Brooklands, I mean."

"Well, since someone had just committed suicide, or been murdered, or whatever —"

"No, apart from that," he said.

He was lighting a cigarette. She watched him from where she was sitting. There was a way in which he would always be a stranger to her, an intimate stranger, this father who for the first two decades of her life had pretended she was not his daughter. And now, suddenly, it came to her, watching him there, the great bulk of him in his too-tight black suit, dwarfing her little room, that without quite realising it she had forgiven him at last, forgiven the lies and subterfuge, the years of cruel abnegation, all that. He was too sad, too sad and wounded in his soul, for her to go on resenting him.

"Tell me more about it," she said, shivering a little. She made herself smile. "Tell me about the widow, and the girl that tried to kill herself. Tell me everything."

David Sinclair felt confused. He was resentful of Quirke for that clumsy attempt tonight to pair him off with his daughter, and resentful of Phoebe, too, for going along with it. And that ghastly restaurant had reminded him of nothing so much as the dissecting room, with plate succeeding plate of pale dank carcasses. He could still taste the sole at the back of his throat, a salty, buttery slime. Why had he accepted the invitation in the first place? He could have made some excuse. He had always known it would be a mistake to let Quirke get any closer than professional etiquette required. What would be next? Outings to the pictures? Sunday morning at-homes? Afternoons at the seaside, with flasks of tea and sandy sandwiches, him and the girl running hand in hand into the waves while Quirke, with the legs of his trousers rolled and a knotted hankie on his head, sat watching from the beach with a smug paternal smile? No, no, he would have to put a stop to this before it started. Whatever *it* was.

And yet, there was the girl. She looked like nothing much, with that stark little face and the hair clawed back as if it were a punishment that had been imposed on her for an infringement of some religious rule. She was a study in black-and-white — the pale face and raked hair, the jet stuff of her dress and its starched lace collar — like the negative of a photograph of herself. And the air she had of knowing something that no one else knew, something droll and faintly ridiculous — that was unnerving. Yes, it was the right word: unnerving. He had tried to remember the story about Quirke and her, something about Quirke pretending for years that she was not his daughter but the daughter of his brother-in-law, Malachy Griffin, the outgoing consultant obstetrician at the Hospital of the Holy Family. He had paid no attention to the gossip — what was it to him if Quirke chose to reject a whole household of unwanted off-spring?

But Phoebe, now, Phoebe; despite everything he could not get her out of his head, and it annoyed him.

He heard the telephone as soon as he came into the hall. His flat was two flights up and he took the stairs two at a time, heaving himself hand over hand up the slightly sticky banister rail. He was convinced it was Quirke calling him, as he had called two days ago, not summoning him to work this time but to something else — what? Another tryst with him and his daughter, already? Surely not. He gained the second-floor landing, out of breath and slightly dizzy, and still the phone was going. Determined, whoever the caller was. He burst into the flat and fumbled the receiver to his ear — why was he in such a state? But he knew, of course; improbable as it was, he was certain it was Quirke calling to talk to him about Phoebe.

In his confusion he did not at first recognise the voice, and when he did he had to stop himself groaning. "Oh, Dannie," he said. "Are you all right?" Knowing that of course she was not.

He let the taxi go at the bottom of Pembroke Street, not wanting to have to get out directly in front of her door, he was not sure why. She was in her dressing-gown when she let him in. She had not bothered to turn on the light on the stairs coming down and they climbed to her flat in the dark. A fanlight on the return held a single star, stiletto-shaped and shimmering. Dannie had not yet said a word. He was filled with foreboding; he could almost feel it sloshing about inside him like some awful oily liquid. Why had he answered the damned phone, anyway? Now he was trapped. Dannie would make a night of it. He had been through this before, the floods of words, the tears, the soft wailing, the pleas for understanding, tenderness, pity. Now they reached the open door of the flat, and when she trailed in ahead of him he hesitated for a second on the threshold, wondering if he had the courage just to turn on his heel and go running off down those stairs as fast as he had run up the stairs at home to answer her anguished call for help.

Her flat had the familiar smell, brownish and dull, that it took on when Dannie was in one of her lows; it was like the smell of hair left long unwashed, or perhaps that was indeed what it was. Dannie had two modes, wholly distinct. For most of the time she was a coolly self-contained daughter of the middle class, fond of her pleasures, a little bored, somewhat spoilt. Then something would happen, some blend of chemicals in her brain would tip the wrong way, and she would sink into what seemed a limitless depth of sorrow and bitter distress. Her friends had learned to dread these lapses, and at the first sign of them would discover convenient excuses to be unavailable. Sinclair, however, was unable to refuse her when she was like this, so sad and helpless. She was infuriating, too, of course. Her relentlessness was hard to bear, and after hours of her hammering on at him he would have the urge to seize her by the shoulders and shake her until her teeth chattered.

Afterwards, when the depression had lifted and she had regained her equilibrium, she would be full of apologies, ducking her head in that childish way she did and doing her mortified laugh. Although they never remarked it outright it was acknowledged between them how much she appreciated the fact that he had never taken advantage of her when she was at her weakest, for when she was like that she would do anything to win even a crumb of sympathy. More than once he had been tempted, when she fell into his arms and clung to him, but always he called to mind the wise but cruel watchword from his student days: never screw a nut. Anyway, he suspected she had not much interest in that kind of thing. She had the air of a debauched virgin, if such a thing were possible. Poor Dannie, so beautiful, so damaged, so pitiful.

In the front room they sat on the bench seat in the bay of the big window that looked down on the deserted street. Though it was almost midnight a bluish glow still lingered in the air, and the street-lights glimmered wanly.

"I'm sorry," Sinclair said, "about your brother." He did not know what else to say.

"Are you?" she said listlessly. "I don't think I am. Isn't that strange?" She was looking down into the street. She seemed calm except for her hands, clasped together in her lap and swarming over each other in a convulsive washing movement. "Or maybe it's not strange," she said, "maybe no one is ever really sad when someone dies, but only pretending. Don't they say it's not the person who's dead that we feel sorry for but ourselves, because we know we'll die, too? And yet people cry at the graveside and I don't think they could be so sorry for themselves that it would make them cry, do you? Have you ever watched children at a funeral, how fed up they look, how angry they seem at being made to do this boring thing, standing in the cold and the rain while the priest says prayers they can't understand and everyone looks so solemn? I remember when Daddy died and I . . ."

Sinclair let his thoughts wander. Despite everything it was almost soothing, sitting here in the gloaming with the young woman's voice pouring over him like some mild balm — soothing, that is, so long as he paid no attention to what she was saying. He was remembering an encounter, if such it could be called, that he had witnessed between her and her late brother. It was an evening in spring. Sinclair and Dannie were walking together down Dawson Street. They had been drinking in McGonagle's and Dannie was a little tipsy, talking and laughing about two writers who had been standing next to them at the bar arguing drunkenly as to whether or not the country still could boast a peasantry worthy of the name. A gleaming chauffeur-driven black Mercedes with a high square rear end had pulled up outside the Hibernian and three men came out of the hotel, talking together loudly and laughing. At the sight of them Dannie abruptly stopped speaking, and although she kept walking Sinclair sensed her faltering, or shying, like a nervous horse approaching a difficult jump. One of the men was Richard Jewell. She had spotted him before he saw her, and then he turned, sensing her gaze, perhaps, and when his eye fell on her he too hesitated for a beat, and then put his head far back, his nostrils flaring, and smiled. It was a strange smile, fierce, somehow, almost a snarl. The two siblings did not greet each other, merely exchanged that swift, intense glance, the one with his smile and the other looking suddenly stricken, and then Jewell turned to his companions and slapped them on the shoulders in farewell, and went forward quickly and climbed into the back seat of the Mercedes, which pulled away smoothly from the kerb. Yes, Dannie said through clenched teeth, yes, that was her brother. She was walking quickly with her back held stiffly straight, staring ahead; she had gone very pale. It was clear that she would say no more on the subject, and Sinclair let it go. But he remembered the look on Dannie's face, taut and stark, and the almost violent manner in which she marched along with her spine rigid and her shoulders thrust unnaturally high, all thought of McGonagle's and those funny drunken scribblers clearly gone from her mind.

". . . And yet it's strange, too," she was saying now, "the way people just disappear when they die, I mean the way they're still here, the body is still here, but *they* are gone. Whatever was them has been extinguished, like a light that's just been switched off." She stopped, and turned her face towards Sinclair, sitting there, a dim figure before her in dusk's last lingering gleam. "I'm glad he's dead," she said, very softly, as though someone else in the room with them might overhear her. "Yes, I'm glad."

He saw that she was weeping, the tears running down her face unchecked, as if she were unaware of them. He tried to think of something to say, something comforting, that she was being too hard on herself, that she was in shock, that kind of thing, but the words would not come, and if they had he knew they would have been inadequate to the moment, fatuous, weak words, ridiculous, even, in the circumstances. He did not know how to deal with the grief of others.

"Tell me what happened," he said.

She had turned away from him and sunk into herself again, and at his words she twitched, as if he had wakened her suddenly from sleep. She frowned. "What happened where?"

"At Brooklands. On Sunday."

She thought for fully a minute before she spoke. "They wouldn't let me see him," she said. "I wanted to but they wouldn't let me. I suppose he would have looked terrible, with blood and everything. It was a shotgun, his own, the one that he was so fond of." She turned to him again and spoke rapidly, urgently. "First they said he shot himself but then there was a policeman, a detective, he said he hadn't, that someone else had done it. But who would come there on a Sunday and shoot him — who would do that?" She reached out in the shadows and groped for his hand where it lay on the bench seat and grabbed it, squeezed it. "Who would do such a thing?"

He went into the kitchen to make coffee for them both. She had all sorts of expensive electric gadgets for cooking with that he was sure she never used. *Poor little rich girl*, he thought, and smiled to himself wryly. While he waited for the coffee pot to come to the boil he went and stood at the window with his hands in his pockets, looking down into the street but not seeing it. He was imagining what had happened at Brooklands, a place he had never seen. Quirke had described the scene to him, the office up the outside wooden steps above the stables, the desk, the body twisted across it, the stain like a huge red blossom on the window. Someone had climbed those stairs without making a sound and crept up behind Richard Jewell, and when Jewell turned at last he would have found himself staring into the twin barrels of the gun he recognised at once, a Purdey twelve-bore side-by-side, twenty-six-inch lump construction barrels, with signature self-opening system and a straight pistol grip of polished Turkish walnut. Sinclair, whose father had worked all his life on the estate of the Earls of Lismore, knew something about guns. Behind him on the stove the coffee pot had begun to rumble.

It was not until the small hours that he at last persuaded Dannie to go to bed. She was exhausted, but still talking, circling round and round the subject of death and the difficulty of knowing how to behave in the face of it. He made her take a pill, selecting one from the troop of little brown bottles that she kept on a shelf to themselves in the bathroom cabinet. She did not pull back the counterpane, but lay on top of it in her dressing-gown, turned on her side with her knees drawn up and a hand under her cheek, staring past him into the shadows. He switched off the bedside lamp and sat beside her for a long time on a straight-backed chair, chain-smoking and drinking the cold dregs of coffee in his cup.

Around them the city was silent. When she spoke she made him start, for he had thought, had hoped, that she was asleep.

"Those poor orphans," she said.

He did not understand, and in the darkness he could not see her face, how she looked. Richard Jewell had only one child, he knew, and besides, the child's mother was not dead. So what orphans did she mean? But she would say no more, and presently the pill began to work, and her breathing took on a slow, shallow rhythm, and he felt her consciousness slipping away. He waited another quarter of an hour, watching the greenly luminous second-hand of his watch sweep round the dial. Then he stood up quietly from the chair, feeling a sudden stab of pain in a knee that had gone stiff, and went out and closed the bedroom door behind him.

On the landing he could not find the light switch and had to feel his way down the stairs, his heart racing from too much coffee and too many cigarettes. In the lunette above the return, the dagger-shaped star still sparkled. Outside the front door he turned left and set off towards Baggot Street. The night air was chill and damp against his face. He thought the street was empty but then a young woman, hardly more than a girl, really, stepped out of a darkened doorway and asked him if he had a light. She could not have been more than sixteen. She had a thin, pale face and pale hands that made him think of claws. At that moment, inexplicably, the clear sharp memory came to him of Phoebe Griffin's face, smiling at him faintly across the restaurant table. The girl, ignoring the box of matches he was offering her, asked if he was interested in doing business. He said no, and then apologised, feeling foolish. He walked on, and the whore cast a soft obscenity after him.

What orphans?

CHAPTER
THREE

Somehow Quirke had known that she would call. Although he had given her his home number, for some reason she chose to phone him at the hospital. "It's Françoise d'Aubigny here," she said, and then added, "Mrs Jewell," as if he might have forgotten. He had known who it was from the first word she spoke. That voice. After the initial exchange neither said anything for some moments. Quirke fancied he could hear her breathing. His forehead had gone hot. This was absurd; he was being absurd.

"How are you?" he asked.

The coroner had returned an open verdict on Richard Jewell, a travesty, of course, but not a surprise; the *Clarion* had reported the judgment in two paragraphs buried on an inside page.

"I feel very strange, as a matter of fact," Françoise d'Aubigny said. "As if I were in a hot-air balloon, floating above everything. Nothing has any weight."

The memory of her had been weaving itself around Quirke's thoughts for days, elusive and insubstantial as a stray strand of cobweb, and as clinging, too. Even lying in Isabel Galloway's bed he saw the other woman's face suspended above him in the darkness,

65

and felt guilty, and then resentful, since there was nothing he was guilty of, or nothing of substance, anyway. *Or not yet*, as a small voice whispered in his head.

"Yes," he said now, "grief is strange."

"Ah — you seem to know how it feels?"

"My wife died. It was a long time ago." She said nothing to that. Again there was a silence on the line. "And your daughter," he asked, "how is she coping?"

"Not badly. She is a very brave little girl. She's called Giselle." Now it was his turn not to know what to say. "She refused to go to the funeral."

"What age is she?"

"Nine. Very young, and yet old enough to know her own mind. I can remember what it was like to be that age, and how sharp the pain of things was then."

Yet again that silence on the line, hollow, slightly unsettling.

"Would you like to meet?" Quirke heard himself ask.

Her reply was instant. "Yes," she said, "I would."

They met for lunch in the Hibernian. There was the usual lunchtime bustle, and as the glass front door kept opening and shutting, it threw a repeated flash of reflected sunlight along the length of the marble floor, among the feet of the people coming and going. She was already at the table when he arrived, sitting up very straight with her shoulders back and her eye fixed expectantly on the door. She wore a thin pale-blue summer dress with polka dots, and a tiny scrap of a hat, stuck with a feather and a pin, that he suspected she might have bought in the Maison des Chapeaux, where his daughter worked — perhaps, indeed, Phoebe had sold it to her. She extended a hand palm down, as if for him to kiss, but he only shook it, and felt clumsy. "I'm a little sorry," she said, glancing about, "that I suggested this place — Richard used to lunch here all the time. In fact, I think I have had one or two disapproving glances. Should I be wearing black, at least?"

She ordered a salad and a glass of iced water. Quirke wistfully considered a half bottle of wine, but thought better of it. He scanned the menu uncertainly and settled for an omelette.

"Yes," Françoise d'Aubigny said, "Richard loved it here. He used to joke that it was his answer to the Kildare Street Club, where of course he would not have been welcome." She looked at Quirke with a searching glint. "You know the family is Jewish? It is not something they speak of."

Had he known it? He was not sure. There was the fact of Jewell's having been circumcised, but that was never conclusive evidence. He did not know what to think of this aspect of things, or what its relevance might be. And what of her? Was d'Aubigny a Jewish name? He could ask Sinclair, who might know. "I doubt the chaps at Kildare Street would have me, either," he said, but did not meet her eye. He thought about wine again; maybe just a glass?

She was still watching him, smiling a little. "I'm thinking, Doctor Quirke, you are not entirely at ease?"

He experienced a sudden flash of impatience, of annoyance, even. She was right: they should not have come here for lunch; probably they should not have met at all. "The thing is, Mrs Jewell, I'm not sure exactly what is happening — I mean, why we are here like this." She was so lovely it almost pained him to look at her.

She lowered her gaze as if to hide her smile. "Yes, as I said, perhaps this was not a good idea." Now she looked up again, and did smile. "But if I recall correctly it was you who issued the invitation."

Their food arrived. Quirke asked the waiter to bring him a glass of Chablis. To his surprise Françoise d'Aubigny said she would have one too. Perhaps she was as nervous as he was, for all her air of coolness and poise.

"That detective," she said when the waiter had gone, "— what is his name?"

"Hackett."

"Yes. Hackett. All the policemen here, are they like him?"

Quirke was glad of a reason to laugh. He leaned back in his chair. "No," he said, "I don't think so. But he's not as dim as he seems."

"Dim?"

"Dull. Slow."

"Ah, no — he did not seem like that to me. On the contrary."

"Yes, he's a sly dog, is Hackett." He was watching the waiter weaving towards them among the tables, bearing aloft a tray with two glasses on it.

"I thought at first that *you* must be the detective from the city," she said, "and that he was — I don't know. Someone local, maybe, down there. I do not know much about Kildare, although we have been at Brooklands for many years."

The waiter set down their glasses. Twin stars of light from some far window glowed in their straw-coloured depths. Quirke did not pick up the glass, but began counting to ten, slowly, in his head.

"He's not very adept on the social side of things," he said, "which is why, I think, he brings me with him." He had been thinking of the wine and not of what he was saying. Now he caught her eye and felt his forehead redden. "Not that I'm so very sophisticated." He lifted his glass. He noted the faint tremor in his hand. He drank. Ah!

"Do you believe as he does," Françoise d'Aubigny was saying, "— I mean, that my husband did not kill himself?"

Quirke, turning the stem of the glass in his fingers, was trying not to smile for simple happiness. The euphoria that blossomed as the alcohol spread its filaments through him, like the roots of a burning bush, was irresistible. He must be careful now, he told himself, he must watch his words. "Mrs Jewell," he said, "I think it is beyond question that your husband was murdered."

She blinked, and he saw her swallowing. "What did you find," she said, "when you — when you did whatever it is you do?"

"The post-mortem, you mean? It was hardly more than a formality. You saw how it was at the scene that day, the way your husband was lying across the desk, with the shotgun in his hands."

"Yes?"

She waited, watching him, and he shifted his weight uneasily on the chair. Surely she could not be in doubt, surely she was just clutching at the hope that — that what? Would she really think it preferable that he should have killed himself?

"This is very difficult to talk about, Mrs Jewell."

Her look hardened. "Difficult for you, or for me?"

"For you, of course, but for me, also."

They were silent, she with her black-eyed gaze fixed on him and he casting about uncomfortably. She had not tasted her salad, or the wine.

"Mrs Jewell," he said, hunching forward over the table with the air of starting again to explain in still simpler terms something that was already obvious, "it's not easy to kill yourself with a shotgun. Think of the length of the barrel, and the awkwardness of getting the gun in position. Certainly your husband couldn't have done it and ended up with the gun held across his chest. As you saw, it was —"

"What did I see?" she snapped, and the couple at the next table stopped in the midst of their conversation and looked at her, startled. "What do you think I saw? My husband lying there in that terrible way — what was I supposed to do, take a note of everything, as if I were someone like you?" Her eyes were fairly glittering.

70

"Do you think I am a monster entirely, that I have no feelings, that I am incapable of being shocked?"

"Of course not —"

"Then please do not speak to me like that, as if you were discussing the matter with your Inspector Hackett."

She stopped, and they both looked down into their wine glasses, hers still full and his nearly empty.

"Please forgive me, Mrs Jewell," he said. "You asked me what I had found, and I tried to explain."

"Yes yes yes," she said, her voice hissing, "of course. I am the one who should say I am sorry." She gave an apologetic shrug and forced the flicker of a smile. "Please, go on."

He opened his hands to show her how empty they were. "What else is there for me to say? Your husband did not kill himself, Mrs Jewell. Inspector Hackett told you that already, and he's right. This was a murder. I'm sorry."

She gazed at him for a long moment, a tiny vein twitching at the side of her chin, then snatched up her glass and drank off half of the wine in one draught. Now it was her hand that was trembling. "What am I to do, Doctor Quirke?" she asked. "Tell me, what am I to do? My life seems suddenly shattered. I cannot pretend that Richard and I were — that we were in the first flush of love, as they say. But he was my husband, he was Giselle's father. And now we are without him."

Her eyes were shining and he was afraid that she was going to weep. His mind squirmed in helplessness. How was he to tell her what to do, how to live? His own life was a mystery to him, an insoluble mystery; how was he to know about the lives of others?

"Have you heard," she said, "of a man called Sumner, Carlton Sumner?"

"Yes, of course. I know of him." He felt his heartbeat slowing.

"You should talk to him. Inspector Hackett should interview him."

"Why?"

She looked about the room, frowning, as if in urgent search of something. "If my husband had enemies — and surely he had — Carlton Sumner was the chief of them."

Everything had slowed down now, along with his heartbeat, and he had a sense of being suspended in some heavy but marvellously transparent, sustaining substance. "Are you saying," he said, "that you think Carlton Sumner may have had something to do with your husband's death?"

She gave her head a quick impatient shake. "I cannot say. But I think that you should know — that your detective friend should know — how things were between that man and my husband."

He looked at the omelette half eaten on his plate, at the single remaining drop of wine glinting in the bottom of his glass. He put his hands to the armrests of his chair and pushed himself to his feet. "Excuse me," he said, "I must —" He walked quickly away from the table and out to the lobby. Where was the lavatory? He saw the sign and headed towards it. Two clergymen, a vicar and what must be his bishop, were conferring by a potted palm. A bellboy in his jaunty little hat caught Quirke's eye and for some reason grinned, and winked. Quirke pushed through the swing-door into the Gents. The place was empty. He went and stood in front of the big mirror behind the handbasins and gazed for some moments steadily into his own eyes, until the look in them, which seemed not to originate in him, made him flinch and turn aside. The dribble of a faulty cistern seemed the sound of the thing talking to itself.

He took a deep breath, then another, hardly noticing the fetid air that he was drawing in. Then he washed his hands and dried them with the towel, risked another glance at himself in the glass, and walked out to the lobby again. At the door of the dining room he paused for a second to look across to where Françoise d'Aubigny sat. She was lighting a cigarette; he thought, with dull inconsequence, that he must ask Phoebe if it was she who had sold her that hat. He took another deep breath, pressing a hand briefly to his breastbone, then made his way forward between the tables. Françoise d'Aubigny looked up at him, blowing cigarette smoke sideways.

"Are you all right?" she asked.

"Yes." He sat down. "I shouldn't drink wine."

"Oh?"

He did not feel like elaborating on that topic, even as an evasion tactic. "Sumner and your husband," he said, "were they in business together?" His voice in his own ears sounded thin and wispy.

Françoise d'Aubigny was leaning forward with her elbows on the table and the cigarette held aloft to one side. Her lipstick was a deep and almost violent shade of scarlet. She still had not touched her salad, and the lettuce had already begun to wilt. "Carlton Sumner," she said, "was trying to *take* my husband's business."

"You mean, he was trying to move in on his market, or —?"

"He was trying to take the business over. He wanted — wants — especially the *Clarion*. He bought some shares in it secretly."

"How many?"

"I do not know — I cannot remember. Very many, I think. Richard was worried. I believe he was afraid of Sumner." One corner of her mouth lifted in a faint ironic smile. "There were not many people Richard was afraid of, Doctor Quirke."

"No," Quirke said, "I don't imagine there were." He lit one of his own cigarettes. He wanted another glass of wine. "So Sumner was making an attempt to take over?"

"I think so. There was a meeting at Sumner's house in the country. Something went wrong, and Richard left."

"Why?"

"I do not know. Richard did not speak to me of these things." Her eyes narrowed and she tilted her head an inch to one side. "You know about this, don't you, about the argument, and Richard walking out?"

"Do I?"

"I can see it in your face."

He signalled to the waiter, and held up his empty glass and waggled it. "My assistant, at the hospital, knows your sister-in-law."

74

She drew back a little, frowning. "Dannie? She has been treated, at your hospital?"

"No, no. He knows her socially. They met at college." It occurred to him to wonder how they had met, for Sinclair was surely two or three years older than Dannie Jewell. Was Sinclair one of those opportunists who prey on younger women in their starting year? "They play tennis together."

"Yes, Dannie is a good player," she murmured; it was apparent she was thinking of something else. "What is his name, your assistant?"

"Sinclair." He paused. "He's a Jew."

"Oh, yes?" she said vaguely. The information did not interest her; indeed, he was not sure that she had properly registered it. "Poor Dannie," she said, frowning into space, "this has been very hard for her, this death."

His second glass of wine arrived. This time he counted to twenty, but counted faster than before.

"Tell me about the war," he said. She blinked, momentarily baffled. "You said your brother was killed."

"Ah. Yes." She turned her face aside briefly. "They took him to Breendonk — it was a camp, a prison fortress, in Belgium."

"Because he was a Jew?"

She stared. "What? No, no, he was not a Jew." Her face cleared. "Ah, I see. You thought —" She broke off and laughed; it seemed to him it was the first time he had heard her laugh. "We are not Jews. What an idea!"

She laughed again, shaking her head. "My father was a great Jew-hater."

"And yet . . ."

". . . And yet I married a Jew, yes?" She nodded, her smile turning bitter. "That was the greatest crime I could have committed. My father — what do you say? — disowned me. I was no longer his daughter, he said. That was a pity, really. He had liked Richard, before he found out that he was Jewish. They are — were — very alike, in so many ways. I did not attend his funeral. I regret that, now. It's why I could not bring myself to insist that Giselle should be there when Richard was buried. I understood."

They were silent. Quirke drank his wine. He should have eaten more of the omelette, it would have helped with the alcohol, but the eggs were cold now, and were developing a sheen, like sweat. It was always the way with him: drink soured his appetite and made him bilious, though it sang so sweetly in his veins. "Your brother," he said, "what happened to him?"

She was lighting another cigarette. Her hand was steady now, he noted. "We never heard from him again," she said, "nothing. Probably he was taken to the east. I do not know which was the greater sorrow for my father, that his son had died, or that he had died among the Jews." She glanced at Quirke and away again swiftly. "I'm sorry," she murmured, "I should not say such a thing. My father could not help being what he was, after all. None of us can help what we are."

They let some moments pass in silence, a mark of respect, of sorts, for the dead, it might be, the father as well as the son. Then Françoise d'Aubigny stirred herself, and stubbed out her cigarette in the glass ashtray on the table. "I think I should go now," she said. Quirke signalled to the waiter again. The woman was watching him, weighing something up. "Will you speak to the inspector about Carlton Sumner?" she asked.

Quirke did not look at her. "Yes, I'll mention it. Be warned, he may need to ask you questions — Hackett, I mean."

She shrugged, but he could see she was not as unconcerned as she pretended. "If my husband was murdered," she said, "then someone did it. We must find out who it was" — she arched an eyebrow, seeking his assent — "must we not?"

The day was blindingly bright when they came out of the hotel, and the glare reflected from the roofs and windows of the passing cars made them squint. They said goodbye on the pavement.

"Thank you for lunch," she said. "It was very pleasant."

"You didn't eat anything."

"Did I not? I hardly notice, these days." Once more she offered him briefly her cool soft hand. "*Au revoir*, Doctor Quirke. We shall meet again, I hope."

He watched her as she walked away in the direction of Nassau Street. She moved quickly but without haste, taking rapid deft steps, with her head bent, looking down, as if scanning the ground for any small obstacle that might rise up in her way. He turned and set off in the opposite direction, not thinking where he was going, not caring.

At the junction of Molesworth Street a warm breeze assailed him, and would have swept off his hat had he not held on to it; the brim flapped and snapped like a duck's bill, and he grinned to himself blearily. The alcohol in his blood — not enough, not nearly enough — was dispersing already, and he clung on in faint and happy desperation to the last of its effect. In Stephen's Green the trees, dusted all over with sunlight, seemed dazed from the heat, their foliage polished and of such a dark-green hue it was almost black. He had a vision suddenly of summer itself, off behind the sticky heat and noise and grime, going blithely about its blue and gold business as always, and at just that moment the awful thought came to him that he had fallen in love. He hoped it was the wine.

CHAPTER
FOUR

But it was not the wine, and in the days following that lunch with Françoise d'Aubigny Quirke's increasingly agitated spirit led him helplessly on into ever deeper excesses of amorous folly. He felt like a stony-hearted old *roué* embarrassingly shackled to a lovesick youth. It was foolish to be like this, at his age. As if the woman herself were too daunting for him to think of directly, he fixed on oblique aspects of her, in the same way that when he was an adolescent and encountered in the street a girl he was sweet on he would look anywhere but at her. France, now, not just France the country but France the idea, suddenly loomed large for him, as if he had been running a magnifying glass idly over a map of the world and had come to a wobbly stop on that big, ghost-shaped mass at the western edge of Europe. He had only to take a sip of claret and he was there, in a Midi of the mind, under dappled vine leaves, smelling the dust and the garlic, or in some sultry *impasse* beside the Seine, with swaggering pigeons and water sluicing cleanly along the cobbled gutters, half the street in purple shadow and the other half blinded by sunlight.

He sidled into Fox's opposite Trinity College and bought a packet of Gauloise, and took it home and sat dreamily smoking by the wide-open window above Mount Street as the evening sky turned yellow along its edge, and the early prostitutes came tottering out on the broad pavements below. He found a newsagent that carried day-old copies of *Le Monde* and bought them up and with his few scraps of French picked his way through reports on the *guerre d'Algérie* and next month's Tour de France. He had not felt like this since the long-ago days when he was courting Delia, and now he was appalled at himself, shame-faced and embarrassed and yet ridiculously happy, all at the same time. He seemed to float through his days in a state of stupefied bliss, all obstacles parting magically before him like weightless water.

They had made no plan to meet again, he and Françoise, but it did not matter, he knew they would meet, that the fates would arrange it. The fates would arrange everything; there was nothing he need do but wait. And all the time, while that young Lothario gambolled in the meadows of his fancy, plucking nosegays and ecstatically calling out his beloved's name, in another, unenchanted, part of his mind, the old dog that he really was shuddered in dismay at the thought of the violent and bloody circumstance that had led him to this love.

On one of those romance-tinted evenings — that apricot sky, those drifting copper clouds! — he arrived home to find Jimmy Minor sitting on the steps outside his front door. Minor was absurdly well named for he was a tiny fellow, with thin red hair that came to a widow's peak and a pinched little bloodless face blotched all over with big, shapeless freckles. He wore faded corduroy trousers and a tweed sports jacket and a tightly knotted narrow green tie that had the look of a wilted vegetable. He was smoking a cigarette with grim distaste, as if it were a task he had been unfairly assigned but which he must not shirk.

Quirke was not surprised: he had been waiting for Minor to come calling. "I hear you're on the *Clarion* now," he said, stopping on the steps while the young man got to his feet. "Didn't think that would be your kind of paper."

"It's a living," Minor answered defensively, and showed for a second a tobacco-stained canine.

Quirke had his key in the lock. "A friend of mine used to say of the *Clarion* that it was all horses and dead priests. I imagine that was in the respectable old days, before the Jewells took over and turned it into a scandal-sheet."

Minor sighed; no doubt this was not the first taunt his new job had elicited. "Some things are easier to attack than others," he said. "I suppose you read the *Irish Times* — sorry, I suppose you 'take' the *Times*."

Quirke, stepping into the hallway, shook his head. "If I take anything I take the *Indo*."

"No shortage of dead priests and horses there."

"Not that I think much of it, mind. I read it for the court cases."

"You like a bit of genteel smut, then."

Quirke blandly smiled. "Come on up," he said, "I need to change out of this suit."

In the flat the air was heavy and stale — he had forgotten to leave a window open. He opened one now, letting down the sash as far as it would go. The sky had turned a deep rose along its edge, with higher bands of orange and creamy white; the little clouds were gone. And there was Venus, dotting the *i* of the Pepper Canister's spire with a spike of greenish ice. "Cup of tea?" Quirke said over his shoulder. "Or shall we go up to the pub?"

"I thought you needed to change."

"I will, in a minute."

Minor was at the bookcase, scanning the titles with his little sharp head thrown back. He had a new cigarette going. "You know why I'm here, of course," he said, in a studiedly distracted tone, still eyeing the books. "I see you like poetry. Lot of Yeats." He turned his head. "He your man, is he, Yeats?" He assumed a chanting voice in imitation of the poet in full resonant flow. "*The fury and the mire of human veins.*"

Quirke gave no reply to that. "How is the *Clarion* managing, without its head?" he asked.

Minor snickered. "Without its head, eh? You're a great man for the gallows humour. Goes with the job, I suppose." He took down a book and flicked through it. Quirke watched the tip of Minor's cigarette, afraid he might spill burning ash on the page. It was a first edition of Yeats's *The Tower*, a thing he treasured. "The headless *Clarion* sounds on its exquisite note," Minor said, his eye still on the page. "Like Orpheus."

Quirke thought he was quoting from the book in his hand but then realised his mistake. "The other way round," he said.

"Hmm?"

"Orpheus ended up only a head, after the maenads had torn the rest of him to pieces."

"Ah. I bow to your superior education, Doctor Quirke."

Now it was Quirke's turn to sigh. He was suddenly bored. He took no pleasure in trading leaden banter with this sour little man. He suspected he had invited him in only because it might give him the opportunity to talk about Françoise d'Aubigny. "I hear you wrote the report on Richard Jewell's death," he said. "No byline, though." He lit a Gauloise. "You know, for days after Stalin died, none of his gang of toadies could work up the nerve to announce the news to the great Soviet public. As if the old monster might come back and liquidate them."

Minor put the book back on the shelf. Quirke grudgingly noted with what delicacy he had handled the volume, and how careful he was to fit it snugly into its original place.

"It wasn't the kind of story that needs a byline," Minor said mildly. "Your pal Hackett of the Yard wasn't giving much away. I take it Jewell's death wasn't suicide?"

"You do?"

"And it could hardly have been an accident."

"Hardly."

Minor came to the window and the two men stood side by side looking out.

"There are a lot of people glad to see Dick Jewell dead," he said.

"I'm sure there are."

"I hear even his widow isn't acting as if she's exactly grief-stricken."

"I think that marriage came to an end a long time ago."

"Is that right?"

"They seem to have led separate lives."

Minor shrugged. "I wouldn't know about that."

"She implied as much."

"Oh, yes?"

"— When we met." It was annoying, but Minor seemed hardly to be listening. "We had lunch, at the Hibernian. A few days after — after the body was found."

Minor was frowning now. "You had lunch with Jewell's wife?"

"Yes." Quirke realised he was sweating lightly. It was dangerous, talking to Minor like this — who knew where it might lead to? And yet he could not stop. It was as if he were clinging by his fingertips to a merry-go-round that was going out of control, spinning faster and faster. "She phoned me up. She wanted to talk."

"About what?" Minor stared, incredulous. "About her husband's *death*?"

Quirke went to the mantelpiece and pretended to be straightening a framed photograph hanging on the wall there. Atget, *Versailles, Vénus par Legros*. The marble statue's poised yet faintly suffering look. Like hers. His mind ran on, gabbling to itself. He felt vaguely unwell, as if he had a chill coming on. *La grippe*. The fevers of love. Absurd, absurd. He turned back to the little man at the window. "How would she not? — talk about him, I mean. About it."

"And what did she say?"

What *did* she say? He could hardly remember, except the one thing, of course. "She mentioned Carlton Sumner."

"Did she, now. And what did she mention about him?"

"That he and her husband had quarrelled at a business meeting at Sumner's place in Wicklow. That her husband had walked out. Know anything about that?"

"Only the rumours. Sumner was making a takeover bid for the papers, Jewell wasn't having it, they had a scrap — what's so remarkable about that? Business is warfare by other means."

"Yes, and people in warfare get killed."

"And you think they don't in business? —" He stopped. They had turned from the window and were facing each other now. Minor was smoking yet another cigarette — how did he do it? They appeared as if conjured straight from the packet already lit. "Are you suggesting what I think you're suggesting?" he asked, with almost a laugh. "That Carlton Sumner —?"

"Let me get changed," Quirke said.

The last of the long evening's sunlight was in the bedroom, a big gold contraption falling down slantways from the window. Quirke stood and took a deep breath, then another. He took off his suit and hung it in the wardrobe — the jacket smelt of stale sweat — and put on a pair of grey slacks that were too tight for him, and found a pale-blue cashmere jumper he did not know he owned, and put that on, too. Then he caught his reflection in the wardrobe mirror, gaudy in pastel shades. He peeled off the jumper and the trousers and put on a pair of khaki bags and an old tweed jacket.

They went up to Baggot Street, to Toner's. It was not crowded. The dreamy bluish summer dusk seemed to penetrate the smoky atmosphere, subduing further what little talk there was. At the bar Quirke sat on a wooden stool while Minor stood, so that they were almost at eye-level. Minor, smoking of course, had one hand in a pocket of his trousers, jingling coins. Quirke thought it advisable not to drink, and asked for tomato juice. Minor ordered a pint of stout, which somehow, when he lifted the big glass to his beaked lips, made him look all the more like a cocky and prematurely aged schoolboy.

"So," he said, wiping his mouth with the back of his hand, "you think Carlton Sumner did in Diamond Dick." He gave a whinnying laugh.

Quirke considered this not worth replying to. "How serious was the takeover bid?" he asked.

"Very serious, so I hear. Sumner owns twenty-nine per cent of Jewell Holdings. That's a lot of shares, and a lot of clout."

"He'll renew the bid, now."

"Maybe not. They say he's lost interest. You know what these big boys are like — they don't hang about at the scene of a defeat. Anyway, what good would it do him to have Dick Jewell done in?"

"Revenge, maybe?"

Minor shook his head. "It doesn't make sense."

"No, it doesn't."

"What does Hackett think?"

"Who ever knows what Hackett thinks?"

They drank their drinks in silence for a while. "What else did she say, the wife — the widow?" Minor enquired.

"She has a daughter, nine years old. She's worried about her. Hard, at that age, losing a father."

"She's French, right, the wife?"

"Françoise d'Aubigny."

"Eh?" Minor gave him a keen look, catching something in his tone, perhaps, an unwarranted warmth. Quirke toyed with his tomato juice.

"She goes by her maiden name," he said. "Françoise d'Aubigny."

"Does she, indeed." He grinned. "Is that what she told you, over the oysters and the vichyssoise at the Hibernian? That must have been a cosy occasion." Minor took a professional pride in going too far. He licked his lips, still grinning. "She'll be quite the heiress, I imagine."

"Do you?"

Minor wore for a second a thin moustache of creamy froth that once again he wiped away with the back of that dainty little freckled hand. "There's a trust,

87

apparently. I don't think she — the wife — I don't think she has any interest in taking it on. She'll probably settle for cash and move back to France. By all accounts she doesn't exactly love it here. They have a place in the south somewhere — Nice, I think, or thereabouts." He peered at Quirke closely. "You seem to have been impressed by her. A looker, is she? Heh heh." Quirke said nothing. "Very strange," Minor went on, "her phoning you up to have lunch and her husband hardly cold in his grave. The French certainly are different."

Still Quirke would not respond. He was sorry now he had not left Minor sitting outside the front door, had not simply stepped over him and gone on about his day, instead of letting him in and giving him the opportunity to talk about Françoise d'Aubigny like this, as if he were running those clammy little hands of his all over her.

A large florid man in a dingy black suit who was passing by stopped and said to Minor, "Jesus, Jimmy, where have you been keeping yourself?" The man leered, swaying; he was blearily, shinily, drunk. The two conversed for a minute in tones of raillery, then the florid man staggered away. Minor had not introduced him to Quirke, and Quirke had not expected that he would. Quirke thought, *This city of passing strangers*. He remembered that he had been supposed to call Isabel Galloway after work and before she went on stage — she was in *Saint Joan* and tonight was the first preview. He felt guiltily in his pocket for pennies and glanced towards the phone booth, a little cabin with a door varnished in a gaudy wood-grain effect and a circular window like a port-hole.

"Is that all she said about Sumner," Minor asked, "that there had been a row in Wicklow?"

Quirke drained the watery pink dregs of the tomato juice. "Have you got something on this?"

"On what?"

"Jewell's death, the row with Sumner. *You* came to see *me*, remember."

"I was hoping *you'd* know something. You usually do. Hackett talks to you, he's your" — he smiled unpleasantly — "your special pal."

Quirke batted aside the gibe. "Hackett is as puzzled as the rest of us," he said. "Why don't *you* go and talk to Carlton Sumner?"

"He won't see me. His people say he doesn't talk to the press. Doesn't need to, I suppose."

Quirke was developing a headache; it set up a beat behind his forehead like that of a small tight drum. He needed a drink, a proper drink, but he did not dare to order one. He stood up from the stool. "I've got to go," he said.

"I'll walk along with you."

The night was mild and soft. Above Baggot Street a haze of stars looked like the bed of a river silted with silver.

"How is Phoebe?" Minor asked. "I haven't seen her for a while."

"She's fine. She moved."

"Where is she now?"

"Up the street there, beyond the bridge. She has what she calls a bed-sitting room." Quirke had often wondered about Minor and his daughter. He presumed they were and always had been no more than friends, but he could not be sure. Phoebe had her secrets. He wondered if Sinclair had called her, after that disastrous dinner at Jammet's. He hoped he had. The thought of Sinclair wooing Phoebe was a spot of warm potential at the back of Quirke's mind.

"The yard manager, Maguire," Minor said. "You know he served a spell in Mountjoy."

Quirke took a second to absorb this. "Maguire?"

"He's the manager at Brooklands — Jewell's place."

"What do you mean, a spell?"

"Three years. Manslaughter."

Sinclair did telephone Phoebe. He invited her to the pictures. They went to *The Searchers*, starring John Wayne, at the Savoy. This second of their meetings was hardly more successful than the dinner at Jammet's had been. The film seemed to irritate Phoebe. As they walked along O'Connell Street afterwards she talked about it dismissively. She did not like John Wayne, she said, he was effeminate — "that *walk*" — despite all his tough-guy posing; really, he was nothing but a phoney. And Natalie Wood, playing the girl who had been stolen by the Comanches — those braids, and that ridiculous shiny mahogany-brown makeup!

Sinclair listened to these complaints in silence. Her vehemence was disproportionate to the topic. Phoebe was a far stranger creature than he had at first imagined. He sensed a darkness in her, he even pictured it, a circular gleaming black pool, as at the bottom of a deep well, perfectly still except for now and then when the surface shivered for a moment in response to some far quake or crack and sent off a flash of cold light. She was really not his type. Usually he liked dim girls, not brainy but with plenty of spirit, raucous and bouncy girls who would pretend to fight him off as he steered them backwards towards a sofa or, on rare occasions, a bed, but then with a gurgle of laughter would give in. He could not imagine making that kind of rough advance to Phoebe, could not imagine making any kind of advance at all. She was thin, too, so very thin. When they were taking their seats in the cinema and his hand accidentally brushed against hers he had been shocked by the chill boniness of it, and despite himself he had been reminded of the dissecting room. Why was he there with her? What was it he wanted, or expected? Where Phoebe Griffin was concerned, he did not understand himself.

To his surprise she asked him if he would like to come back to her place for coffee. The invitation was issued so unaffectedly and with such directness that he said yes straight off, without thinking. Almost immediately, however, he began to have doubts. It was as if they were children and she had asked him to come and play house with her, but they were not children, and the kind of play he might join her in would not be childish. This was his boss's daughter. Yet it was Quirke who had invited him to dinner to meet Phoebe, and what was he to think that was, if not an encouragement to . . . to what? He did not know. This was all very puzzling. What did Quirke expect of him? What did Phoebe expect of him? — what did he expect of himself? And why, anyway, had he phoned her in the first place? As he walked along beside her, the two of them silent now, he saw himself a little like a condemned man walking towards his fate.

They were silent on the bus, too. Before he could fumble the money from his pocket Phoebe had paid for both of their tickets. She folded the slips of paper and pressed them into his hand, smiling complicitly, as if it were a secret code she was entrusting to him. They sat on the top deck and watched the glimmering streets going past. Although it was only ten thirty and still warm there was no one about, for the pubs had not shut yet. The trees in Merrion Square were darkly massed, their upper leaves splashed garishly with lamp-light at fixed intervals. Sinclair disliked the night-time, always had, since a child; it gave him an obscure sense of desolation. He thought with longing of his own place: the armchair by the window, the curtains drawn, the record-player waiting to be turned on.

Phoebe reached up and pulled the cord and they heard the ping of the bell downstairs in the driver's cab.

Her room was well proportioned, with a high ceiling and a picture-rail that ran all the way round the walls, but it was very small to be living room, bedroom and kitchen all in one. While she brewed the coffee he walked about with circumspection, looking at her things, trying to seem interested but not inquisitive.

92

There was a photo in a silver frame on the mantelpiece of Quirke as a young man, with a young woman on his arm — his long-dead wife, no doubt.

"Their wedding day," Phoebe said from across the room, making him start. She came and brought him his cup, and together they stood looking at the picture of the happy couple. "Her name was Delia," Phoebe said. "Isn't she beautiful, even in that quaint outfit? I never knew her — she died having me." She gave him an oddly impish glance. "So imagine my life of guilt," she said, in a film star's drawl. He did not know what to say to that.

There was only one chair, beside the fireplace, and she made him take it, while she went and sat on the bed. There were cardboard boxes on the floor; he remembered Quirke saying that she had recently moved. He drank his coffee. It was too strong, and had a scorched, bitter taste; it was bound to keep him awake for hours.

"Do you like my father?" Phoebe asked. He stared at her, widening his eyes. She was sitting on the bed with her legs folded under her and her back resting against the wall. She wore a dark dress with a white collar — was it the same one she had worn that other night, at Jammet's? Her hair gleamed in the lamp-light, blue-black, like a crow's wing. She was very pale. "Sorry," she said, and gave a little laugh. "I suppose that's not the kind of thing one should ask. But do you?"

"I don't know that it's a matter of liking," he said carefully.

"He walks a bit like John Wayne, have you noticed that?"

"Does he?" He laughed. "Yes, I suppose he does, a little. Maybe all big men walk like that."

"What's he like to work with?"

He had the distinct impression that these questions were not about her father at all, but about him.

"He's very professional. And we work well together, I think." He paused. "Does *he* like *me*?"

"Oh," she said gaily, "we don't talk about such things."

He did not smile. "What things *do* you talk about?" Few, he supposed, knowing Quirke.

She considered, tilting her head, bird-like, to one side. "Well, he does talk to me about the work itself. This latest business, for instance — that man Jewell, who was shot." She was silent for a moment, looking into her cup. "He tells me you know his daughter — no, his sister, is it?"

"Yes, Denise — Dannie, she's called. I've known her since college."

"Do you know her well?"

He hesitated. That question again, the same one Quirke had asked him. "We play tennis together now and then," he said.

"Hmm." She studied him with a closer intent. "I'm sure," she said, "you'd be a good friend to have." She uncurled herself from the bed and went to the little stove in the corner and poured more coffee for herself. She turned to him and lifted the percolator enquiringly but he shook his head. She went back and crawled on to the bed and composed herself as before.

94

He wondered if he might risk a cigarette, and as if she had read his thoughts she said, "You can smoke if you like. There's an ashtray on the mantelpiece." She watched him fetch out his cigarettes and light one, and then stand up to take the ashtray and set it on the floor beside his chair. "What's it like, being a Jew?" she asked.

Again he stared, expelling a surprised quick stream of smoke. It was a question he had never been asked before, a question he had never expected to be asked. He gave a brief helpless laugh. "I don't think I do think about it. I mean, you don't think about what you are, do you?"

"But *I* don't think I am anything, you see. I'm just like everybody else, here. But you — you have an identity, a race."

"It's not really a race."

She waved an impatient hand. "I know, I know," she said. "I know all about that, the Semitic peoples, and so on. But the fact is, you are a Jew, a member of a tiny, a *tiny*, minority. That must feel like something — I mean you must be aware of it, part of the time, at least."

He saw what it was. Despite what she claimed she did not think she was like everybody else, not at all; she thought she was like him, or what she took him to be, an outsider, an outcast, even, a paleface among the Comanches.

"My people weren't religious," he said, "and if you're not at least a little bit religious then you're not really a Jew."

"But in the war, you must have been — you must have felt . . .?"

He set his cup, which still had coffee in it, on the floor beside the ashtray. "I'll tell you a story," he said. "The war was ending, and the news of the concentration camps was starting to come out. It was Easter-time, when the Catholic Church collects a yearly offering from parishioners, you know? One dark night there was a knock at our front door and my mother sent me to answer it. There, on the threshold, was the biggest, reddest-faced priest I had ever seen, a real clodhopper, his neck bulging over his collar and his little pig-eyes popping. He looked down at me along the length of his soutane, and in the thickest Cork accent you can imagine said, '*I'm here for the Jews!*' " She put her head to the side again, frowning uncertainly. "The *dues*, he meant," Sinclair said, "the Easter dues, only a Cork *d* always comes out as a *j*."

"What did you do?" she asked, laughing now. "— What did you say?"

"I shut the door in his face and ran into the kitchen and told my mother it was a travelling salesman selling Bibles."

"Were you frightened?"

"I suppose so. They were always frightening in those days, priests and so on — anyone official from *their* world."

She pounced. "You see?" she said, triumphant. "*Their* world. You did feel different."

"Every child feels different, Jew or otherwise."

"Only children?"

"What do you mean?"

"*I* feel different, always will. I suppose you'll think that's vanity, but it's not. Can I have a cigarette?"

He rose quickly from the chair, reaching into his pocket for the packet of Gold Flake. "I'm sorry," he said awkwardly, his dark brow turning darker. "I didn't think you smoked."

"I don't. I used to, but I've given up."

She took a cigarette, and he snapped open his lighter and she leaned forward to the flame and touched a fingertip briefly to the back of his hand for balance. Behind the smoke he caught a faint breath of her perfume. She looked up at him, her eyelashes moving.

He was suddenly aware of the night all around them, vast and still. "I should go soon," he said.

She leaned back, and folded one arm and cupped her palm under the elbow of the other. She picked a fleck of tobacco from her lower lip. He backed away, turned, walked to the armchair by the fireplace and sat. "If I didn't know better," she said, in almost a conversational tone, "I'd say you were a little frightened of me."

He gazed at her owlishly, then suddenly laughed. "Well, of course I am," he said. "What man isn't frightened when a girl gets him into her room?"

"Isn't it supposed to be the other way about?"

"Of course," he said, "but it never is, really, as you know. We're the weaker sex, after all."

"Yes," she said, pleased, "you are. Aren't you?"

And so they sat for a long moment fairly beaming at each other, neither of them knowing what exactly had happened between them just now, but certain that something had.

CHAPTER
FIVE

What the fates arranged, or what the fates in the form of Françoise d'Aubigny herself arranged, was, of all things, a party. She did not call it that: on the little gilt-edged invitation card it said *Memorial Drinks*, which to Quirke's ear had an almost comical ring. The event was to be at five in the afternoon at Jewell's — now Françoise d'Aubigny's — townhouse at the top of St Stephen's Green. It was a very grand house, with a big gravelled Japanese garden at the back, and here the guests were gathered. No one had known quite what to wear to such a bizarre occasion. The men were properly sober-suited, but the women had been forced to improvise, and there was a great deal of black silk on show, and many black feathers in night-blue toques, and one or two of the more mature ladies wore elbow-length black cotton gloves. Waiters in frock-coats and white ties moved among the crowd bearing aloft silver trays of champagne in crystal flutes; a trestle table, covered with a blindingly white tablecloth, offered canapés and bowls of olives and pickled onions and, at its centre, a mighty salmon, succulently, indecently, pink, arranged on a nickel salver and dotted all over with dabs of mayonnaise and a glistening beady

without distraction, those moments he and Françoise d'Aubigny had shared beside the trestle table with its coy little bowls of glistening savouries and its shameless salmon. There was an ancient judge who had known his adoptive father whom he had to stop and listen to for a painful five minutes — the old boy was deaf, and spoke in bellowing tones as if everyone else shared his disability — and an Abbey actress who gave him a playfully reproving eye and enquired, in a voice dripping with saccharine sweetness, why Isabel Galloway was not with him. Now and then, when a gap opened among the gabbling heads, he had a tantalising glimpse of Françoise — in his mind he had at last been able to drop the formality of the surname — but manoeuvre his way as he might through the crowd he somehow could not manage to put himself directly in her vicinity. He drank a third glass of champagne, and then took a fourth, and stepped through the french windows with it and wandered into the house.

He entered a big modern kitchen, where he was ignored by the hired-in catering staff, busy at their work, and then a long passageway that in stages, through two successive green-baize doors, widened to become the front hall. This part of the house seemed deserted. He noted paintings — a couple of insipid Paul Henrys and a dubious oil portrait of a prissy fellow in a periwig — and an antique oak side table with, over it, a big gilt-framed mirror that leaned out at an angle from the wall and gave an impression of vigilance and faint menace. To right and left two tall white doors faced each other. The one on the right, to his vague surprise, was locked. The other opened on to a square high-ceilinged drawing room ablaze with early-evening sunlight. He stepped inside.

Here there were two enormous windows that looked across the road to the Green and its trees, and the light pouring in through them had a leafy verdant tinge. A big old grandfather clock with a ponderous and hesitant tick stood against one wall. On a sideboard there rested a bowl of glowing yellow roses. He went and stood at one of the windows; lifting his face, he bathed in the sky's calm soft radiance. The champagne had set up a mild and not unpleasant buzzing in his head. *Disenchanted*, she had said. Yes, it was a beautiful word, and yes, it carried a weight of sadness, but there was something hard in it, too, hard and unyielding. He pondered the dark fact that it was due to a violent death that he was here, tipsy on the dead man's champagne and overflowing at the brim with infatuation for that man's enchanting and dangerous widow. He knew the perils of the situation he had blundered into, and he accepted them, more than accepted them — what was passion without risk, without transgression? Although he knew himself guilty of many unforgivable lies and evasions in his life, he had never tried to hide from himself his taste for the hazard of sin. And that was what Françoise d'Aubigny represented for him now.

He began to notice a faintly uncomfortable sensation in the back of his head. He turned. A slight, pale, plain little girl with a long narrow face and circular steel-framed spectacles was regarding him from an armchair by the fireplace. The chair was expensively upholstered in yellow silk with a subtle fleur-de-lis pattern, and yellow too, or gold, rather, was the girl's dress, an unsuitably formal gown with bows and flounces suggestive of the eighteenth century, which made her look like a grown-up woman viewed from the wrong, too distant perspective. Her hair was done in two heavy black braids tied at the ends with gold ribbon that matched her dress. She seemed quite composed, and her gaze was direct and unblinking, and he felt, standing there in the suddenly hard-edged, green-tinged light, like a specimen set up and arranged specifically for her scrutiny.

"Hello," he said, his voice sounding unnaturally loud under the lofty ceiling.

The girl did not respond at once, but continued examining him, the lenses of her glasses two rounds of opaque light. At last she spoke. "Are you one of Daddy's people," she asked, "or are you a friend of Maman?"

He found it peculiarly difficult to devise a satisfactory, or even plausible, answer to this perfectly reasonable question. "Well, I don't think I'm either," he said. "I only spoke to your father once, some time ago, although I've met your mother a number of times."

He frowned, and saw her absorbing this; it was obvious she considered his reply to be as unsatisfactory as he did. "Are you a detective?" she asked. She had the faintest, lisping trace of an accent.

"No," he said, laughing, "no, I'm a — I'm a sort of doctor. And you must be Giselle, yes?"

"Yes, of course," she said dismissively.

She had a book open on her lap, a large volume with illustrations done in muted tones.

"What are you reading?" he asked.

"*La Belle et la bête*. Maman brought it back for me from Paris."

"Ah. And you read French, do you?"

This question too she seemed to consider not worth replying to, and merely shrugged, as if to say again, *of course*.

Always in moments of social awkwardness Quirke became acutely aware of his bulk; standing there under the unblinking gaze of this small, unnerving person he felt like the lumbering giant in a fairytale. Now the child closed her book and pushed it firmly down between the cushion and the arm of her chair and stood up, smoothing the front of her gold frock. "Why aren't you at the party?" she asked.

"I was. But I came in to — to look at the house. I haven't been here before. It's a very nice house."

"Yes, it is. We have another one in the country, Brooklands — but you probably know that. And another one in France. Do you know the Côte d'Azur?"

"Not very well, I'm afraid."

"Our place is in Cap Ferrat. That's just outside Nice. Our house is on a hill above the bay at Villefranche." She frowned thoughtfully. "I like it there."

She came forward until she was standing before him. She was not small for her age yet the top of her head barely reached the level of his diaphragm. He caught her child's smell; it was like the smell of day-old bread.

Her hair was a deep, gleaming black, like her mother's. "Would you like to see my room?" she asked.

"Your room?"

"Yes. You said you came in to see the house, so you should see the upstairs, too." He tried to think of a way of declining this invitation but could not. She was a strangely compelling personage. She put her right hand in his left. "Come along," she said briskly, "this way."

She led him across the room and opened the door. She had to use both hands to turn the great brass doorknob. In the hall she took him by the hand again and together they climbed the stairs. Yes, that was what he felt like, the misunderstood ogre, monstrous and lumbering but harmless at heart.

"How did you know who I was?" she asked. "Have you seen me before?"

"No, no. But your mother told me your name and I thought you could not be anyone else."

"So you know Maman quite well, then?"

He thought about this for a moment before answering; somehow she compelled serious consideration. "No, not very well," he said. "We had lunch together."

"Oh, did you?" she said, without emphasis. "I suppose you met her when Daddy died, since you're a doctor. Did you try to save his life?"

Her hand was dry and cool and bony, and he thought of a fledgling fallen from the nest, but this a fallen fledgling that would without doubt survive. "No," he said, "I'm not that kind of doctor."

"What other kinds of doctor are there?"

She was leading him now across a broad landing spread with a Turkish rug in various shades of red from rust to blood-bright.

"Oh, all sorts," he said.

This answer she seemed to find sufficient.

Her room was absurdly large, a great square space painted white all over, with a white ceiling and a spotless white carpet and even a white cover on the small narrow bed. It was alarmingly tidy, not a toy or an article of clothing in sight, and not a single picture on the walls. It might have been the cell of a deeply devotional but incongruously well-to-do anchorite. It made Quirke shiver. The only splash of colour was in the single tall sash window opposite the door that gave on to Iveagh Gardens, a rectangle of blue and gold and lavish greens suspended in the midst of all that blank whiteness, like a painting by Douanier Rousseau. "I spend a lot of time here," the child said. "Do you like it?"

"Yes," Quirke said, lying. "Very much."

"There are not many people I invite to come up here, you know."

Quirke did his newly learned Frenchman's bow. "I'm honoured."

She gave a small sigh and said matter-of-factly, "You don't mean that."

He did not try to contradict her. They walked together to the window.

"I like to watch the people in the gardens," she said. "All sorts of people come. They walk about. Some of them have dogs, but not all. They bring picnics, sometimes. And there's an old man. I believe he lives there — I see him all the time, going along the pathways or sitting on the grass. He has a bottle in a brown-paper bag. I tried waving to him once but he couldn't see me."

She stopped. Quirke tried to think of something to say, but could not. He pictured her here, leaning at this window, silent, looking out through her big spectacles at life going by.

"Would you like to play a game?" she asked.

She was standing very close to him, looking up at him gravely, those round lenses shining and the heavy braids hanging down. She had a very immediate physical presence, or, rather, she created a strongly tangible sense of the physical, for in fact it was not her nearness that pressed in on him, he realised, but the sense of his own fleshliness, the blood-heat of himself. "What kind of game?" he asked warily.

"Any kind. What games did you play, when you were little?"

He laughed, though it did not sound to him like a laugh, but more a sort of nervous gasp. "You know," he said, "I can't remember. It's such a long time ago. What games do *you* play, with your friends?"

Something passed behind those shining lenses, a brief flash of irony and amusement that made her look much older than her years, and for the first time he saw a resemblance in her to her mother. "Oh, the usual," she said. "You know." He felt himself mocked.

She was still gazing up at him, standing with one foot resting on the instep of the other and swaying her meagre hips slightly. He could not think what might be going through her head.

"Hide-and-seek," he said, somewhat desperately, "that's one game I remember."

"Yes, Daddy and I used to play that. He was too good at it, though, and always found me, no matter where I hid."

There was a silence, in which she seemed to be waiting for some particular and marked response. The carpet under his feet might have been a sheet of creaking ice. Should he try to say something to her about her father, try to offer some comfort, or just to give her the opportunity to go on talking about him? He was an orphan, he did not know what it would be like to lose a parent suddenly and violently, yet this child's calmness and self-possession seemed to him unnatural. But then, children to him were a separate species, as unfathomable as cats, say, or swans.

"There is one thing you could do for me," she said.

"Yes?" he said, eagerly.

"There's a thing Daddy gave me that I can't find. You might look on top of that wardrobe" — she pointed — "and see if it's there. I'm sure you're tall enough."

"What kind of thing is it?"

"Just a toy. A glass globe, you know, with liquid in it, and snow."

She was watching him with a keener light now, curious, it seemed, to see what he would do, how he would respond to her request. He went to the wardrobe she had indicated — it was made of some almost white wood, birch, or ash — and ran a hand around the top outer edge of it. He felt nothing, not even dust. "There's nothing, I think," he said. "A snow-globe, you say? Is there a little town in it? —"

"It might be at the back. You haven't searched at the back."

"It's too high," he said. "I can't reach."

"Stand on this chair." She brought it to him. It had curved legs and a white satin seat. He looked at it doubtfully. "Go on," she said, "stand on it. If you dirty it the maid will clean it."

He could not think how to put a stop to this . . . this what, exactly? Was it a game she was playing, was she making sport of him? The look in her eye was almost avid now, and he felt more than ever mocked. He lifted his right foot — no part of him had ever looked so large or inappropriate to its surroundings — and set it on the chair and prepared to hoist himself aloft. At that moment the door opened and Françoise d'Aubigny put her head round it, saying her daughter's name. All froze into a tableau, the woman at the door with her hand on the doorknob, the man teetering on one foot, the little girl standing before him with her hands clasped demurely before her. Then Françoise d'Aubigny said something in French; the words had an angry, even a violent sound. Quirke took his foot from the seat of the chair and lowered it to the carpet as if it were not his own, but something burdensome that had been fastened to him.

"I'm sorry," he said, not knowing what it could be, exactly, that he was apologising for, but the woman brushed his words aside.

"What are you *doing*?" she said. "Why are you here?" Her blazing eye was fixed on Quirke — it seemed to him she had not so much as glanced at the child. He did not try to speak again — what would he have said? She strode forward from the door and set a hand claw-like on the girl's shoulder, but still all her attention was directed at Quirke. "For God's sake!" she hissed. He realised he still had the champagne glass in his hand, though it was empty now; was he perhaps a little drunk, was that what she was so angry about? She had become transformed on the instant into a harpy, her narrow face as white as the walls, her mouth a vermilion slash. What had he done, what outrage did she think him guilty of? The situation she had surprised him in was surely no more than absurd. He took a step forward, lifting a placatory hand, but Françoise d'Aubigny quickly turned, and turned the child with her, and marched her off to the door. There the girl hung back for a second and turned her head and threw back at Quirke a glance of what seemed to him pure, smiling malice. And then she was gone, and he stood, baffled and shaken, making a goldfish mouth.

Presently he was descending the stairs, stopping on every third or fourth step to listen down into the house, he did not know for what — recriminations, tears, the pained cries of a child being beaten? But he heard nothing except the distant buzz of voices from outside where that grotesque memorial party was continuing. He was walking past the drawing room when the door opened and Françoise d'Aubigny was there, looking no longer angry but haggard and spent. "Please, don't go," she said, stepping back and opening the door wider and motioning him to enter. He hesitated, feeling a flicker of angry resistance — was he to forget how not three minutes ago she had flared at him in fury as if he were an interloper or, worse, some sort of child molester? Yet he could not make himself pass by: the draw of her beauty, of her — yes — her magnificence, was too strong for him. When he stepped through the doorway he was relieved to see that the child was not there, though he spied her book still lodged down the side of the armchair where she had left it. The sunlight had shifted in the window, was thinned now to a blade of deepest gold.

Françoise d'Aubigny walked to the fireplace, wringing a lace handkerchief spasmodically in her hands. "Forgive me," she said. "You must think me a terrible person, to speak to you like that."

"No, I'm the one who should apologise. I didn't mean to invade the privacy of your home. It didn't feel like that, when I was doing it. Your daughter is very charming."

She glanced at him quickly. "Do you think so?" It seemed a real question, requiring a real answer.

"Yes, of course," he said lamely, lying again. "Charming and . . . irresistible." He tried out a winning smile, not knowing what there was to be won. "She insisted on showing me her room."

Françoise appeared to have stopped listening. She stood by the mantelpiece, gazing into the empty marble fireplace with a haunted expression. "It has been so difficult," she murmured, as if speaking to herself, "so difficult, this past week. What does one say to a child whose father has — has gone, so suddenly, in such a terrible way?"

"Children are resilient," Quirke said, aware how lumpish and banal it sounded. "They get over things that would kill us."

She went on staring wide-eyed into the grate, then came back to herself with a start and turned to him. "Do they?" she said.

He faltered. "So I'm told."

"You have no children?"

"No — I mean yes. I had — I *have* a daughter. She's grown-up. I didn't really know her when she was a child."

She began to weep, without preamble, without fuss, making no sound, her shoulders shaking. He did not hesitate, but crossed to where she stood and took her in his arms. She was so thin and, suddenly, so frail, a tall, bereft bird. Through the satin stuff of her dress he could feel the twin sharp flanges of her shoulder-blades; her sobs made them twitch like tensely folded wings. At his approach she had pressed her fists against each other with the handkerchief between them and held them to her breast, and now they were against his breast, too, though they were not a barrier, he felt, but on the contrary a sign of need, a gesture of supplication. Somehow he found her mouth, and tasted her tears, hot and sharp. He kissed her, but she did not kiss him back, only suffered his lips on hers, unwilling, it seemed, or perhaps even unnoticing. She might have been a sleepwalker, bumping up against him in the dark

112

and not waking. She detached herself from his embrace and took a step back.

"I'm sorry," he said, although he was not.

She blinked, he could see her making herself concentrate. "No, no," she said, "please, do not keep apologising. I'm glad. It was" — she smiled with an effort, the tears still shining on her cheeks — "inevitable."

Strange, how for him all the uncertainty and doubt, all that feeling of adolescent fumbling, how it was all gone, rid of in an instant, replaced by something deeper, darker, of far more weight, as if that kiss had been the culmination of a ceremony he had not been aware of as it unfolded, and that had ended by their sealing, there by the cold hearth, a solemn pact of dependence and fraught collaboration, and it was not the nearness of the fireplace, he knew, that was giving to his mouth a bitter taste of ashes.

CHAPTER
SIX

When the Hospital receptionist called to say he had a visitor, Quirke at first did not recognise the name. Then he remembered. "Tell her I'll come up," he said, and slowly replaced the receiver.

It was usually cool down here in his basement office, but the heat of this day reached even to these depths. He took a last quick couple of puffs at his cigarette and crushed the stub in the glass ashtray on his desk and stood up. He had not been wearing his white coat but now he put it on; it was as good as a mask, that coat, lending anonymity and authority. He walked along the curving green-painted corridor, then climbed the outlandishly grand marble staircase that led up to the entrance lobby of the hospital — the place had been built to house government offices in a past century, when governments could still afford that kind of thing.

She was waiting by the reception desk, looking nervous and a little lost.

"Mrs Maguire," he said. "How are you?"

She wore an ugly little hat held at an angle on the left side of her head with a pearl pin. On her arm she carried a caramel-coloured leather handbag. Quirke noted the cheap sandals.

She spoke in a rush. "Doctor Quirke, I hope you don't mind me coming here like this, only I wanted to talk to you about —"

"It's all right," he said quietly, touching a fingertip to Sarah Maguire's elbow to move her out of earshot of the two receptionists, who were eyeing her with frank speculation. He had intended to bring her to the canteen but now decided it would be better to get her away from the building altogether — there was a touch of hysteria to her manner, and he did not relish the prospect of a scene. He took off and folded his white coat and asked one of the receptionists to look after it until his return. "Come along," he said to Mrs Maguire. "You look like a person who could do with a cup of tea."

He walked her out into the noise and heat of mid-afternoon. The air had a blue tint to it and felt leaden and barely breathable. Buses brayed and the humped black roofs of cars gave off a molten sheen. They stopped at the Kylemore café on the corner. There were few customers at that hour, women, mostly, taking a break from shopping and looking hot and cross. Quirke led the way to a table in a shaded corner. He had a cigarette going before they were seated. The waitress in her chocolate-brown uniform came and he ordered a pot of tea with biscuits and a glass of soda water for himself. Mrs Maguire in her chair shrank back into the corner, looking much like a mouse crouching in the dim entrance to its hole. There was a cold sore at one corner of her mouth. Her eyes were so pale it would have been hard to say what colour they were; Quirke thought of those marbles made of milky glass that were much prized when he was a boy.

"So," he said, "tell me what it is you want to talk to me about."

As if he did not know.

"It's about William, my husband. He —"

Suddenly, when she said the name, Quirke remembered. How was it he had forgotten, when Jimmy Minor told him of Maguire having served a sentence in Mountjoy, that he had given medical evidence at the trial? Billy Maguire — of course. Ten years ago, it was — more, fifteen. A cattle dealer killed in a brawl after a fair-day in Monasterevin. Blow of a fist to the throat, the carotid artery crushed, and then, as if that were not enough, the fellow had fallen back and smashed his skull on a kerbstone. Billy Maguire had not known his own strength, or, it seemed, his uncontrollable temper. The court had pitied him, this desolate and frightened young man slumped in the box day after day in his Sunday suit, trying to follow the proceedings of the trial like the slowest child in the classroom. Five years he got, three, as it turned out, with good behaviour. Had Dick Jewell known of the conviction when he hired him to run the yard at Brooklands? Quirke thought not. Jewell the social philanthropist was largely a skilfully got-up figment of the imaginations of the *Clarion*'s colour writers.

"— But that's no reason to be casting slurs on him now," Maguire's wife was saying, leaning forward intently with her thin defenceless neck thrust out.

"William is a good man, and all that is past history, isn't it, Doctor Quirke?"

"Slurs?" Quirke said. "What slurs?"

She cast a quick bitter glance to one side. "Oh, in the town, of course, they're saying Mr Jewell didn't do away with himself at all, that it was only made to look like that by someone who was there that day. But it was suicide, wasn't it, Doctor?"

Quirke made his smile as kindly as he could manage. "You haven't touched your tea," he said. "Take some, it'll calm your nerves."

"Oh, my nerves!" she said, with a harsh little laugh. "— My nerves are long past calming."

Quirke sipped his soda water, the bubbles going up his nose and popping tinily, making him want to sneeze. "What is it you think I can do, Mrs Maguire?"

"You could maybe talk to him, tell him to stand up for himself and not be heeding all them in the town prattling behind his back. He remembers you from the — from the trial, how sympathetic you seemed."

He looked away from her, from the awful imploring gaze that to his shame was setting his teeth on edge. "And what does *he* think happened that day?" he asked.

She drew her head back and sank her chin into her throat and stared. "What do you mean?"

"Your husband — does *he* think Richard Jewell killed himself?"

The stare wavered and slid aside. "He doesn't know what happened, any more than anyone else" — she turned back to him and now her eyes narrowed — "any

117

more than the guards themselves know, when you read between the lines in what the newspapers say, even the *Clarion*." Again that rasping little laugh. "Especially the *Clarion*."

He poured more tea. She watched his hands as if he were performing an exotic and immensely delicate manoeuvre.

"How long have you been at Brooklands," he asked, "you and your husband?"

"Since a year after he — after he got out. Mrs Jewell took him on."

"*Mrs* Jewell?" he said sharply. "Françoise? I mean —"

"Yes, her. She's the joint owner at Brooklands, you know. She's always run the place."

"And she took your husband on as yard manager. Did she know about . . .?"

She gave him a pitying look. "That he'd been in jail? Do you think you could keep a thing like that hidden, in that place?"

"You didn't think of moving away, to somewhere else?"

This time she shook her head in disbelief of his naïvety. "And where would we have moved to?" She took a sip from her cup and grimaced. "It's gone cold," she said, but when he offered to order a fresh pot she said no, that she could not drink tea anyway, she was that upset. She brooded for a while, absently probing that cold sore with the tip of her tongue. "He didn't have much of a chance from the start, poor William,"

118

she said. "His mother died when he was seven and his father put him in St Christopher's."

"St Christopher's," Quirke said, his voice gone flat.

"Yes. The orphanage." She looked at him; his expression too was blank. "That was some place. The things he told me! Call themselves priests? — Ha!"

He looked aside. Cigarette smoke swirled lazily in the sunlight pouring in at the doorway, and the scuffed legs of the tables glowed, and dust moved on the floor.

He said again, "Tell me, Mrs Maguire, what it is you think I can do for you."

"Not for me," she said sharply, giving him a quick stare.

"Well, for your husband, then."

"I told you — you could talk to him."

"I don't really see what good that would do. If he has nothing to feel guilty about then —"

"*If?*" Again that stare. There was a faint cast in her left eye that gave her a lopsided and slightly unhinged aspect. Why, really, had she come to him?

"As I say, if he has nothing to feel guilty for then I don't see why he should need me or anyone else to talk to him. Are you worried about *his* nerves?"

"He's under a terrible strain. He takes that job of his very seriously, you know. It's a big responsibility, running the yard. And now, of course, there's the worry about what will happen. There's talk of her selling up and moving off to France." Her. When she spoke the word her thin mouth grew thinner still. "Mr Jewell's brother in Rhodesia is going to come back and run the business, but Mr Jewell left his half of Brooklands to her to do with as she likes."

"I'm sure she won't see you and your husband go hungry."

"Are you?" She did her cold laugh. "I wouldn't be sure of anything, with that one."

He lit a cigarette.

"You were at the house that morning, weren't you?" he asked. "Did you hear the gunshot?"

She shook her head. "I heard nothing until William came down from the office and told us what had happened."

"Us?"

"Her and me — her ladyship, Mrs J."

"I thought she came later, from Dublin?"

"Did she?" Her eyes grew vague. "I don't know, I thought she was there. It's all gone blurred in my mind. I couldn't believe it, when William said what had happened. And then the guards, and that detective . . ." She fixed her offcentred stare on him again. "Why would Mr Jewell do such a thing, shoot himself like that?"

He stubbed out his cigarette in the tin ashtray. He was trying to devise a way of ending this conversation, if that was what it was, and getting back to work. The woman irritated him, with her manner that was at once obsequious and bitter as gall. "I don't think," he said, "that he did shoot himself."

"Then what —?"

"Someone else, Mrs Maguire," he said. "Someone else."

120

She breathed slowly out. "So what they're saying in the town is true, then."

"That he was murdered? I think so. The police think so."

Suddenly she reached out and grasped him by the wrist. "Then you'll have to talk to that detective and tell him it wasn't William. My William wouldn't do such a thing. That other business, that was an accident — you testified as much yourself, in court. You helped him then — will you help him again, now?"

She released her hold on his wrist. He looked at her, trying to conceal his distaste. "I don't know that I can help him. I don't see that he *needs* help, since he's not guilty of anything."

"But they're saying —"

"Mrs Maguire, I can't stop people gossiping. No one can."

She sagged, expelling a long breath that seemed to leave her deflated. "It's always the way," she said, with quiet venom. "The grand ones do as they like and the rest of us can go hang. She'll sell up, I know she will, and take herself and that rip of a daughter of hers off to the sunshine in France, and leave us where Jesus left the Jews."

"I'm sure you're wrong," he said, in a voice that sounded unintentionally harsh. He could not deny it, he found this woman repellent, with her whining voice and crooked eye and that sore on her lip. He told himself it was not her fault, that she was one of life's natural victims, but it did no good: he still wanted, violently wanted, to be rid of her. "And now," he said, with exaggerated briskness, pushing back his chair and fishing out a half-crown for the bill, "I must get back to work."

He stood up, but she sat on, staring with narrowed and unseeing eyes in the direction of his midriff. "That's right," she said, a vehement murmur, "go on back to your big job. You're all the same, the lot of you."

She gave a stifled sob and, snatching up her handbag, slid sideways out of the chair and hurried to the door with her head down and was gone, swallowed in the dusty sunlight of outdoors. He set the coin on the table, and sighed. Was the woman right? Would Françoise sell up and go to France? After all, what was to keep her here?

He walked out into the day, and despite the heat his heart felt chilled. All at once he could not imagine this place without Françoise d'Aubigny in it.

On Saturday he and Inspector Hackett travelled to Roundwood. Hackett had asked Quirke to come with him "and see what you make of this Carlton Sumner fellow". They sat in the back of the big unmarked squad car, in companionable silence for the most part, watching the parched fields opening around them like a fan as they drove along the narrow straight roads. Sergeant Jenkins was at the wheel, and when they looked forward they had a view of the narrow back of his head and his large pointed ears sticking out.

"You've no car yourself at all now, Doctor Quirke?" Hackett enquired.

Quirke said nothing. He knew he was being teased. The Alvis he had owned, a magnificent and breathtakingly expensive beast, had toppled into the sea one snowy afternoon last winter, with a dead man inside it.

They went by way of Dundrum and set off from there on the long climb into the mountains. The gorse was struggling to bloom but the drought had stunted everything. It had not rained for weeks, and the pines and firs that marched in squared-off ranks across the hillsides drooped at their tips. "There'll be fires," Hackett said, "and that'll be the end of these plantations. Good riddance, too, I say — we should be planting oak and ash, not those ugly bloody things." At Enniskerry the picturesque little village was crowded with weekend traffic on its way to Powers-court and Glencree. Jenkins was a nervous driver, and kept treading heavily on the brakes and jerking the gear-stick, so that the two men in the back were thrown back and forth like a pair of manikins; neither commented.

Quirke described the visit from Sarah Maguire.

"Aye," Hackett said, "I went back through the files on your man, the husband. You gave evidence at the trial."

"Yes," Quirke said, "I had forgotten."

"He got a soft ride from you."

"And from the judge. It was a bad affair; no one came out of it undamaged."

The detective laughed shortly. "Especially the poor lummox that died." He offered a cigarette and Quirke brought out his lighter and they lit up. "What did she want, the missus?"

"I don't know," Quirke said. "She asked me to talk to you, tell you it wasn't her Billy that did in Diamond Dick."

Hackett said nothing, only looked sideways at Quirke with a lopsided grin.

The Sumner place had the look of a ranch, a big ugly rectangle of flat-roofed one-storey buildings ranged around a central courtyard with scrubby sun-browned grass. They entered by a wrought-iron gate that should have been surmounted by emblematic cow's horns and a crossed pair of six-shooters. At the end of a short, dusty drive they passed under a low archway into the courtyard, where a woman in slacks and a sky-blue blouse was waiting for them. Quirke recognised her. Gloria Sumner had not changed very much in the quarter of a century since he had last seen her. She was tall and blonde and broad-shouldered, with a strong face that had once been beautiful in a squarish sort of way, and was handsome now. She came forward, extending a hand. "Inspector Hackett, yes?"

Hackett introduced Quirke. The woman's bland smile of welcome did not alter: did she remember him and had decided not to show it? The time when they had known each other was probably not one she cared to recall — girls of her class and standing did not get pregnant before marriage — and anyway their acquaintance had been of the slightest. "Doctor Quirke," she said, "you're very welcome."

She led the two men through a glass porch into the house — Jenkins had been ordered to wait in the car — and down a low, broad corridor to a kind of lounge, also glassed on one side, and furnished with low-slung armchairs and a big leather-upholstered sofa. There were cactuses in pots, and a rug on the floor fashioned from the pelt of a wolf, complete with head and fiercely glaring glass eyes. Gloria Sumner saw Quirke looking at these things and gave him a droll smile. "Yes," she said, "my husband likes to be reminded of the Canuck wilderness of his youth." She turned to Hackett. "Tea, Inspector?" Her eye took on a playful light. "You look to me like a man in need of a good strong cuppa."

She must have pressed a hidden bell for almost at once there appeared a girl or young woman — it was difficult to guess her age — wearing rough corduroy trousers and a checked shirt. She was short and stocky and had fair, almost colourless hair and a bony sun-roughened face. She was no wraith yet moved with eerie soundlessness, trying to be invisible and looking at no one. "Ah, Marie," Gloria Sumner said. "Tea, please." She turned to Quirke. "And you, Doctor Quirke — tea, or something else?"

"Nothing, thank you," Quirke said. "A glass of water, maybe."

The girl Marie nodded once mutely and departed, as silently as she had come.

"Sit down, gentlemen," Gloria Sumner said. The two men took to the armchairs while the woman settled herself, half reclining, on the sofa, and regarded them with calm interest. She was wearing Greek sandals, with thongs crossed above her ankles. "My husband is riding," she said. "He expected to be back by now. I hope he hasn't fallen off." Again she smiled drolly in Quirke's direction. "He does that rather a lot, I'm afraid, though he wouldn't want you to know it."

They spoke of the weather, the great heat, the lack of rain. "The horses hate it," Gloria Sumner said. "The dust is dreadful for them — I hear them coughing in their stables half the night. Do you know about horses, Doctor Quirke?"

By now Quirke had decided that she did remember him, and that for some reason it amused her not to admit it. "No," he said, "I don't. Sorry."

"Oh, don't apologise. I hate the brutes." She turned to Hackett. "What about you, Inspector — are you a man of the turf?"

"Not really, ma'am," Hackett said. He had taken off his hat and was balancing it on one knee; the rim had left a shallow red groove across his forehead under the hairline. His suit was a shade of electric blue in the room's harsh light. "My uncle kept a couple of plough-horses when I was young. And there was an old hinny on his place that we used to ride around on."

The woman looked blank. "A hinny?"

Hackett smiled benignly on her ignorance. "A cross between, I believe, a stallion and a she-ass, ma'am."

"Oh."

Marie sidled in with the tea and the glass of water for Quirke. Still she was careful to meet no one's eye. She handed the glass to Quirke and when he thanked her she blushed. She was quickly gone, seeming only with an effort to stop herself from breaking into a run as she went.

"I imagine," Gloria Sumner said, looking from one man to the other, "you're here to talk about Dick Jewell? What a thing. I couldn't believe it, when I heard. I can hardly believe it now."

"Did you know the man?" Hackett enquired. He had transferred his hat to the floor between his feet and held the cup and saucer balanced on his knee.

"Well, yes, of course. Believe it or not, we used to be quite friendly with the Jewells, Carl and I, at one time."

"And what was it that upset that grand state of affairs, if I might ask?"

She smiled. "Oh, you'll have to ask my husband that, Inspector."

Quirke had been hearing, or feeling, rather, a slow set of heavy, dull thumps approaching, and now suddenly in the blazing light just outside the glass wall there reared up a gold man on a huge black glistening horse. Gloria Sumner twisted about to look, a hand shading her eyes. "Here he is," she said, "the *chevalier* himself. More tea, Inspector?"

Carlton Sumner was a large man with a head shaped somewhat like a shoebox and almost the same size. He had brown curly hair and a black square-cut moustache and round, somewhat droopy eyes of a surprisingly soft shade of baby-brown. He wore a short-sleeved gold-coloured wool shirt and fawn jodhpurs and very tight, highly polished though now dusty riding boots, and spurs, real cowboy spurs, that clinked and jingled as he walked. His forearms were exceedingly hairy. "Christ," he said as he entered. "This heat!"

His wife made the introductions, and had not finished when Sumner turned to Hackett and said, "You're here about Dick Jewell — he was murdered, wasn't he?"

"That's how it seems, all right," the detective said. He had risen to his feet, and was holding the cup and saucer in his left hand. He smiled his thin-lipped froggy smile. "You don't seem very surprised at that, Mr Sumner."

Sumner laughed, slowly, richly. "Surprised?" he said. "I'm surprised, all right — surprised someone didn't do it years ago." His Canadian accent gave his words a harsher edge than it seemed he had intended. He turned to his wife. "Where's Marie? — I need a drink, something long and cool, unlike Marie."

Gloria Sumner sketched a small sardonic bow. "I'll go and prepare it myself," she said, "if Your Lordship can wait a moment or two."

Sumner shrugged aside the irony and turned his attention to Quirke. "You are —?"

"Quirke," Quirke said. "I'm a pathologist."

"A *what?*" He looked to Hackett. "You work together?" he said, flicking a pointing finger from one of them to the other. "You're some kind of a team, are you?" He turned again. "What's your name — Quirke? — you'd be Doctor Watson, right? Back-up for the sleuth here." There was nothing to be said to that. Sumner was shaking his head and laughing to himself. "This country," he said. His wife returned, bearing a tall glass of pale-pink stuff with ice cubes and a sprig of something green sticking out of it.

"What the hell's this?" Sumner said, taking the glass from her and holding it up to the light and squinting at it.

"Pimm's," his wife said. "Tall and cool, as you ordered."

Sumner took a swig, swallowed, grimaced. "Cissy drink," he said. "Look, can we all sit down? I'm bushed."

Quirke could not but admire the performance, the brash carelessness, the casual aggression.

They sat, except for Gloria Sumner. "I'll leave you men to your talk," she said. She glanced at Quirke as she turned away, and there was something in her look that he found faintly unsettling. Had he kissed her once, back then, when they were young, kissed her in rain, under trees, in the dawn at the end of some party? Was it she or someone else he was thinking of? He had kissed many girls, in many dawns, back then.

"Well, gents?" Sumner said, when she had gone. He was unbuckling his spurs, and now he threw them, jingling and clattering, on to the low table in front of the sofa. "What can I do for you?"

He sprawled back on the sofa with an ankle crossed on a knee and his tall drink lifted. Beads of moisture were squiggling down the side of the glass. His hair and the bristles of his moustache gleamed and glinted as if each strand had been gone over with dark-brown boot-polish.

"You had a meeting here with Richard Jewell a week or so before he — before he died," Hackett said. "Is that right?"

Sumner shut one eye and trained the other on Hackett as if he were aiming along the barrel of a gun. "I suppose you heard about him throwing a tantrum and walking out."

"We did," Hackett said, "we heard that. What was the trouble?"

Sumner lifted a hand and let it fall again. "Business," he said. "Just business."

"You were making a takeover bid for his company," Quirke said.

"Was I?" Sumner drawled, not bothering to look at him. "I was negotiating a merger. Dick was reluctant. Words were spoken. He stormed out. That was it."

"You didn't see him again, after that?" Hackett asked.

"No. Or wait, yes, of course, I was forgetting: there was the day I went out to his place and blew his head off with his own shotgun."

"How did you know," Hackett enquired in a conversational tone, "that it was his shotgun?"

Sumner clamped a hand to his mouth and stared at the policeman with rounded eyes. "Oh, Lord," he exclaimed, "now I've done it — I've let slip a vital clue." He leaned back again and took a large gulp of his pink drink and smacked his lips. "In this country, everybody knows everything," he said. "— Haven't you realised that yet, Mr Holmes?"

The water in Quirke's glass had gone tepid and slightly cloudy. He was remembering Sumner as a young man, how he had looked, the things he had said. He had been a bully then, too, the rich man's son, cocksure and careless of his words. He had money when everyone else was penniless, and liked to flaunt it, drinks all round, flash suits, lunches lasting the afternoon, fast cars and fast girls; and then there was Gloria and the baby. Surprising that they were still together, if they were, in anything other than appearance.

"Look," Sumner said to Hackett, "I can't help you with this. I don't know what the hell happened to Dick. First they said he shot himself, then the rumour mill started and now it seems he was murdered. It was murder, yes?" Hackett said nothing, and Sumner turned to Quirke. "You'd know, even if he doesn't, right? Given that you're a pathologist and all." He waited. "No? Nothing to divulge? Don't tell me — you're bound by a solemn oath."

He chuckled, and drank more of his drink, and plucked out the green sprig and ate it, the stem as well as the leaves, and they heard his teeth chomping. "What does it matter, anyway?" he said. "Dick is dead, the rest is noise." He stood up and walked to the wall of glass and stood in the sunlight, vigorously scratching his groin. "Françoise would sell to me," he said, looking out into the courtyard and the burned-up grass. "The brother, though, what's his name, Rhodesia Ronnie, he won't deal. But I'll find a way round him." He turned and looked at them. "I want those newspapers. I need a voice. I'll get them."

A clock chimed in a distant room. With the cactuses and wolf's fur and the beating light they might have been in some desert place, far away on the other side of the world.

"Mrs Sumner tells me," Hackett said, "that you and her used to be great friends with the Jewells. Is that so?"

Sumner drew himself away from the sunstruck glass and sat down on the sofa again. "Jesus," he murmured, darting his nose towards one armpit and then the other, "I stink." He looked up. "You fellows going to need me much longer? I've got to go have a shower." Hackett gazed at him impassively, and Sumner heaved a sigh and flung himself back once more against the leather cushions. "Yes, we were friendly," he said, in a weary voice. "I kept a couple of horses at Brooklands for a while, and we'd go over, Gloria and me, for dinner or whatever. The two wives got into charity work together — Dick was funding that kids' place, Saint what-do-you-call-it. We even went on holiday together one time, down to their place in the South of France." He snickered. "Not a success. Dickie and I didn't fit so easily together in a confined space."

"Was there a fight?" Quirke asked.

"What, you mean with fists, the old one-two? Naw, of course not. Squabbles. Bickering. Françoise is very French, especially when she's in France. There were" — he laughed incredulously, remembering — "there was a problem over towels. Imagine — towels! We left early, came home to the old homestead and vowed never to go anywhere as house guests ever again. We realised we were home-bodies, to the core —" He stopped. He had been studying Quirke, and now, frowning, he said, "Wait — I know you. Quirke. You were at college when I was there, weren't you?" Quirke nodded. "Why didn't you say? I knew I knew you when I came in, but I couldn't place you. Quirke. Jesus. It must be, what, twenty-five years? More? So you made it through, you got your qualifications. None of us believed you would, you know."

He laughed, and still Quirke said nothing. "Well," Sumner said, lifting his glass, "here's to old times, *Doctor* Quirke." He turned to Hackett. "Look here, why don't you fellows stay for lunch? You can regale us with tales of the sleuthing life, tell us about the master criminals you've tracked down, all that. What do you say?"

Marie the maid returned to collect the tea things. Sumner said, "Marie here knew Diamond Dick — didn't you, Marie?" She gave him a startled look. "Mr Jewell," he said to her. "Your benefactor." He liked the sound of this, and laughed and said it again. "Your beloved benefactor. Ha!"

She took up the tray with the teapot and Hackett's empty cup on it. "Will you want anything else?" she asked of Sumner, and when he shook his head she scurried off.

"What was it that Jewell did for her?" Quirke asked.

"For Marie the mouse? Sprang her from that orphanage he funded — what's it called? — St Christopher's. She was some sort of slavey there."

133

"Did she work for him — for him and his wife?"

"For a while. Then something happened and Françoise dumped her on us. She's all right — not too smart, but all right."

"What was it that happened, Mr Sumner?" Hackett asked. "Do you know?"

"Naw. Some kerfuffle. No one stays long with Françoise. You've met that guy who runs the place, him and his wife, the other mouse? Talk about long-suffering. What's their name?"

"Maguire," Quirke said.

"That's it. Hey" — he lifted a finger — "I just remembered. Maguire killed a guy, years ago, broke his neck or something in a bar fight. Did you know that, Doc?"

Quirke nodded. "I was involved in the case."

"Were you, now." He drained the last of his drink. "What do you think? — maybe he's the one that pulled the gun on old Dickie." He looked from one of them to the other. "Have you thought of that? Couldn't take the heat any longer and upped and shot the boss. Though I guess he would have gone for Françoise first."

"Mr Sumner, I'd really appreciate it," Hackett said, "if you'd tell us what the disagreement was that you had with Richard Jewell here that day."

"I told you — it was business. There's always fights when business is being done, it's the nature of the game." He scratched at his moustache with a forefinger, making a rasping sound. "Okay," he said then, and sighed. "I own a chunk of his company. I made him an offer of a partnership, he told me to go to hell, things

134

got heated, he left. That was it. If you think I sat here brooding for a week and then went over to his place one morning and blew his head off — well, come on."

"You didn't see him again, after that day?" Hackett asked.

"No." He stood up. "No, I didn't see him again, or talk to him, or hear from him — nothing. Now if you don't mind, I've really got to take that shower — I'm beginning to steam."

Hackett was still sitting, with his hat on the floor between his feet. He picked it up and examined the brim. "And I suppose you've no idea of who might have wanted him dead."

"Are you kidding? I could give you a list of names as long as your arm. But listen" — he lifted a hand and laughed — "maybe Françoise did it. Christ knows she hated him."

Quirke was standing now, and Hackett too got to his feet at last, turning his hat in his hands. "How is your son, Mr Sumner?" he asked.

Sumner went very still, and lowered his boxy head and glowered out from under his thick black brows. "He's fine — why?"

The air between the two men seemed to crackle, as if a strong charge of electricity had passed through it. Quirke watched them, looking from one to the other.

"I just wondered," Hackett said. "He's in Canada now, is he?"

"No, he's back."

"Doing what?"

"Working for me."

"That's good," the detective said. "That's very good." He smiled. "Well, we'll leave you to go and have your wash. Maybe you'd say goodbye to Mrs Sumner for us."

But Gloria Sumner was already in the doorway. "These guys are leaving," Sumner said to her. His mood had turned, all the arrogant brightness had gone and his voice was thick with rancour.

"I'll show you to the door," Gloria Sumner said, and led the two men along the low corridor to the glassed-in porch, where the heat hammered. "Goodness," she said, "your driver will have baked, poor fellow. I could have sent Marie out with a cool drink."

"How long," Quirke asked, "has she been with you, the maid?"

"Marie? Funny, I never think of her as 'the maid'. Three, four years, I suppose. Why do you ask?"

Quirke did not answer, only shrugged.

"Good day to you now, ma'am," Hackett said, and put on his hat.

"Goodbye. And goodbye, Doctor Quirke. Nice to see you again, after all these years." She smiled into his face. "You thought I hadn't remembered you, but I did."

Jenkins had moved the squad car into the scant shade of a birch tree, and had all the windows wide open, but he was sweating and had taken off his jacket and his tie. He greeted Hackett with a wounded look and started up the engine. Gloria Sumner was still standing in the doorway of the porch, and waved one hand slowly as they departed.

"What was that about the son?" Quirke asked.

"Teddy Sumner," Hackett said. "A bit of a boyo. He has a record. Gave a girl a hiding after a party over at Powerscourt one night. Would have done time if his father wasn't who he was. They packed him off to the family's place in Canada. Now, it seems, he's back."

They passed through Roundwood village. Among trees off to the right the reservoir was a glint of pewter. Quirke was eyeing the backs of Jenkins's large pink ears. "Sumner didn't like being asked about him," he said.

"No, indeed, I noticed that."

Quirke waited, but nothing more was forthcoming. "You think there might be a connection, with Dick Jewell?"

"Oh, hardly," Hackett said, putting on the mild and vacant look that he did when he was doing his hardest thinking. "But I wonder if Teddy was there the day that Jewell and Sumner had their row. I should have asked."

"Yes," Quirke said. "You should have."

CHAPTER
SEVEN

Even as it was occurring to Sinclair the idea seemed crazy, and yet it had a peculiar and a nagging appeal. He had gone out a third time with Phoebe, on what he afterwards supposed must have been their first real date, for although she did not invite him in, the evening had ended with a prolonged and serious, indeed, a solemn, kiss on her doorstep, and now he found that the thought of her was never far from his mind. He had come to see her unconventional prettiness — it was in the delicacy of her slim hands, in the slightly feline angle of her jaw, in the almost transparent paleness of her skin. Also he had begun to appreciate her humour, the amused and subtle mockery in her attitude to things, him included, perhaps him especially. She had a bright mind; he wondered how she had ended up working in a hat shop. He could not stop himself imagining her without her clothes, reclining on a bed and turning towards him on the pivot of one braced arm, a lock of hair across her cheek, all her bared flesh agleam like a knife-blade. Yes, all that was on his mind, and more. But now the wild thought had occurred to him that he would introduce her to Dannie Jewell, he did not know why. Perhaps he wanted to see what the two of them would make of each other. *Or perhaps*, a sly voice said in his head, *you want to make mischief.*

They had arranged a Sunday-afternoon outing, Phoebe and he, to go and see the rhododendrons on the slopes behind Howth Castle. They would take a picnic, and a bottle of wine. As the day approached he dithered as to whether he dared ask if Dannie might come with them, and more than once he dialled the number of the telephone in the hallway of the house where Phoebe had her bedsit, but hung up before anyone answered. The idea *was* crazy, surely. What was it supposed to achieve, what purpose was it supposed to serve? Phoebe would most likely resent Dannie's presence, and Dannie would not much care to be a gooseberry. Probably Dannie would not come, anyway, even if Phoebe were to say that she could. Finally he worked up the courage and telephoned them both, Phoebe first, then Dannie. They both said yes. And straight away, of course, he regretted the whole thing, and cursed himself for his foolishness.

He called for Dannie first, and they walked together to Phoebe's place. The morning was sunny and hot but a faint fresh breeze was coming down from the mountains and the air had lost some of the heaviness that had weighed on it in recent days. Dannie was hardly recognisable as the same girl he had last seen curled forlornly on her bed in a drugged sleep that night after her brother had died and she had phoned him for help. Today she wore a white dress that the breeze made balloon around her, and a light cashmere jumper was draped over her shoulders with the sleeves knotted loosely in front. She had put on lipstick, and wore perfume. When she had answered the door to him she had seen the anxiousness in his eyes and had put a hand reassuringly on his arm and said, "Don't worry, I'm all right, I won't break down or anything." Now they stopped outside the front door of the house where Phoebe lived, and stood smiling at each other vaguely as they waited for her to come down, and the plane trees on the other side of the street rustled their leaves excitedly as if they were discussing these two young people standing there in the midst of a Sunday morning in summer.

To his surprise, they got on together from the start, Phoebe and Dannie. As he was introducing them he saw how alike they were. Not that they looked alike, but there was something definite that they shared, though he could not say exactly what it was — a quality of things endured, perhaps, of troubles not surmounted but absorbed, with grit and determination, painfully.

They took the bus to Sutton and then mounted the little tram that whirred and rattled its way up the long slope of Howth Head. Phoebe had packed the picnic, ham sandwiches on brown bread with lettuce and sliced tomatoes, and a cucumber cut in four lengthways, and pickles in a jar, and a fancy tin of biscuits from Smyths on the Green. Sinclair and Dannie had each brought a bottle of wine, and Dannie had a basket with three glasses wrapped in napkins. They kept meeting each other's eye and smiling, a little bashfully, for they felt suddenly childish and exposed, to be on an outing, like ordinary people, and ordinarily happy. Seagulls were circling above them in the blue, and far in the distance the sun sparkled on the sea, and no one mentioned Richard Jewell.

They got off near the summit and walked down the road, but no one knew the way to the castle, and for a while they got lost, and in the end gave up on the rhododendrons and sat down at the corner of a field and unwrapped their sandwiches and opened the wine. Sinclair's bottle of Liebfraumilch had lost its chill but they did not mind; they drank it first and then drank the much grander Bordeaux that Dannie had brought. When the wine was finished the girls went off to find a secluded place to pee, and Sinclair lay back in the soft lush grass and shielded his eyes with his arm and briefly dozed, and had a sort of dream in which Phoebe and Dannie, merged into a single person, came to him and touched his face and confided to him some profound piece of knowledge that he forgot the moment the voices of the real girls woke him up. He sat up and watched them picking their way towards him through the grass. They had found the wood with the rhododendrons in it: it was just across the next field. "The blossoms are nearly finished, though," Phoebe said, sitting down beside him, and smiling at him with a particular intent that he could not fathom, and he thought again of his strange little dream.

He lit a cigarette and offered the packet around, but Dannie shook her head, and Phoebe reminded him that she had given up smoking.

There were cows at the other side of the field, black and white, some standing and some lying down. A black bird, rook or crow, flew across in a ragged sort of way, cawing.

"Look," Phoebe said, "those boats are in a race." They shaded their eyes to peer down to where the yachts were plying their way against the wind, and sure enough there came to them up the length of the hillside, delayed by distance, the boom of the starting signal. "Such white sails," Phoebe murmured. "Like wings, look."

Dannie had lain down on her front in the grass with her chin propped on her hands. She was chewing a blade of grass. Three flies circled above her head, round and round, tracing the ghostly outline of a black halo. Sinclair saw again how beautiful she was, with that broad face and delicate chin, more beautiful than Phoebe, though not half so fascinating, he told himself.

"Isn't it strange to think," Dannie said, "that people who are old now were young once, like us? I meet an old woman in the street and I tell myself that seventy years ago she was a baby in her mother's arms. How can they be the same person, her as she is now and the baby as it was then? It's like — what do they say? — the headless axe without a handle. Something that's there and yet impossible."

Sinclair had the impression of a tiny speck of darkness, a beam of black light, piercing the sunlit air, infinitesimally fine but thickening, thickening.

Orphans. The word came to his mind unbidden. *Those poor orphans,* she had said. But what orphans? He would not ask, not now.

Quirke that same Sunday afternoon was in bed with Françoise d'Aubigny. She had telephoned first and then come to his flat. Giselle was at Brooklands, being looked after by Sarah Maguire. There were no preliminaries. He let her in at the front door and they climbed the stairs in silence and once inside the flat she turned to him and lifted up her mouth to be kissed. Their lovemaking at first was not a success. Quirke was uncertain and Françoise seemed preoccupied — it was as if she were conducting an experiment, or an investigation, of him, of herself, of the possibilities of what they might be to each other. Afterwards they sat up in bed in the hot, shadowed room, not speaking, but forgiving of each other. Quirke smoked a cigarette and Françoise took it from his fingers now and then and drew on it, and when he offered her one of her own she shook her head and said no, she wanted to share this one, because it tasted of him.

"When did you know this was going to happen?" he asked.

She gave a soft laugh. "Oh, the day we met, I suppose. And you?"

"Not so quickly. Women always know long before men."

Her breasts were like pale apples, her ribs plainly visible under their sheath of silky skin. She was, he realised with a kind of happy dismay, not his kind of woman at all — at least Isabel Galloway had some flesh on her bones.

"You have someone already?" she asked. She had that gift of reading his thoughts.

"Yes," he said. "Sort of."

"Who is she?"

"An actress."

"A famous one? Would I know her?"

"I doubt it. She works mostly at the Gate."

"Tell me her name."

"Isabel."

"And do you feel very guilty about her, now?"

"Yes."

"Ah. I'm sorry."

"Don't be — I'm not."

She took the cigarette again and put it to her lips, shutting one eye against the smoke. "Shall we continue together, you and I, do you think?" she asked mildly. "Will there be more times like this?" She smiled, and gave him back the cigarette. "Or will you be" — she put a theatrical quiver into her voice — "overcome by your guilt?"

"There *will* be more times. There'll be all the time in the world."

"*Alors*," she said, "is that what they call a declaration?"

"Yes," he said. "It is."

She turned and put her arms around him. He crushed the last of the cigarette in the ashtray on the bedside table. His eye fell on the telephone there,

144

hunched, black and gleaming, a reminder of all that was outside this room: the world, and Isabel Galloway.

Two days after his outing with Phoebe and Dannie, in the middle of an otherwise ordinary morning, Sinclair received a telephone call at the hospital. This was unusual: hardly anyone phoned him at work. The nurse who put the call through from Reception sounded odd, she seemed to be trying not to laugh, and then the voice that came on was strangely muffled, as if the speaker were speaking through a handkerchief.

"Listen, Jewboy," the voice said, "you keep sticking that big fat nose of yours into places where it's not wanted and you'll get it lopped off. Then your prick and your Jew face will be a nice match." This was followed by a cackle of laughter and then the line went dead.

Sinclair stood looking at the receiver. He thought it must be a prank, some so-called friend from college days, maybe — it had been a young man's voice, he was sure of that — doing it for a bet, or out of some long-remembered grudge, or even just for a moment's amusement. Despite himself he was shocked. He had never experienced this kind of thing before, certainly not since school days, but then it had been a matter of malicious teasing, not abuse like this, not hatred. The effect was first of all physical, as if he had been punched in the pit of the stomach, then the rage came, like a transparent crimson curtain falling behind his eyes. He had an urge too to tell someone, anyone. Quirke was in his office — he could be seen through the glass panel in the door; he was doing paperwork and smoking a cigarette in the ill-tempered way that he did, blowing the smoke out swiftly sideways as if he could not bear the stink of it. Sinclair knocked on the door and walked in. Quirke looked at him and lifted his eyebrows. "Christ," he said, "what's the matter with you? One of the stiffs come back to life?"

Suddenly, to his intense surprise and puzzlement, Sinclair was overcome by shyness. Yes, shyness, it was the only word. "I had a — I had a call," he said.

"Oh? Who from?"

"I don't know."

"You don't know?"

"No. A man."

Quirke leaned back in his chair. "A man phoned you and didn't give his name. What did he say?"

Sinclair pushed back the wings of his white coat and shoved his hands into the pockets of his trousers. He stared through the long window that gave on to the dissecting room, garishly lit under the big white neon lamps in the ceiling. "It was just . . ." He touched a finger to his forehead. "Just abuse."

"I see. Personal or professional?"

"Personal. But it could have been professional, I don't know."

Quirke rotated the open packet of Senior Service on his desk until the cigarettes, arrayed like the pipes of an organ, were facing in Sinclair's direction; Sinclair took one, and lit it with his Zippo.

"I've had those calls," Quirke said. "No point in telling you not to mind, they're always a shock." He

146

stubbed out his own cigarette and took a fresh one, and leaned back further. "Phoebe tells me you and she went to Howth. Nice, out there?"

Sinclair thought about being indignant — did she tell Quirke everything she did? did she tell him about that kiss, too? — but the anger was not there sufficiently. "Dannie Jewell came with us," he said.

Quirke looked surprised. "Did she? Phoebe didn't say. Do they know each other?"

"No, they hadn't met before. I thought it would be good for Dannie."

"And was it?"

Sinclair looked at him. The cold light that had come into Quirke's eye, what was that? Was he worried Phoebe would be affected by Dannie and her troubles? Sinclair suspected Quirke did not know very much about his daughter. "She's doing well, Dannie. She's coping."

"With her grief."

"That's right."

Something had tightened between them, as if the atmosphere had developed a kink.

"Good," Quirke said briskly. He was rolling the tip of his cigarette back and forth in the ashtray, sharpening it like the point of a red pencil. "You're aware that Phoebe, too, like Dannie Jewell, has things to cope with, things that happened, in the past."

Sinclair nodded. "She doesn't talk about it — at least she hasn't so far, to me."

"She's seen more than her share of violence. And in America she was — she was attacked."

Sinclair had heard all this: it was talked about in the hospital, a fact he hoped Quirke was not aware of.

"If you're telling me to be careful," Sinclair said, "you needn't. I like Phoebe. I think she likes me. That's as far as we've got." He wanted to say, *And, besides, you're the one who put us together,* but did not.

Quirke's cigarette was spent already; he crushed it in the ashtray among the remains of a dozen others. The subject of Phoebe, Sinclair could see, was closed.

"This fellow on the phone," Quirke said, "did he mention names?"

Sinclair had walked to the window and was leaning against it, one foot lifted behind him and the sole of his shoe pressed against the wall. "How do you mean, names?"

"Sometimes when they're bereaved they call up mad with grief and complain about their loved ones being cut up. God knows why the switch puts them through."

"No, no, nothing like that. He told me I'd get my Jew nose cut off if I stuck it in other people's business."

"Your Jew nose."

They both smiled.

"All right," Sinclair said. "I'll forget about it."

He came forward and stubbed out his cigarette in the crowded ashtray and made for the door. Behind him Quirke said, "Phoebe and I are having dinner tonight. It's our weekly treat. It used to be Thursday, now it's a movable feast. You want to join us?"

Sinclair stopped, turned. "Thanks," he said, "no. I have a thing to do. Maybe another time." He set off again towards the door.

"Sinclair."

Again he stopped. "Yes?"

"I'm glad that you and Phoebe are — are friends," Quirke said. "And I appreciate your — your concern for her." He suddenly looked vulnerable there, wedged in the chair that was too small for him, his big hands resting palm upwards on the desk as if in supplication.

Sinclair nodded, and went out.

CHAPTER
EIGHT

St Christopher's was a gaunt grey mock-Gothic pile standing on a rocky promontory that looked across to Lambay Island. The more sophisticated among the priests of the Redemptorist Order who administered the place referred to it jocularly as the Château d'If, though the inmates called it something else. It was an orphanage, exclusively for boys. Those who passed through it remembered most vividly of all the particular smell of the place, a complex blend of damp stone, wet wool, stale urine, boiled cabbage, and another odour, thin and sharp and acidic, that seemed to the survivors of St Christopher's the stink of misery itself. The institution had a formidable reputation throughout the land. Mothers threatened their miscreant sons that they would be sent there — for not all the inmates were orphans, not by any means. St Christopher's welcomed all comers, and the mite of state subsidy that each one brought. Overcrowding was never a problem, for boys are small, and St Christopher's boys tended to be smaller than most, thanks to the frugal diet they enjoyed. Passengers on the Belfast train were offered the best view of the great house standing upon its rock, with its sheer granite walls, its louring turrets, its bristling chimneys dribbling meagre plumes of coal-smoke. Few going past looked on it for long, however, but turned their eyes uneasily aside, and shuddered.

Quirke travelled by train to Balbriggan and at the station hired a hackney car that drove him down along the coast to Baytown, a huddle of cottages abutting St Christopher's and looking like so many lumps of weathered masonry left over after the construction of the house had been completed. The day, though heavily overcast, was hot, and had a sulky look to it, determined as it was on withholding the rain that the fat clouds were full of and that the parched fields so sorely craved. At the tall gates Quirke pulled the bell-chain and presently an old man came out of the gate lodge bearing a great iron key and let him in. Yes, Quirke said, he was expected. The old man eyed his well-cut suit and expensive shoes and sniffed.

The driveway Quirke remembered as much longer, and much wider, a great curved sweep leading majestically up to the house, but in fact it was hardly more than an unfenced track with a ditch on either side, dry now. He supposed this would be the general tenor of his visit this afternoon, everything misrecalled and jumbled up and out of proportion. He had spent less than a year here, on his way to Carricklea, the industrial school, so-called, in the far west, where he had been sent because no one could think what else to do with him. He had not been very unhappy at St Christopher's, not if his unhappiness were measured against the scale of the things he had experienced up to then in his short life, and certainly not if measured against what had awaited him at Carricklea. One or two of the priests at St Christopher's had been kind, or at least had shown an intermittent mildness, and not all of the bigger boys had beaten him. Yet it gave him an awesome shiver to be walking up this dusty way, in this sullenly radiant light, and at every step his legs seemed to sink deeper into the ground before him.

A lanky boy with cropped blond hair, a trusty of the place, led him along a soundless corridor to a high dim room with an oak dining table that had probably never been dined on and three windows that were enormous and yet seemed to let in only a trickle of light from outdoors. When he was here he had not known of the existence of such a room, so grand, as it would have seemed to him, so richly appointed. He stood with his hands in his pockets, looking out blankly — a bit of lawn, a gravelled path, a far patch of sea — and listening to the faint and seemingly apprehensive poppings and pingings deep in his gut. His lunch was not sitting well with him.

Father Ambrose was tall and thin and grizzled, like one of those pared-down selfless priests who till the mission fields or care for lepers. "Good afternoon, Doctor Quirke," he said, in the strained and reedy voice of an ascetic. "St Christopher's is always glad to see old boys." A fan of fine wrinkles opened at the outer corner of each eye when he smiled. His hand was a bundle of thin dry twigs in a wrapping of greaseproof paper. He gave off a faint aroma of candle-wax. He was an implausibly perfect specimen of what a priest should look and sound and even smell like, and Quirke wondered if he was kept in a cell somewhere and brought out and pressed into service whenever a visitor called.

"I wanted to enquire," Quirke said, "about a girl — a young woman — called Marie Bergin." He spelled the surname. "It seems she worked here, for a time, some years ago."

Father Ambrose, still absently holding the hand that Quirke had given him to shake, stood very close to him and was examining his features minutely, running his eyes rapidly here and there, and Quirke had the eerie sensation of being not looked at but rather of being palped, softly, delicately, as if a blind man were feeling all over his face with his fingertips.

"Come, Doctor Quirke," he said, in his breathily confidential voice, "come and sit down."

They sat at a corner of the dining table, on two of the high-backed chairs that were ranged around it like effigies of ancient priests, the founders of the place. Quirke was wondering if he might be permitted to smoke when the priest delved into a fold of his cassock and brought out a packet of Lucky Strike. "One of the fathers over in America sends them to me," he said. He tore the silver foil and tapped with a finger expertly on the underside of the pack and a cigarette popped out. He offered it to Quirke, then tapped out another. The first breath of the exotic-tasting smoke brought Quirke back instantly to a big house near the sea south of Boston, years before.

"Do you recall your time here?" the priest was asking.

"I was very young, Father, seven or eight. I remember the food."

Father Ambrose did his crinkly smile. "Our cooks were never famous for their culinary skills, I'm afraid." He drew on his cigarette as if he were tasting some fabulous and costly vintage. That was another thing Quirke remembered, from the various institutions he had endured, the way the priests and brothers smoked, like eager debauchees, indulging all their senses in one of the very few permitted pleasures. "That would be quite a while ago, then, way before the war. We have changed a great deal since those days. This is a happy home, Doctor Quirke." His tone was not defensive but his eye took on a quickened light.

"I didn't mind it, here."

"I'm glad to hear it."

"But, then, my expectations were modest. I was an orphan, after all." Why, really, had he come here today? Making enquiries about the Sumners' maid was only a pretext. He was kneading an old wound.

"And you were brought to St Christopher's. The Lord tempers the wind to the shorn lamb, as the Psalmist tells us. Where had you come from?"

"I have no origins, Father. I have a suspicion of what they were, but if what I suspect is the case, I don't want it confirmed."

The priest was studying him closely again, running ghostly fingers over the braille of Quirke's soul. "There are some things, indeed, that it's better not to know. This girl, this — what did you say her name was?"

"Marie — Marie Bergin."

"That's right." The priest frowned. "I don't recall her. Did she work in the kitchens?"

"I think so."

"Yes. Because of course we don't have maids, the lads shift for themselves. It's a good discipline for life, knowing how to make a bed properly and how to keep your things in order. We've sent out many a fine young independent man into the world. You say this Marie Bergin is working now for someone you know?"

Had he said that? He did not think he had. "Yes, she worked for the Jewell family, and then —"

Father Ambrose threw up his hands. "The Jewells! Ah!" His face darkened. "Poor Mr Jewell. What a tragedy."

"He was one of your benefactors, I believe."

"He was. And he's a great loss to us, a tragic loss."

"He raised funds for the place?"

"Yes, and contributed himself, very generously. There's a little unofficial committee" — he pronounced it *comity* — "that he set up, you know, himself and a few friends, businessmen like himself. I can hardly think what we would do without the Friends of St Christopher's — that's what they call themselves — and certainly this is a worrying time for us, a time of uncertainty, with Mr Jewell gone." He turned his eyes to the window, his saintly profile sharp against the light. "Such a good man, especially so, considering he was not of our persuasion. But then, you know, there's a

155

history of quiet co-operation between the Jewish community here and Holy Mother Church. Mr Briscoe, our new lord mayor, is a great friend of Rome, you know, oh, yes." He paused to look at the cigarette packet on the table before him, reached for it, then drew back his hand. He smiled apologetically. "I ration myself to ten a day," he said. "It's a little mortification of the flesh I make myself indulge in. If I smoke another one now I won't have one for after my tea — but forgive me, Doctor Quirke, I didn't offer you anything. Would you like some tea, or maybe a glass of sherry? — I'm sure there's a bottle somewhere about."

Quirke shook his head. "Nothing, thank you." Despite himself he was warming to this gentle, simple man. How did such a sensibility manage to survive, in a place like St Christopher's? "Do you think," he asked, "there might be someone in the kitchens who would remember Marie Bergin?"

The priest made an o of his mouth. "I doubt it, Doctor Quirke. There's a big turnover of staff here, the girls rarely stay more than a few months. We try to find them places with good families, outside. A boys' orphanage is no place for a young woman. So many of them are innocents, you know, up from the country with not a notion in their heads of the perils awaiting them in the wider world."

"She's working for Mr and Mrs Sumner now," Quirke said.

"Is she, indeed? There's another name I know well."

"Oh?"

"Yes — Mr Sumner is one of the Friends of St Christopher's."

"He is?"

Father Ambrose smiled and bowed his narrow head. "Surprising, yes, I know. But there you are, often the unlikeliest turn out to have a saintly side. Would you like to see something of our work here? I could give you a little tour. 'Twill not take more than a quarter-hour of your time."

The great house, as they walked through it, was eerily quiet. Quirke had the impression of a hushed multitude corralled behind locked doors, listening. What boys they met shuffled past with eyes downcast. Here were the workshops, with rows of shiny tools neatly laid out, where crucifixes and framed pictures of the saints were manufactured for distribution among the faithful in Africa, in China, in South America; here was the recreation room, with dart-boards and a ping-pong table; in the refectory, long pine tables were set out in rows, their surfaces scrubbed white and the grain of the wood standing up like polished veins. They viewed the kitchen garden, where boys in brown aprons lurked like worker gnomes among the potato drills and the stands of runner beans. "We grow so much produce," Father Ambrose confided proudly, "that often the surplus has to be sold to the shops round about — a source of much-needed income, I can tell you, in the summer months." They crossed the lawn that ran to the very brink of the sea, and stood on the edge and looked down at the black rocks where even on this calm day the waves exploded in great bursts of heavy white spray.

"This is what I don't remember from when I was here," Quirke said, "the sea. And yet it must have been a constant presence."

He felt Father Ambrose beside him scrutinising him again. "I hope you'll forgive me saying it, Doctor Quirke," the priest said, "but you seem to me a troubled spirit."

Quirke was surprised not to be surprised. He said nothing for a moment, then nodded. "Do you know any spirits that aren't troubled, Father?"

"Oh, yes, many."

"You move in different circles to the ones I move in."

The priest chuckled. "I'm certain that's true. But you're a medical man, you must know nurses, nuns, fellow doctors, whose souls are at peace."

"I'm a pathologist."

"Even so. There is great peace to be found, after all, among the dead, whose souls have gone to their eternal reward."

"If there is, I haven't found it." He watched a gannet dive like a white dart and pierce the water's surface and disappear with hardly a splash to mark the spot. "Maybe I'm looking in the wrong place, or from the wrong angle."

Far out, a pallid sun broke through the clouds and set two burly pillars of light standing astride the sea.

"Maybe you are, indeed," the priest said. They turned back towards the house. "This young woman, this Marie Bergin — is she in trouble?"

"No, not that I know of."

The green turf underfoot was as taut and resilient as the skin of a trampoline. The sea mists must water it, Quirke thought.

"May I ask why you're enquiring after her?"

They were on the gravelled pathway. Quirke stopped, and the priest stopped, and they stood facing each other. "It seems, Father, that Richard Jewell didn't kill himself, but was killed."

"Killed?"

"Murdered."

The priest put a shrivelled hand quickly to his mouth. "Oh, dear Heaven. And you think Marie Bergin is in some way involved?"

"Not directly, no. What I'm trying to understand, Father, is *why* Dick Jewell was killed."

"But surely some poor maid that once worked for him . . .?"

"She didn't kill him, of course she didn't. But she might be part of the reason why someone else did."

"I'm sorry, Doctor Quirke, I don't understand."

"No, neither do I."

Presently he was walking down the dusty drive. The iodine smell of the sea was stronger now, or perhaps he had not taken note of it when he was walking up, earlier. At the gate he thought of asking the old man with the key if he had known Marie Bergin, but from the guarded look in the fellow's rheumy eye he did not think he would get much out of him even if he had known who she was. The hackney driver, whom Quirke had asked to wait, was asleep behind the wheel, his head lolling to one side and his mouth part-way open and trailing a dribble of dried spit. The air inside the car was heavy with the man's stale reek. They set off along the coast. That far rent in the clouds had been mended and the sky was once again a seamless grey-blue upside-down plain stretching all the way to the horizon.

Why had Carlton Sumner not said he was one of the Friends of St Christopher's? And who, apart from him and Dick Jewell, might the other Friends be?

Rose Crawford, or Rose Griffin, as she was now, took Phoebe to lunch in a little wine bar off Dawson Street that Rose had discovered and treated as a secret to be jealously guarded. Phoebe, although she would not say so, did not think much of the place. It was poky and dim, and there was a distinct smell of drains. The décor was heavily nautical, with lengths of fishing net draped about the walls, and seashells glued everywhere, and a real ship's wheel attached to the desk on which the cash register stood. The owner, or perhaps she was just the manager, a blowsy blonde in a black wool dress and fishnet stockings, herself exuded an air of the waterfront, and even moved with something of a sailor's bow-legged roll. Rose sat in the midst of this marine fantasy with a satisfied, proprietorial air. It all made Phoebe feel slightly seasick. Rose, she had to admit to herself, was prone to surprising lapses of judgement.

Phoebe ordered steak, not because she wanted it but because it was the only alternative to fish on the menu.

"Well, my dear," Rose said, in her twangiest Southern-belle drawl, "tell me all about him."

Phoebe stared, beginning to laugh. "All about who?"

"Don't act the innocent with me, young lady. I know that look. You have a beau, haven't you?"

Phoebe put down her fork. "Oh, Rose, there's no hiding anything from you."

"There. I knew it. Who is he?"

Stalling, Phoebe took a slow draught from her wine glass. There were other people at the tables around them, couples, mostly, but in the dimness — the red-shaded lamps on the tables seemed to shed not light but lurid shadows only — they were indistinct and somewhat sinister-looking, crouched over their plates and speaking in what sounded like nothing but asides. "He's nobody very exciting, I'm afraid," she said.

"I'll be the judge of that. Come — tell."

"He works with Quirke."

"Does he? He's a doctor, then."

"Yes, a pathologist, or training to be, I'm not sure. He's Quirke's assistant."

"Oh, so he's that young man, what's his name . . .?"

"David Sinclair."

"That's the one. Well."

Now it was Rose's turn to lay down her fork. She sat back on her chair, straightening her spine and elongating her already long, slender neck. Rose's exact age was a matter of sporadic speculation in the family, though no conclusion was ever reached. Phoebe suspected that even her latest and very recent husband, Malachy Griffin, did not know the figure for certain.

Rose's choice of Malachy had surprised many, and appalled not a few, including Phoebe, though she had covered up her dismay. They were an unlikely match — Rose the mature blossom of old Dixie and Malachy the mole. He was consultant obstetrician at the Hospital of the Holy Family, a position from which he had been ditheringly and for what seemed a very long time in the process of retiring. He was also the man who, for the first nineteen years of her life, had passed as Phoebe's father, for Quirke had secretly handed her over to him and his wife after her mother died giving birth to her. This subterfuge, after the vicissitudes she had suffered since it had been revealed to her — by Quirke, as it happened, one horribly memorable snowy day in that house south of Boston — seemed to Phoebe now not so much a cruel and unnatural betrayal, but rather an aspect of the design, of the blueprint, of Quirke's conception of life and how it might be conducted.

Rose had drawn her mouth down at one corner in a clownish grimace. "I don't know," she said, "that I approve."

"You mean you don't approve of David, or of my seeing him?"

"I haven't said I *dis*approve. I haven't decided."

"Do you know David?" Phoebe asked gently.

"Do I? I may have met him. I've certainly heard him spoken of."

"He's Jewish."

"Ah. Is he."

This brought a brief and thoughtful hiatus, during which Phoebe addressed herself to the rather tough and overcooked piece of beef on her plate. She drank more wine; she felt in need of its fortifying effect. "Do you disapprove of *that?*" she asked, keeping her eyes lowered.

"Of what?"

"You know very well what — of David's being a Jew."

"I have nothing but regard for the Jewish people," Rose said piously. "Industrious folk, careful with money, clever, resourceful, ambitious for their children. I confess I didn't know you had any, in this country."

"I didn't either, really," Phoebe said, laughing, "but we have."

Rose's face took on a dreamy look. "The Jews I know, or at least know of, are New Yorkers, mostly, doctors and dentists and the like, and their wives, large-sized ladies with moustaches and piercing voices."

"You see?" Phoebe cried, laughing again. "You *are* bigoted."

Rose was calmly dismissive, lifting her nose at an angle and gazing off to one side. "Some of the most charming and cultivated men I have known were bigots to the bone."

"Anyway," Phoebe said, "you needn't think you're going to put me off David by being horrible about him. In fact, he's no more Jewish than I am."

"And what's that supposed to mean, may I enquire?"

"Jewishness is a state of mind —"

"It most certainly is more than a state of mind, my girl. There's such a thing as blood."

163

"Oh, please," Phoebe said, groaning and laughing at the same time. "You're so old-fashioned. Blood! You sound like someone in the Bible."

"Which, I would remind you, was written by Jews. They know about such things."

"Such things? — what things?"

"Might I ask, my dear young woman, if by any chance you are familiar with the word *mis-ceg-en-ation?*"

Phoebe put down her cutlery, with a restrained bang this time. "I don't want to talk about this any more," she said, but found it impossible really to be angry with Rose, who she knew anyway was only amusing herself by talking about these things in this provocative way. Rose did not care much about anything; it was one of the reasons Phoebe was so fond of her. "Speaking of my father," she said, "I suspect he's on the way to getting himself into trouble again."

"If you think you can change the subject, I can tell you that you won't."

"I just have. You're not eating your fish, by the way — is it all right?"

"I'm too distracted, as you should know. This Sinclair —"

"This *trouble*," Phoebe said firmly, "that Quirke is manoeuvring himself into, has to do with that man who died, who was shot, Richard Jewell."

"Shot?" Rose repeated, diverted despite herself. "Didn't he shoot himself? That's what the papers implied."

"Quirke thinks someone else did it."

"Lord" — in her accent it was *Lawd* — "don't say he's playing at detectives again?"

"I'm afraid he is. He's teamed up with that Inspector Hackett —"

"Oh, my!"

"— and they're going about interviewing people, and all the rest of it, and generally behaving like a pair of schoolboys."

Phoebe had her eyes on her plate again, and kept them there. Despite the lightness of her tone she knew very well, and so did Rose, that the crimes that Quirke had involved himself in solving had not been schoolboy fare; terrible things had been done, and the doers of them had not all been brought to justice. The world, so Quirke and Inspector Hackett had taught Phoebe, is more darkly ambiguous than she would have guessed a few short years ago.

"And how," she asked, changing the subject again, "is my erstwhile father?"

"Erstwhile? What a way you people have of talking over here — it's like being in a Shakespeare play all the time. If you mean Malachy, my present spouse, well, my dear, I have to tell you he is getting more weird every day." Phoebe delighted in an accent that could put three distinct and separate syllables into the word *weird*. "He is loving-kindness itself, of course, and I treasure him, but Lordy, if I thought that after marrying him I could shape and mould the man, I was very, *ve-ry* mistaken. Stubborn as an old mule, that's my Mal. But then" — she sighed — "I wouldn't have him any other way." She pushed her plate away with one finger.

Despite being distracted, as she claimed, she had eaten every morsel on it save the fish-bones. Rose had been poor when she was young, before she married a rich man, and she had the old habit still of letting nothing go to waste. "You do know," she said, "that I once had a notion of your — what's the opposite of erstwhile? — well, of your *real* father, the impossible Doctor Quirke?"

"Yes, I know," Phoebe said, keeping her voice steady; she too had once had a notion of Rose as her stepmother, and had been bitterly disappointed and resentful when Rose had fixed on Malachy Griffin instead.

"It would have been a disaster, of course — a *dis-aster*, my dear."

"Yes, it probably would."

"Quirke, you see, would have stood up to me, and there would have been fights — oh, my, there would have been *fights*."

"But you said Malachy is stubborn too."

"Stubborn is one thing, relentless is another. And ruthless. You know Quirke."

Did she? Somehow, she doubted it. Somehow, Phoebe thought, there would be no knowing Quirke, not really. He did not even know himself.

"Relentless," Phoebe said, "yes, I suppose he is."

Rose was scanning the dessert menu intently; she had a sweet tooth, which she tried to resist, with not much success. She ordered meringues with cream and raspberry sauce. Phoebe said she would have coffee only; she was feeling slightly queasy, after her struggle with that steak.

"And this business about the man that was shot," Rose said, "I suppose he won't let that alone until he's caused the usual mayhem and annoyed powerful people and got himself roughed up and set everyone against him? He's a kind of innocent, you know, in spite of everything. That's what your late grandfather used to say about him. *Quirke's a damn fool*, Josh would say. *He thinks a good man can set the world to right, all the while not seeing that the last thing folks want is the world to be as it should be.* And he knew about the world, and about folks, did my Josh."

Rose's meringues arrived, they looked like soiled snow splashed with blood. Phoebe averted her eyes. "Yet you said Quirke also is ruthless," she said.

"And so he is, when it comes to getting what he wants, for himself. That's what they're all like, these self-appointed knights in shining armour — inside all that gleaming steel they're just like the rest of us, greedy and selfish and cruel. Oh, don't mistake me" — she waved her dessert spoon — "I love Quirke dearly, I surely do. I was *in* love with him, once, for a while, but that didn't stop me from seeing him as he is." She gave Phoebe a piercing look, and grinned. "I know what you're thinking — it takes one to know one. And it's true. I ain't no saint" — suddenly she was a hillbilly — "but I don't pretend otherwise. Now do I?"

"You're better than you think," Phoebe said, smiling. "And Quirke is better than you think, too."

"Well, my darling, you may be right, but oh, dear, you have so much to learn. By the way, this meringue is just *dee-licious*."

A leaden dawn was struggling to break when the telephone on Quirke's bedside table rang. He reared up in fright, fighting an arm free from the tangle of sheets, his heart pounding. In his haste he knocked the receiver off its stand and had to fumble for it on the floor. He feared and hated telephones. It was Isabel Galloway; he knew it was she almost before she spoke. "You bastard," she said breathily — her lips must have been pushed against the mouthpiece — and immediately hung up. He kept the receiver to his ear, listening to the hollow hum inside it, his head hanging and his eyes shut tight. Dear God.

The room was hot and airless and smelt of himself. He found his cigarettes on the table, lit one. He got out of bed and drew the curtains all the way open. Three floors below, the long narrow garden that no one ever tended was a riot of sullen green under the grey light of day. The cigarette smoke made him cough; he doubled over, hacking and wheezing. He needed a drink — what he would not give for a drink, right now, despite the hour and his cotton-wool morning mouth. He sat down on the side of the bed and dialled her number. Engaged — she would have left it off the hook. He pictured her, in her silk tea-gown with the big flowers printed on it, lying across the bed with her face in the pillows, sobbing, and cursing him between sobs.

How did she know? How had she found out?

He realised, later, what a mistake he had made in not going straight away to her house in Portobello, however early it was when she had called him. Now it was his turn to curse himself. He was cutting open the rib-cage of an old woman who had died under suspicious circumstances in the care of her spinster daughter when Sinclair came to tell him he was wanted urgently on the phone — the phone, again! — and something inside him instantly turned to ice.

She had been brought to St James's. Of all the city's hospitals it was the one he disliked most. Whenever he thought of the place he recalled with a shiver a night of storm and black rain when he had stood sheltering in a bleak porch under the wildly swaying light of an oil lamp — an oil lamp? surely he was mistaken? — and waited for a nurse who worked in the casualty department, who was supposed to be going on a date with him, but who in the end stood him up. How Isabel had got there he never discovered — maybe she had called for an ambulance herself, before she took the pills. He would not have put it past her.

She was in a tiny room with a narrow brick window that looked down on a brick boiler-house. The bed too was narrow, much too narrow, it seemed, to accommodate a normal-sized person, even one as trimly made as Isabel. Her face was drawn and had a greenish cast. She had on what he could see was a hospital smock. Her arms were outside the blankets, stretched rigid at her sides. *At least*, he thought, *she did not cut her wrists.*

169

"You know," he said, "this kind of thing is terribly bad for your health."

She gazed at him in silence. She had the look of an El Greco martyr. "That's right, laugh," she said. "A joke for every occasion."

She was hoarse, he supposed from the effect of the tubes they would have forced down her throat when they were pumping her stomach. He had spoken to the ward sister, a raw-faced nun in a white wimple, who had not met his eye but tightened her lips and said Miss Galloway had been very careless, swallowing all those pills by accident; no, she had not been in serious danger; yes, they would keep her in tonight and probably she could go home tomorrow.

"Do you want me to open this window?" he asked her now. "It's stuffy in here."

"Jesus," Isabel said, "is that all you can say, that it's stuffy?"

"What do you want me to say?"

He felt sorry for her, and yet he felt remote from her, too, remote from everything here in this shabby little room, as if he were floating high up under the ceiling and looking down on the scene with no more than mild curiosity.

"I didn't think you could be so cruel," she said.

"I didn't think you could be so stupid." He winced; the words had come out before he could check them. He lifted his shoulders and let them droop again. "I'm sorry."

She stirred in the bed, as if something somewhere had delivered her a stab of pain. "Yes, well, you're not half as sorry as I am."

"How did you find out? Who told you?"

She tried to laugh, but coughed instead, drily. "Did you think you could climb into bed with the widow of what's-his-name — Diamond Dick, is it? — while he was still fresh in his grave and that half the city wouldn't know before you'd got your socks back on? You're not only a louse, Quirke, you're a fool, too." She turned her face to the wall.

He did not want to see her suffer, really, he did not, but he felt paralysed and did not know how to help her. "I'm sorry," he said again, more weakly than ever.

She was not listening. "What's she like, anyway?" she asked. "Which kind of French is she — sultry and smouldering, or cool and detached?"

"Don't."

"You'd prefer cool, I imagine. You don't go in much for passion, do you?"

He wished she would stop: he did not want to be made to pity her. "I'm sorry I've hurt you," he said. "These things happen. It's no one's fault."

"Oh, no," she said bitterly, "no one's to blame, of course, least of all you. Give me a cigarette, will you?"

"I don't think you should smoke."

"Bad for my health?" She had turned from the wall and was watching him narrowly, searching for a way to wound, he could see. "You know she's been through every half-presentable man in this town, don't you? Or did you think you were the first? She hated that husband of hers — it's probably her that shot him. She must have a taste for bastards — first him and now you. God, what are we like — women, that is? Such fools."

"I'll come for you in the morning," he said. "I'll take you home."

"Don't bother." She struggled to sit up. He made to help her with the pillows but she slapped at him with both hands and told him to get away from her. "You never loved me, Quirke."

"I don't think I've ever loved anyone," he said mildly.

"Except yourself."

"Myself least of all."

"What about that wife you had of yore that you talk about so much? What's her name? — Delia?"

"She died."

"Oh, that's not allowed, is it, dying?" She looked at him, the sad spectacle of what he was. "I almost feel sorry for you," she said.

"I'd rather you didn't."

She turned her face aside again. "Goodbye, Quirke."

As he walked away down the long corridors he was aware of a faint sharp pain, as if he had been pierced by a bolt shot from another planet, a wounding so fine it could hardly be felt.

The smell of hospitals, he realised, was the smell of his life.

In the street he huddled in a telephone booth and called Françoise.

"What's wrong?" she asked. He told her. There was a long silence on the line. Then she said, "Come to the house."

CHAPTER
NINE

On Sunday mornings when the weather permitted Quirke bought an armful of the English newspapers and sat with them on a bench by the canal below Huband Bridge. There he read, and smoked, and tried to forget for a while the emotional complications into which over the years he had allowed himself to stumble. Today the papers were full of menacing news. It was some comfort to Quirke, but not much, that the world was in so much more of a sorry state than he was.

The morning was hot still but at least the cloud cover of recent days had lifted and the sun was shining out of what seemed a freshly lacquered sky. On the water a moorhen paddled busily about with five chicks veering in a line behind her, like feathered balls of soot, and an iridescent dragonfly was prancing among the tall shoots of sedge. Gamal Abdel Nasser had been appointed president of Egypt. Polio was still on the increase. He lit another Senior Service and leaned back and closed his eyes. *Gamasser appointed pres. Egypt on the increase. Gamdel Abel Nassolio . . .*

"Doctor Quirke — am I right?"

He emerged with a start from his doze.

Who?

Blue suit, horn-rimmed specs, oiled black hair brushed fiercely back from a pock-marked brow. He was sitting at the other end of the bench, one arm laid easily along the back of it and one knee crossed on the other. Familiar, but who was he?

There was an inch and a half of ash on Quirke's forgotten cigarette; it detached itself now and tumbled softly to the ground.

"Costigan," the man said, and took his arm from the back of the bench and laced his fingers together before his breast. When he smiled he bared the lower front row of his teeth; they were yellow, and overlapped. "You don't remember me."

"Sorry, I don't recall . . .?"

"I knew your adoptive father, Judge Griffin. And Malachy Griffin, of course. And we had a drink together, once, you and I, in McGonagle's public house, if I'm not mistaken. A drink and a chat." Those teeth again.

Costigan. Yes, of course.

"I remember," Quirke said.

"Do you?" Costigan looked exaggeratedly pleased.

Yes, Quirke remembered. Costigan had padded into the pub that day and delivered a warning that Quirke had ignored, and afterwards he had been attacked in the street and given a beating that had left him with a broken knee and a limp for life. He remembered, all right. Now he ground the butt of his cigarette under a heel and began gathering up the newspapers. "Nice to see you again," he said, beginning to rise.

"Very sad," Costigan said, "about poor Dick Jewell." Quirke slowly sat down again. He waited. Costigan had turned his attention to the moorhen and her brood. "Lovely spot, this. You live nearby, don't you?" He jerked a thumb over his shoulder. "Mount Street? Number thirty-nine?"

"What do you want, Costigan?"

Costigan put on a look of innocent surprise. "Want, Doctor Quirke? I was just strolling along here and saw you sitting and thought I'd stop and say a word. How are you, these days? Did you recover from that mishap you had? A fall, wasn't it, down some steps? Very unfortunate."

Costigan was a leading light in the Knights of St Patrick, a shady and powerful organisation of Catholic businessmen, professionals, politicians. It was the Knights, among others, that Quirke had provoked, which was why he had ended up with a smashed knee at the bottom of those steps that night — three years ago, was it, four? He said, "Why don't you say what you have to say, Costigan?"

Costigan was nodding, as if he had come to an agreement with himself on something. "I was just thinking," he said, "walking along here this lovely morning in the sunshine, how different things often are from the way they seem. Take the canal, there. Smooth as glass, with those ducks or whatever they are, and the reflection of that white cloud, and the midges going up and down like the bubbles in a bottle of soda water — a picture of peace and tranquillity, you'd say. But think what's going on underneath the surface, the big fish

175

eating the little ones, and the bugs on the bottom fighting over the bits that float down, and everything covered in slime and mud."

He turned his bland gaze to Quirke, smiling. "You might say that's how the world is. You might say, in fact, that there are two distinct worlds, the world where everything seems grand and straightforward and simple — that's the world that the majority of people live in, or at least imagine they live in — and then there's the real world, where the real things go on."

He took out a gold cigarette case and opened it on his palm and offered it to Quirke. Quirke shook his head. "No, thanks." He should stand up now, he knew, he should stand up and walk away from here. But he could not.

Costigan struck a match and lit his cigarette, and dropped the spent match on the ground beside Quirke's right shoe.

"I needn't ask which is your world," Quirke said.

"Ah, but that's where you're wrong, Doctor Quirke. That's where you're wrong. I don't operate in either world exclusively, but somewhere in between the two. I acknowledge them both. I have, you might say, a foot in both. People must have sunshine and calm water with baby ducks on it, if they're not to sink into despair. Deep down they know how things really are, but they pretend not to, and manage to convince themselves, or to convince themselves enough to keep the pretence going. And that's where I come in, me, and a few others of a like mind. We move between the worlds, and it's our job to make sure the appearances are kept up — to

176

hide the dark stuff and emphasise the light. It's quite a responsibility, I can tell you."

There was silence then between them. Costigan seemed quite calm, cheerful, almost, as if he were greatly pleased with his little speech, and were thinking back over it admiringly.

"Did you know Dick Jewell?" Quirke asked.

"I did."

"I wouldn't have thought he was the kind of person you and your cronies would find congenial. You're not going to tell me he was a member of the Knights, and him a Jew?"

"I didn't say I knew him well."

"He certainly lived in the second world, among the big fish."

"And he was also a benefactor of many of our projects."

"Such as St Christopher's?"

Costigan smiled and slowly nodded. Quirke wondered if he might be a spoiled priest, for he had a priestly manner, bland and soft but with an interior hard as stone. "Such as St Christopher's," he said, "yes. Where I believe you spent a little time when you were small, and where I believe you visited again the other day. Might I ask, Doctor Quirke, what exactly it was you were after?"

"What business is it of yours?"

"Just curious, Doctor Quirke, just curious. Like yourself, I imagine. For I know you are an inquisitive man — you have that reputation."

Quirke made himself stand up. The bundle of newspapers under his arm was the size and heft of a schoolbag, and he felt for a dizzying moment as if he were a small boy again, standing accused before the Head Brother, or the Dean of Discipline. "Have you come to threaten me, like the last time?" he asked.

Costigan lifted his eyebrows and his hands in unison. "Quite the contrary, Doctor Quirke," he said. "Like the last time, I'm giving you a friendly tip, so you can avoid getting into — what shall we say? — a threatening situation."

"And what is it, this tip?"

Costigan was gazing up at him with what seemed a lively and sympathetic air, though stifling a smile. "Leave off this amateur detective stuff, Doctor Quirke. That's my tip. Leave it to the real detective, to — what's his name? — Hackett. Dick Jewell, St Christopher's, the Sumners —"

"The Sumners? What about the Sumners?"

"I'm telling you" — a touch of weary exasperation had come into his voice — "you'd be best advised to lay off. You're a very inquisitive man, Doctor Quirke, very inquisitive. It got you in trouble before, and it'll get you in trouble again. And speaking of trouble: what is it the French say? — *cherchez la femme*? Or should I say, give up *cherchezing la femme*. If you'll take my advice. Which I hope you will, if you're wise."

The two men gazed at each other, Costigan calm as ever, Quirke turning pale with outrage and anger. Costigan chuckled. "As you see," he said, "you find out a lot of things, moving between the two worlds."

178

Quirke began to walk away. Behind him, Costigan called his name, and despite himself he stopped and turned. The man on the bench made an undulant swimming motion with one hand. "Remember," he said, "the little fish, and the big fish. And the mud at the bottom."

Dannie Jewell had known Teddy Sumner since they were children, when the Sumners and the Jewells were still friends. She did not like Teddy, really — he was not an easy person to like — but she felt something for him. They both had things to cope with, their respective families, for a start. But Teddy was peculiar, with peculiar ways. There was the fact that he had no interest in girls. Dannie often asked herself if it was just that he had no interest in *her*, but no, she believed it was a general indifference. This she considered a point in his favour. It was positively restful to have someone around that you did not have to watch every word with, and who, when you did say something, did not take it as *significant* in the way that fellows almost always did. In fact, she, for her part, had not much interest in boys. They were all right for playing tennis with, or calling up when you felt low, as she did with David Sinclair, but when they started getting soppy or, worse, when they tried something on and were rebuffed and then got angry, they were either frightening or a bore.

But she did not think Teddy was the other way inclined, either.

He was hirsute and muscular, like his father, but about two-thirds the size, a hairy little fellow with a low forehead and a square chin. He had meltingly soft brown eyes, again like his father, and a bandy gait that was oddly endearing. His temper was terrible and he was quick to take offence, which made him impossible, sometimes. He despised himself, Dannie supposed, but that hardly made him unique.

He was wicked, she knew, wicked, and probably dangerous. She indulged herself in him, as she might in some awful, secret sin. He made her feel gleeful — it was the only word — and at the same time ashamed. Even the shame, though, was enjoyable. Just to be with Teddy was already to have gone too far. He was like a child, wilful and cruel, and in his company she allowed herself to be childish, too. Teddy was dirty, and she could be dirty with him.

She knew she should not have told him about the afternoon on Howth Head with David Sinclair and Phoebe Griffin. But she also knew that Teddy was fascinated by the things other people did, the simple things that make up a life, for those who are capable of living. He was like a creature from another planet, charmed and baffled by the doings of these earthlings among whom he was forced to carry on his precarious existence.

They were on an outing of their own, she and Teddy, when she described the visit to Howth to him in hilarious detail. She knew she was betraying David Sinclair by talking like this but she could not stop herself — it was a guilty pleasure, like wetting the bed when she was little.

Teddy had a Morgan that his parents had given him for a present on his twenty-first. It was a gorgeous little car, green like a scarab beetle, with cream-coloured leather upholstery and spoked wheels. In it they would spend happy afternoons cruising the outskirts of the city with the hood down, Dannie with a wind-blown silk scarf at her neck and Teddy wearing a cravat and Italian sunglasses. They favoured the more characterless suburbs for these expotitions, as they called them — she was Pooh Bear and he was Eeyore — where the lower classes lived, dreary new housing estates of pebble-dashed three-ups, two-downs that were all alike, or pre-war council estates struggling to become gentrified, in which the Morgan must have appeared as outlandish and expensive as a spaceship. They would point out to each other the more pathetic efforts the householders had made to add a bit of class to their properties, the fancy name-plates screwed to wrought-iron gates, with names like Dunroamin, or Lisieux, or St Jude's; the venetian blinds proudly displayed in every single window, no matter how tiny or narrow; the preposterous built-on porches, with leaded panes of stained glass and miniature plaster statues of the Sacred Heart or the Blessed Virgin or the Little Flower presiding in niches over the front door. And then there were the garden ornaments, the fake fountains, the plastic Bambis, the jolly, red-cheeked gnomes peeping out among the beds of hydrangeas and snap-dragon and phlox. Oh, how they laughed at all this, a hand pressed over their mouths and their eyes bulging. And how soiled this made Dannie feel, how gloriously soiled.

They played amusing games. They would stop outside a house where a pensioner was mowing the lawn, and simply sit and stare at him until he took fright and fled indoors, where they would see him, a reddened old nose and one wild eye, lurking behind the lace curtains like some burrowing creature scared into its hole. Or they would fix on a housewife coming home from the shops loaded down with bags of groceries, and drive along in first gear at a walking pace a couple of yards behind her. Children they tended to leave in peace — it was not so long since they had been children themselves, and they remembered what it was like — but now and then they would pull up at a kerb and Dannie would ask the way of a fat boy in bulging short pants, or a washed-out girl in pigtails, speaking to them not in English but in French, and pretending to be puzzled and offended that they did not understand her. When they tired of these games they would drive back into the city and stop for afternoon tea at the Shelbourne or the Hibernian, and Teddy would amuse himself by submerging halfpennies in the sugar bowls and the little pots of jam, or squashing out cigarette butts under the little vases of flowers that adorned the tables.

Today Teddy was agog to hear every detail of the afternoon in Howth. He knew David Sinclair slightly, and professed to think him altogether too slippery and sly, "like all the Jews", as he said darkly; Phoebe he had not met, but clapped his hands and crowed in delight at

182

Dannie's malicious description of her, the little pale pinched face and the mouse-claws, the bobbed black hair, the sort of dirndl thing she had worn with the elasticated bodice and convent girl's lace collar.

"But weren't they on a date?" Teddy asked. "— Why did Sinclair bring you along?"

Dannie paused. She did not like the dismissive way he said it. Why would David not ask her to come with him and Phoebe, even if it was a date? "It wasn't like that," she said sulkily. "It wasn't a *date* date."

They were driving slowly down a long road of featureless houses somewhere in Finglas, she thought it was, or Cabra, maybe, on the lookout for likely victims to follow and stare at.

"Do you think they're — you know — doing it?" Teddy asked.

"She doesn't seem the type. Besides, I think something happened to her, in America."

"What sort of something?" Teddy asked. He was wearing a blue yachting blazer with brass buttons and a crest on the pocket, and fawn slacks. She had noticed that he had begun to use perfume, though she supposed he would say it was shaving lotion.

"I think she might have been . . ." She hesitated: this was too much, too much; she should stop now and say not another word on the subject.

"Might have been what?" Teddy demanded.

"Well" — she could not stop — "ravished, I think."

Teddy's brown eyes widened to the size of pennies. "Ravished?" he said, in a hoarse whisper. "Do tell."

"Can't," she said. "Don't know. It was just a remark she made, about being caught in a car with somebody when she was over there. It was years ago. As soon as she saw I was interested she changed the subject."

Teddy pouted disappointedly. "Did you ask the Rabbi Sinclair?"

"Did I ask him what?"

"If they're doing it or not!"

"Of course I didn't. I suppose you would have."

"I certainly would."

There was nothing Teddy would not ask about, nothing he would not ferret into, no matter how private or painful. He had got her to describe to him that Sunday morning at Brooklands, the blood, and the horror. He had envied her, she had seen it in his eyes, the almost yearning expression in them.

"Oh, look," he said now urgently, "look at the fat lady hanging up her bloomers on the clothes-line, let's pull over and have a good gander at her." He drew the car to the kerb and stopped. The woman had not noticed them yet. She had a clutch of clothes pegs in her mouth. "A laundry-line on the front lawn," Teddy murmured, "that's a new one."

Dannie was glad that he was diverted. She was feeling more and more guilty for talking as she had. She liked Phoebe: Phoebe was funny, in a clever, understated way, a way that Dannie could never be. And Phoebe was fond of David Sinclair, that was obvious, and perhaps he was fond of her, though it was always hard to tell, with David. She wanted him to be happy. She wondered if she might be a little in love

184

with him herself. But in that case would she not be jealous of Phoebe? She knew she did not understand these things, love, and passion, and wanting someone. That had all been stopped in her, long ago, tied off, the way a doctor would tie off her tubes so as to keep her from having babies. In fact, that was a thing she was going to have done as soon as she could find somewhere to go; it would have to be in London, she supposed. She would ask Françoise; it was the kind of thing Françoise would know about.

The fat woman was a disappointment: when she had finished hanging up the laundry she merely threw them a look and chuckled and waddled off into the house.

"Cow," Teddy said in disgust, and drove them away.

They did not go for tea that day, but went to the Phoenix Park instead. Teddy parked the car by the Wellington monument and they strolled over the grass, under the trees. The sunlight seemed vague somehow and diffused, as if it were weary after so many hours of shining without stint. A herd of deer grazing in a cloud of pale dust stopped at their approach, and lifted their heads, their nostrils twitching and stumpy ears waggling. Stupid animals, Dannie thought, and only pretty from a distance; up close they were shabby, and their coats looked like lichen.

"You know," she said, "they're saying now that Richard was murdered."

Teddy did not seem surprised, or even much interested, and she was sorry she had spoken. It was when she was bored that she blurted things out. She remembered how when she was a child, at Brooklands, she would squat by the pond at the bottom of the Long Field and poke a stick into the muddy shallows and watch the water bugs swimming and scurrying frantically away. How nice it was the way the mud would swirl up in chocolatey spirals, and then spread itself out until all the water was the colour of tea, or turf, or dead leaves, and nothing more was to be seen of all that life down there, all that squirming, desperate life.

"Who did it?" Teddy enquired casually. "— Do they know?"

He seemed so calm, indifferent, almost. Had he known about Richard, what he was like, the things he did? Perhaps everyone knew. She felt a little thrill of terror. She remembered at school those curious periods of suspended waiting, after she had done something bad and before it was found out. They gave her the same kind of thrill, those breathless intervals, and she would feel as if she were floating weightlessly in some medium lighter even than air and yet wonderfully sustaining. But what, now, had she done that she was waiting to be discovered? And how would they punish her, since she was not guilty, not really?

"No," she said, "they don't know who killed him. At least no one has said, if they do." She giggled; it was a real giggle; it startled her. "Françoise is trying to make them think it was your father."

Teddy stopped and bent to detach a twig from the leg of his slacks. "Trying to make who think?"

"The police. And that doctor fellow, Quirke, that David works with."

"Quirke."

"Yes. He's Phoebe's father, as a matter of fact."

He straightened. "Didn't you say her name was Griffin?"

"She was adopted or something, I don't know."

"He's a doctor?"

"A pathologist. He came down with the guards, that day."

"But why would your sister-in-law be trying to convince him of anything?"

Dannie stopped and made him stop with her, and they stood facing each other.

"Teddy Sumner," she said, "tell me why you aren't shocked that Françoise should be trying to make people think your father murdered my brother?"

"Were you trying to shock me?"

"Yes — of course."

He smiled his sly smile. "You should know by now that I'm unshockable."

"Your father didn't, by the way — do it."

"Well, I hardly thought he had."

"Oh, I don't know. He might have. They were always fighting, Richard and your father."

But Teddy was thinking of something else. "Do you talk about all this to Sinclair?"

"A little. Not much. He doesn't ask."

"But you do talk to him about it." She walked on and he trotted after her. "You do tell him secrets, I'm sure you do."

"I don't. I don't tell anyone my secrets."

"Even me?"

"Especially you." They stopped on a rise from where there was a view over the roofs of the city sweltering in the quivering heat haze. "I wish this weather would break," Dannie said.

"You know I knew your brother quite well," Teddy said, in a tone of studied diffidence.

"Did you? How?"

"There's a sort of club we were in — I mean, that he was in, and that I'm still in, I suppose."

"What club?"

"It doesn't matter. More a sort of an organisation. He got me in, Richard did. He said it would be" — he gave a bleak little laugh — "just the thing for me."

"And was it — is it?"

He kicked moodily at the grass with the toe of his two-toned shoe. "I don't know. I feel a bit out of my depth, to tell the truth."

"What do they do, in this club?"

"Nothing much. They visit places . . ."

"Like, abroad?"

"No, no. It's a charity thing. Schools." He whistled briefly, softly, squinting out over the city. "Orphanages."

"Yes?" She felt herself grow pale. What did he mean? "I wouldn't have thought that was quite *you*, Teddy," she said, forcing a light tone, "visiting schools and being nice to orphans."

"It isn't me," he said. "At least, I didn't think it was. Until your brother convinced me."

188

She could not go on looking at him, and turned her face towards the city. "When did you join this club?" she asked, her voice wobbly.

"When I left college. I was at a loose end, and Richard — Richard encouraged me. And I joined up."

"And started visiting places."

"Yes."

He turned to her, and there was something in his look, a kind of anguish, and suddenly she understood, and now she did not want him to say any more, not another word. She turned on her heel and set off back in the direction of the car. There were those deer again, in their moth-eaten pelts, with those disgusting black channels at their eyes as if since birth they had been weeping, weeping, weeping.

"Pooh Bear," Teddy called after her softly, pleadingly, in his Eeyore voice, "oh, Winnie!" but she went on, and did not look back.

She was glad he did not try to catch up with her. She hurried down the hill to the park gates and crossed the river and got a taxi outside the railway station. Her mind was blank, or rather it was a jumble of things — like an attic in an earthquake, was how she thought of it. For she knew this state well, the state that she always got into when one of her anxiety attacks, or whatever they were, was coming on.

She must get back now to her own place, and be among her own things.

So hot, the evening, so hot and close, she could hardly breathe.

The taxi man had bad breath — she could smell it from the back seat. He was talking to her about something over his shoulder but she was not listening.

Orphanages.

When she got to the flat in Pembroke Street she filled a tepid bath and lay in it for a long time, trying to calm her racing mind. There were pigeons on the sill outside the window: she could hear them, cooing in that soft secretive way that they did, as if they were exclaiming over some amazing piece of scandal that was being told to them.

After her bath she sat in her dressing-gown at the kitchen table and drank coffee, cup after cup of it. She knew it was bad for her, that the caffeine would make her thoughts race all the faster, but she could not stop.

She went into the living room and lay on the sofa. She felt cooler now, after bathing in the cool water. She wished she had something to hold on to, to hug. Phoebe Griffin had confessed she still had her teddy bear from childhood. Something like that would be good — but what? She had nothing like that; she had never had anything like that.

Thinking of Phoebe's bear made her think of Teddy Sumner, even though she did not want to. Silly name, Teddy. And yet somehow it suited him, even though he was nothing like a teddy bear.

In the end she called David Sinclair. She knew it was not fair, calling him when she was like this. It was not as if she were anything more to him than a friend. David was kind — what other man would come and take care of her, as he did, without getting something in return?

He was not at home, so she looked up the number of the hospital where he worked and phoned him there. When he heard who it was he said nothing for a moment or two, and she was afraid he might hang up. She could hear him breathing. "I'm sorry," she said. "I can never think who else to call."

He arrived at the flat an hour later, and sat with her and held her hand. He gave her the old lecture about "seeing" someone, about "talking" to someone, but what good would seeing or talking do? The damage had been started so long ago, and the marks of it were scored so deeply into her that she pictured them, like jagged grooves gouged in some kind of stone, marble, or what was that other one, alabaster? Yes, alabaster. She liked the sound of it. Her alabaster skin. For she was beautiful, she knew it, everyone had always told her she was. Not that it helped her, being beautiful. A doll could be beautiful, a doll that people could do anything with, love or cuddle or beat or — or anything. But David was so good to her, so patient, so kind. He prided himself on being a tough guy, she knew, but he was not tough, not really. Guarded, that was what he was, wary of showing what he felt, but behind the hard front that he put up he had a soft heart. Some day she would tell him all the things that had happened to her, that had made her as she was, this shivering creature huddled on a sofa with the curtains pulled while everyone else was outside enjoying the summer evening. Yes, some day she would tell him.

He stayed, as he always did, until she was asleep. She did not take long to drop off — he was her sedative, he ruefully told himself — and it was still early, not yet nine, when he slipped out of the house and turned left and walked up towards Fitzwilliam Square. The car that had been parked on the other side of the road when he arrived — a green Morgan, with the hood up, and someone inside it, a shadow behind the wheel — was no longer there. He walked on.

There was a hazy green glow over the square and mist on the grass behind the black railings. The whores were out, four or five of them, two of them keeping each other company, both skinny and dressed in black and starkly pale as the harpies in Dracula's castle. They gave him a look as he passed by but made no overture; maybe they thought he was a plainclothes man out to trap them. One of them had a limp — the clap, most likely. One day, not so far in the future, he might fold back the corner of a sheet and find her before him on the slab, that thin face, the bluish eyelids closed, her lip still swollen. He wondered, as he often wondered, if he should leave this city, try his luck somewhere else, London, New York, even. Quirke would never retire, or by the time he did it would be too late to be his successor; something that was in him now would have been used up, a vital force would be gone.

He had walked up this way, rather than going down to Baggot Street, to avoid being tempted to call on Phoebe. He did not know why he was reluctant to see her. She was probably not at home, anyway: he thought he remembered Quirke saying he would be taking her to dinner tonight. It struck him that he had no friends. He did not mind this. There were people he knew, of course, from college days, from work, but he rarely saw any of them. He preferred his own company. He did not suffer fools gladly and the world was full of fools. But that was not what was keeping him from Phoebe, for Phoebe was certainly no fool.

Poor Dannie. Was there to be no help for her? Something had happened in her life that she would not speak about, something unspeakable, then.

He walked around two sides of the square and turned up towards Leeson Street. Maybe he would call into Hartigan's and drink a beer; he liked to sit on a stool in the corner and watch the life of the pub going on, what people took to be life. As he was passing by Kingram Place a fellow in a windcheater stepped out, waggling a cigarette at him. "Got a match, pal?" He was reaching for his lighter in his jacket pocket when he heard a rapid step behind him, and then there was a crash of some kind, and a burst of light, and after that, nothing but blackness.

Quirke had been to dinner, but not with Phoebe. Françoise had invited him to the house on Stephen's Green. She had said that she would be alone and that she would cook dinner for them both, but when he arrived Giselle was there, which surprised and irritated him. It was not that he felt any particular antipathy towards the child — she was nine years old, what was there to take against? — but he found her uncanniness

193

hard to deal with. She made him think of a royal pet, so much indulged and pampered that it would no longer be acknowledged or even recognised by its own kind. He had, too, when she was about, the sense of being sidled up against, somehow, in a most disconcerting way.

Françoise did not seem to think anything of the child's presence, and if she noticed his annoyance she did not remark it. This evening she wore a scarlet silk blouse and a black skirt, and no jewellery, as usual. He noticed how she kept her hands out of sight as much as possible; women of a certain age, he knew, were sensitive of their hands. But surely she could be no more than — what, thirty-eight? forty? Isabel Galloway was younger, but not by much. The thought of Isabel brought a further darkening of his mood.

They ate asparagus, which someone at the French Embassy had sent round; it had come in from Paris that morning in the diplomatic bag. Quirke did not care for the stuff, but did not say so; later on his pee would smell of boiled cabbage. They ate in a little annex to the overly grand dining room, a small square wood-panelled space with a canopy-shaped ceiling and windows on two sides looking on to the Japanese garden. The calm grey air, tinted by reflections from the gravel outside, burnished the cutlery and made the single tall candle in its pewter sconce seem to shed not light but a sort of pale fine haze. Giselle sat with them, eating a bowl of mess made from bread and sugar and hot milk. She was in her pyjamas. Her braids were wound in tight coils and pinned at either side of her head like a pair of large black earphones. The lenses of her spectacles were opaque in the light from the windows and only now and then and for a second did her eyes flash out, large, quick, intently watchful. Quirke wondered wistfully when it would be her bedtime. She talked about school, and about a girl in her class called Rosemary, who was her friend, and gave her sweets. Françoise attended to her with an expression of grave interest, nodding or smiling or frowning when required. She had, Quirke could not keep himself from thinking, the air of one playing a part that had been so long and diligently rehearsed that it had become automatic, had become, indeed, natural.

His mind drifted. He had been wrestling anew, for some days now, with the old problem of love. There should be nothing to it, love: people fell in and out of it all the time. Countless poems had been written about it, countless songs had been sung in its praise. It made the world go round, so it was said. He imagined them, the hordes of enraptured lovers down the ages, millions upon millions of them, lashing at the poor old globe with the flails of their passion, keeping it awhirl on its wobbly axis like a spinning-top. The love that people spoke of so much seemed a kind of miasmic cloud, a kind of ether, teeming with bacilli, through which we move as we move through the ordinary air, immune to infection for most of the time but destined to succumb sooner or later, somewhere or other, struck down to writhe upon our beds in tender torment.

With Isabel Galloway it had not been difficult. She and Quirke had both known what they wanted, more or less — a little pleasure, a little company, someone to admire and be admired by. It was a different matter with Françoise d'Aubigny. The heat that Quirke and she generated together gave off a whiff of brimstone. He knew the kind of fire that he was playing with, the damage it could do. Isabel had been the first victim; who would be next? Him? Françoise? Giselle? — for she was in it too, he was sure of it, lodged between them like a swaddled bundle even in their most intimate moments together.

He caught himself up — Isabel the first victim? Ah, no.

The child now had finished her pap and Françoise rose from the table and took her by the hand. "Say goodnight to Doctor Quirke," she said, and the child gave him a narrow look.

When they had left the room, Quirke pushed his plate away and lit a cigarette. The dying light of evening had taken on a grey-brown tinge. He was uneasy. He had not reckoned on the child being in the house — though where else would she be? — and he was not sure what to expect of Françoise, or what she would expect of him. He imagined the child lying in that narrow white bed in that ghostly white room, sleepless and vigilant for hours, listening intently for every smallest sound around her. He had not slept with Françoise in this house, and thought it unlikely that he would, this night, anyway. Yet he could not be sure. He was not sure of anything, with Françoise. Maybe she had only slept with him at his flat that one time in a moment of weakness, because she had needed a body to hold on to for a little while, in an effort to warm herself back to life. For when her husband died she must have felt something in herself die, along with him. How could she not? Thinking about these things, Quirke would frequently experience a sort of violent start, like the sensation of missing a step in sleep and being jerked into wakefulness, breathless and shocked — shocked at himself, at Françoise d'Aubigny, at what they were doing together. How, in such circumstances, he would ask himself, how could he imagine himself in love? And again he would seem to catch that sulphurous whiff rising up out of the depths.

What would he do now, tonight, if she asked him to stay? Along with Giselle there was another presence in this house, a listening ghost as vigilant as the living child would be.

He had finished his cigarette and started another when Françoise came back and took her place opposite him again — he always found stirring that way women had of sweeping a hand under their bottoms to smooth their skirts when they sat down — and smiled at him and said that there were two escalopes of veal in the kitchen that she should go and cook.

"Sit for a minute," Quirke said. "I'm not very hungry."

He offered her a cigarette and then the flame of his lighter. She said, "I can see you disapprove of Giselle being allowed to stay up so late."

"Not at all. You're her mother. It's not my business."

"It is that she has bad dreams, you see."

He nodded. "And you?"

"Me?"

"What are your dreams like?"

She laughed a little, looking down. "Oh, I do not dream. Or if I do, I do not remember what I dreamed about."

There was a pause, and then he asked, "What are we doing, here, you and I?"

"Here, tonight?" Her black eyes had widened. "We are having dinner, I think, yes?"

Quirke leaned back in his chair. "Tell me about Marie Bergin," he said.

She started, as if at a pinprick. "Marie? How do you know Marie?"

"I went to see Carlton Sumner, as you recommended. Inspector Hackett and I went out to Roundwood."

"I see." She was looking at the burning tip of her cigarette. "And you spoke to him — to Carlton."

"Yes."

She waited. "And?"

Quirke looked through the window behind her to the sky's darkening blue over Iveagh Gardens. "He said you and your husband used to be friends with him and his wife. That they stayed with you, at your place in the South of France."

She made a quick, sweeping gesture with her left hand. "That was not a successful occasion."

"Something about towels."

"Towels? What do you mean, towels? Carl Sumner tried to make love to me. Now I am going to cook our food."

She stood up and walked from the alcove and quickly across the dining room and out, shutting the door behind her. She had left her cigarette half smoked in the ashtray. A lipstick stain on a cigarette, that was another thing that excited him, every time, whatever the circumstances. He thought of Carlton Sumner's bristling moustache, the sweat-stains at the armpits of his gold-coloured shirt. He rose from the table and went to the door through which Françoise had gone. Silence hung in the hallway like a drape. He remembered coming through the kitchen the day of the memorial party, and set off again in that direction.

She was standing by the sink, holding a glass of white wine with the fingers of both hands wrapped around the stem. The veal was on a plate by the stove, and there were carrots and broccoli on a wooden chopping board, waiting to be prepared. She did not turn when he came in. Blueblack night was in the window now. "I do not know what we are doing," she said, still without turning.

"I'm sorry," he said. "It was a stupid thing to say, to ask." He went and stood beside her and looked at her in profile. There were tears on her face. He touched her hands holding the glass and she flinched away from him. "Forgive me," he said.

She took a sharp breath and wiped at the tears with the heel of a hand. At last she turned. He saw that she was angry. "You know nothing," she said, "nothing."

"You're wrong," he said. "I know a great deal. That's why I'm here."

She shook her head. "I don't understand."

199

"Neither do I. But I am here."

She put down the wine glass and took a step towards him and he held her in his arms and kissed her, tasting the wine on her breath. She moved her face aside and leaned her cheek against his shoulder. "I do not know what to do," she said.

He did not know, either. With Isabel he had been free, or as free as it was possible to be with anyone; but now, here, what had seemed silk cords had turned out to be the rigid bars of a cage in which he was a captive.

He led her to a small plastic-topped table and they sat down, he on one side and she on the other, their hands entwined in the middle. "Tell me about Sumner," he said.

"Oh, what is there to tell? He tries his luck with every woman he meets."

"But you were friends, you and Richard and he."

She laughed. "You think that would make a difference, to a man like Carlton Sumner?"

"Did Richard know about this pass that Sumner made at you?"

"I told him, of course."

"And what did he do?"

"He asked them to leave."

"And they left."

"Yes. I don't know what Carl told Gloria, how he explained the sudden departure. I imagine she guessed."

"Could this have been the cause of the fight your husband had with Sumner at that business meeting?"

She gazed at him for a moment, then suddenly laughed. "Ah, *chérie*," she said, "you are so quaint and old-fashioned. Richard would not care about such a thing. When I told him, he was amused. The truth is, he was glad of a reason to ask them to leave, for he was bored with their company. I suspect, by the way, that Gloria had made a pass, as you say, at *him*. They were, they are, that kind of people, the Sumners." She took her hands from his, and he brought out his cigarettes. "What did he say to you, when you spoke to him?" she asked. "You tell me the policeman was there too? Carlton would have enjoyed that, a visit from the police."

"He said very little. That he had made your husband an offer of a partnership that day, and that your husband walked out."

"A partnership? That is a lie. He wanted — he *wants* — to take over the business entirely. He wanted Richard out, with some silly title — executive director, or something — that was his idea of a partnership." She turned and gestured vaguely towards the food on the counter. "We should eat . . ."

"I told you, I'm not hungry."

"I think you live on cigarettes."

"Don't forget alcohol — that, too."

They left the kitchen and went back to the nook in the dining room. The night was pressing its glossy back against the window. The candle had burned halfway, and a knobbly trail of wax had dripped down the side and on to the table. Quirke lifted the bottle of Bordeaux. "You were drinking white, in the kitchen . . . ?"

"Red will do, it doesn't matter — I never notice what I am drinking." She watched him pour. "Why did you ask about Marie Bergin? Did you see her at the Sumners'? Did you speak to her?"

"I saw her, yes. I didn't speak to her. She doesn't seem to say much. She looked frightened, to me."

"Frightened of what?"

"I don't know. Sumner, maybe. Why did you let her go?"

"Oh, you know what servants are like —"

"No, I don't."

"They come and they go. They always think they are being treated badly, and that things will be so very much better elsewhere." She was leaning forward with her hands clasped on the table before her and as she spoke her breath made the candle-flame waver, and phantom shadows leaped up the walls around them. "Marie was nice, but a silly girl. I don't know why you are interested in her."

He too leaned forward into the wavering cone of candlelight. "I'm trying to understand," he said, "why your husband was killed."

It struck him that each of them rarely spoke the other's name.

"But what has this servant girl to do with it?" Françoise demanded.

"I don't know. But there has to be a reason why he died." To that she said nothing. The prancing shadows around them grew still. "I think," he said, "I should go home."

202

His hand was resting on the table, she touched the back of it with her fingertips. "I hoped you would stay."

He thought of that sprite lying in her white room, staring into the darkness, attending.

"I think it's better that I go," he said.

She pressed her nails lightly into his skin. "I love you," she said, as matter-of-factly as if she were telling him the time.

His footsteps echoed on the granite pavement as he walked along by the side of the Green. Behind the railings the trees were still; they stood in the light of the street-lamps, these vast living things, seeming to lean down as if watchful of his passing. What was he to do? His mind was a swirl of doubts and confusion. He did not know himself, he never had; he did not know how to live, not properly. He put a hand to his face and caught a trace of her perfume on his fingers, or was he imagining it? He could not get the woman out of his head, that was the simple fact of the matter; the thought of her had infected him, like a worm lodged in his brain. If only he could shake free of her, if somehow she were to cease to exist for him, even for a minute or two, he would be able to think clearly, but he was at the middle of a maze, and whichever way his thoughts turned her image was there before him, blocking all paths. What was he to do?

The Shelbourne was lit up like an ocean liner. He walked along Merrion Row past Doheny & Nesbit's, and at Baggot Street turned into the broad sweep of Merrion Street and passed by Government Buildings.

His city, and yet not. No matter how many years he might live here there would always be a part of him that was alien. Was there anywhere that he truly belonged? He thought of the far west, where he had been an orphan child, that land of bare rock and crackling heather and stunted, wind-tormented trees. The trees, yes, they all leaned inland, frozen in perpetual flight, their thin bare branches clawing to be gone from this fearsome place. That was his west. They were trying to sell it now to the Americans as the land of trout streams and honey-bees and Paul Henry skies. Any day now they would drive all the orphans and the miscreants out of Carricklea and turn it into a luxury hotel. Carricklea, Carricklea. The name tolled in him like the dark tolling of a distant bell.

Mount Street was deserted. At number thirty-nine there was something white tied to the door-knocker. It was an envelope, crumpled and stained, with a bit of string through one corner and tied in a neat bow to the knocker. His name was on it. He shrank from it, he did not want to touch it, but how could he not? He reached out and tugged with squeamish delicacy at the loose ends of the bow and the loops of string slipped apart slackly as if they had been dipped in oil. There was something in the envelope, a thing — could it be? — of flesh and bone, by the feel of it.

He went back down the steps to the pavement and stood under the light of the street-lamp. His name, lacking the final e, had been scrawled in shapeless block capitals, as if by a child. He ripped open the flap. The thing inside was wrapped in what, from the smell that floated up, he recognised as a torn-off scrap of a chip bag. When he saw the thing inside he instinctively threw it into the gutter. He squatted, peering, and twisted the torn envelope into a baton and poked at it. He saw with relief that it was not what he had first thought it to be. It was a finger, cheese-pale, crooked a little, as if beckoning. It had been cut off at the point where it joined the hand, and there was blood, and the white glint of bone. He unrolled the torn envelope again and looked inside. No message, nothing. He straightened up. He was aware of his heartbeat, a heavy dull slogging, and for a moment he felt light-headed and was afraid he might fall over. He looked up and down the street in the darkness, and saw no one. A car went past, but the driver did not give him a glance. He bent again and picked up the finger from the gutter and dropped it into the torn half of the envelope, folded it quickly and put it in his pocket.

In the flat he went into the kitchen and put the envelope in the sink. He supposed he should not feel so shaken, given that he dealt with dead flesh every day in work. It was a man's finger, which was a relief — when he had first seen it he had thought at once of Phoebe, whom he had led so many times unwittingly into harm's way. Back in the living room he picked up the telephone receiver and, only half knowing what he was doing, dialled the number of Hackett's office. He had still not switched on the light. Why would Hackett be there, at this hour? But he was. The familiar voice seemed to rise out of a hole in the darkness.

"Doctor Quirke," he said, "I was trying to call you myself."

Quirke could not grasp this. He was calling Hackett — why would Hackett be calling him? He stared into the receiver. "When?" he asked dully. "When were you calling me?"

"The past hour. It's your chap Sinclair. He was attacked."

"Attacked? What do you mean?"

"He's in the hospital."

Quirke closed his eyes and pressed a thumb and two fingers to the bridge of his nose. "I don't understand — what happened?"

"He's all right. He took a going over, but he's not bad. Only . . ." Hackett paused, and his voice sank a tone ". . . he lost a finger."

CHAPTER
TEN

The pain had been a surprise, and a corrective, too, of a radical kind. It was as if a great brusque arm had swept away all the toys and coloured baubles that he had mistaken for the stuff of a grown-up life and left him with only the stony bare floor. This, he suddenly saw, *this* was reality, all else but pretence and play. Everything had narrowed to a few crucial points, the main one located at the third knuckle of his left hand.

When he woke to find himself dumped like a sack of refuse on the cobbles in a corner of that lane, he was aware at first only of a huge confusion, and thought a great mistake must have been made but one that in a moment would be set right. Nothing made sense. He was not supposed to be lying here like this — how had it happened? It was dark, and there was someone leaning over him, breathing foul fumes of alcohol and general bodily rot. He felt a hand scrabbling inside his jacket and instinctively clamped his arm against his side, and the figure above him reared back. "Whoa, Jesus!" a rough voice said in fright. "I thought you were dead."

He was not dead, certainly not, for if he were he would not be feeling this remarkable, quite remarkable, pain. There was a pounding in his head, too, and something was wrong with his back, and his left ankle was twisted under him, but none of this compared to what was happening in his hand. Before he looked at it he imagined it surrounded by a pulsing crimson fireball, as if such pain must be visible. When he lifted it to his face there was no flame, but the perspective was wrong, or the angle, and it did not look like his hand. Was that blood? Yes, a great deal of blood. And a part of his hand, unaccountably, was missing.

"You're in a bad way, Captain," the foul-breathed voice said. "Can you get up on your feet, at all?"

He was worried about his wallet. That must have been what this fellow leaning over him had been searching for inside his jacket. He kept it in his right-hand breast pocket, which meant he would have to reach for it with his left hand, but that would not be possible, not with his left hand in the state that it was. He tried with his right hand, but it was too awkward, and the effort made him feel dizzy, which in turn made him feel sick. He leaned aside and vomited briefly on to the ground. "Jesus," the voice said again, in sympathetic wonderment. That this stinking fellow was still here was a good sign, for if he had found the wallet he would surely have run off.

A cat was sitting on top of the wall on the other side of the lane; he could see it outlined against the last faint luminance in the western sky. What must the animals make of us and our doings? he found himself wondering; we must seem to them mad beyond measure.

The figure above him was a young man with a wispy beard and no front teeth. He smelt like a Christmas dinner gone bad. Somehow, together, they got themselves to their feet — it seemed to Sinclair that he was helping the young man as much as the young man was helping him. This was funny, and if he could have managed it he would have laughed. Clinging to each other, the two lurched up the lane and out on to Fitzwilliam Place. It was nearing midnight and the street was empty. He gave the young man a half-crown which he found in the watch pocket of his waistcoat, and the fellow saluted smartly, and called him "Captain" again, and asked him if he would be all right, and shuffled off.

Now what? He tried flagging down a taxi but when the driver drew close enough to see the state he was in he shook his head and drove on. He could try walking home, but he had definitely pulled something in his back, and the ankle that had been twisted under him felt as delicate as glass and at the same time heavy and hot as a lump of smouldering wood. His left arm he held close across his chest, the hand with the missing finger pressed protectively into the hollow of his shoulder. The pain in it made an enormous steady dull beat. He wondered how much blood he had lost — a lot, given the light-headedness he was feeling.

He crossed to the square and hobbled along by the railings, under the silent trees, assailed by the heartlessly tender perfumes of the night. A girl was standing in inky shadows at the corner. As he approached her he caught the wary flash of an eye.

"It's all right," he said, "I was in an accident. Will you help me?"

She was no more than sixteen or seventeen, painfully thin, with a peaky face under a black scrap of a hat pinned at an angle meant to be jaunty but that only increased the overall melancholy of her aspect.

She was still eyeing him with misgiving. He asked her again to help him and she said that she was a working girl, and what kind of help did he want, anyway? He said he needed an ambulance, and that his hand was injured, and that he had taken a tumble and was finding it difficult to walk; would she telephone for an ambulance?

"What happened to you, anyway?" she asked. "You don't look to me like you were in an accident."

Her fear was abating, he could see.

"No, you're right," he said. "I was attacked."

"Was it that fellow that was helping you? I know him, he's a drunken bowsy."

"No, I don't think it was him — in fact I'm sure it wasn't."

"He wouldn't be able to, anyway, that fellow."

He closed his eyes briefly. "My hand is paining very badly," he said. "Will you telephone for me, will you ring nine-nine-nine?"

She hesitated. She was no longer afraid, now, only impatient and put out, but still, she was a woman and therefore, as he guessed, could not be entirely unsympathetic. "There's a box down at the corner," she said. "Have you pennies?"

He gave her the coins, and waited, watching her walk down to Baggot Street, wobbling a little on her high heels, and step into the lighted phone booth. The pain in his hand made him grind his teeth. He was worried that he might faint. Presently the girl came back. "They're sending the ambulance," she said. "You're to stay here."

He leaned his back against the railings and she began to move away. "Will you wait with me?" he said. He suddenly felt very sorry for himself, but at a remove, as if he were not himself but some suffering creature that had come crawling to him for help, as he had come to the girl. "Please? I'll pay you — here." He reached his right hand fumblingly under the right flap of his jacket, and managed this time to find his wallet, which amazingly was there, untouched. He held it open to her. "There's a five-pound note in there," he said. "Take it."

She looked at him and narrowed her eyes. "Give us a fag," she said. "I don't want your money."

He got out his packet of Gold Flake and turned so that she could reach into his pocket and find his lighter. When they had lit up he asked her name. "Teri," she said. "With one *r* and an *i*."

"Teri," he said. "That's nice." The first lungful of smoke made his head swim.

"It's Philomena, really," she said. "Teri is my professional name. What about you?"

"John," he said without hesitation.

She gave him another narrow-eyed look. "No, it's not," she said.

He was about to protest, but her expression stopped him. "I'm sorry," he said. "It's David. Really it is."

"David. That's a good name. Not Dave, or Davy?"

"No. Just David."

They heard a siren starting up in the distance.

"I'd have let you into my room," Teri said, "only my fellow might have arrived in on top of us."

"Your fellow?"

She shrugged. "You know."

He was astonished all at once to feel his eyes prickle with tears. "I wish you'd take that fiver," he said, with sorrowful fervour. "It's only a way of saying thanks."

She considered him for a moment, and her eyes hardened. "Saying thanks to the whore with the heart of gold, eh?" she said, sounding all at once far older than her years. Way down at the end of the long avenue a flashing blue light appeared. "Here's your ambulance."

She turned and walked away, her heels clicking.

His hand throbbed.

And then there was the strangeness of being in hospital, where everything was familiar and at the same time topsyturvy. The ambulance brought him to the Holy Family — of course, where else, given the grotesqueness of all that was happening? His place of work was in the basement but they put him upstairs, in the new wing, in a big ward with thirty or more beds in it. He had been treated first in Emergency by an Indian intern, whom he knew from seeing him about the place, a whimsical fellow with a high-pitched laugh and remarkably beautiful slender hands that were the colour of cocoa on the backs and brick-pink in the palms. "Oh dear oh dear," the Indian said when he saw the wound. "What happened to you, my friend?"

He did not know what to answer. There had been two of them: the fellow in the windcheater and the one who had come up behind him and hit him expertly behind the right ear with something solid but pliant — a cosh, he supposed, if there really were such a thing outside gangster pictures. He had been unconscious when they lopped off the ring finger of his left hand, not with a knife but with some kind of metal shears, for the skin at the knuckle was bruised and the bone had been crushed and severed rather than cut clean through. The Indian gave him a shot of morphine and cleaned up the wound. Then he was taken into theatre where he was given a local anaesthetic. The surgeon, a red-faced fellow by the name of Hodnett, trimmed back the stub of bone and pulled the skin forward in a flap and sewed it along the rim of the palm, all the while discussing with the anaesthetist the Royal St George regatta due to take place the following Sunday in Dun Laoghaire. Sinclair was offered no sympathy, the fact that he was himself a Holy Family man precluding it, apparently. At the end Hodnett had leaned over him and said, "Someone certainly doesn't like you, Sinclair my lad," and laughed grimly and departed with his surgeon's slouch, whistling.

Upstairs, he slept, thanks to exhaustion and the effects of the morphine. He woke at four, and that was when the pain went to work on him in earnest. His heavily bandaged hand was suspended in a sling attached to a metal stand, so that he had to lie on his back with his left arm lifted straight before him as if he had been felled and left frozen in the act of delivering a martial salute. Pain was a dark giant that seized him wordlessly and pummelled him, slowly, methodically, monotonously. Never before in his life, he realised, had he known what it was to concentrate, to the exclusion of all else, on one particular, relentless thing. The noises that the other patients made, the moans and mutterings, the fluttery sighs, came to him as if from somewhere high above him, on another level of existence. He and the giant were at the bottom of what might be a deep ravine, a secret cleft cut into the ordinary landscape of the world, and it seemed there was to be no getting free.

Yet at dawn the pain abated somewhat, or perhaps it was just that the light of day gave him more strength of spirit to cope with it. The night nurse had largely ignored him and his pleas for painkillers. Her successor on the morning shift was a bright-faced girl whom he had danced with at a staff party the previous Christmas; he could not recall her name, but thought the other nurses called her Bunny. She remembered him, and with his morning tea gave him clandestinely a large purple capsule, even the name of which she would not divulge — "The ward sister would have my hide!" — but which she assured him would do the trick, and winked, and went off, swinging her hips.

Quirke arrived first thing, accompanied by the detective, Hackett. It was all very awkward. Sinclair, blissfully groggy after taking the purple pill, was reminded of the time when he was at the Quaker school in Waterford and contracted mumps and his parents came to visit him. They were led into the infirmary by the form master, a nice man with the apt name of Bland. Sinclair's mother had thrown herself on to the bed and wept, of course, but his father had kept himself at a safe distance, saying that the "doctors" — as if there had been a team of them, grave men with beards and white coats — had cautioned him not to approach too near to the patient for fear of consequences that he did not specify but that would be, it was understood, very serious indeed.

Quirke sat on a metal chair beside the night locker while Inspector Hackett loitered at the foot of the bed with one hand in a pocket of his trousers and the other hovering pensively near his blue-shadowed chin. Sinclair described what little he remembered of the attack, and the two men nodded. Quirke, for all his questions and commiserations, seemed distracted. "Was it the fellow on the phone?" he asked.

Sinclair knew who it was he meant. "No," he said, "he had an educated voice — this one was just a thug."

Hackett spoke up. "What fellow on the phone was that?"

"Someone called him at work the other day," Quirke said, still sounding distracted.

"And?"

"Called me a Jewboy," Sinclair said drily, "told me to keep my Jew nose out of other people's business or I'd get it cut off. At least they settled for a finger."

This brought a silence. Then Hackett said, "The fellow that waylaid you in the lane, this thuggish fellow, what did he look like?"

"I don't know — ordinary. In his twenties, thin face."

"And the accent?"

"Dublin."

"And the second one, who came up behind you?"

"Him I didn't see at all," Sinclair said. He lifted his good hand to touch the aching place behind his ear. "Felt him, though."

Quirke offered Sinclair a cigarette but he said he would prefer one of his own. "In my jacket, in the locker there."

Quirke brought the packet of Gold Flake and held out the flame of his lighter.

"The one on the phone," Hackett said, "— you had no idea what he meant by 'other people's business'? What did he say, exactly?"

Sinclair was growing tired of what felt like an interrogation, and besides, the effect of Nurse Bunny's magic purple philtre was wearing off. "I can't remember," he said shortly. "I thought it was just some joker playing tricks."

The detective glanced at his bandaged hand. "Some trick, though," he said.

An old man in one of the beds opposite began to cough, making a noise like that of a suction pump hard at work in some particularly deep and viscous sump.

"Was there no one around, when these two buckos tackled you?" Hackett asked.

"I saw no one. When I woke up there was a tramp there, a wino, trying to get my wallet."

"You still had your wallet?" The detective looked surprised. "The other two hadn't taken it?"

"They took nothing. Except my finger, of course."

"So there was this tramp," Quirke said. "That's all?"

The old man had stopped coughing and was gasping for breath. No one seemed to be paying any heed to him.

"There was a girl," Sinclair said.

"A girl?"

"On the corner, waiting for business. It was her that phoned for the ambulance."

"What was her name?" Hackett asked.

"She didn't say." One *r* and an *i*. He wished she had taken the fiver he had offered her, the whore with the heart of gold.

The two men left shortly after that, and a nurse came to look at the ancient cougher opposite, and then a doctor was fetched and the curtain was pulled around the old man's bed and everyone else lost interest.

He fell into a restless doze and dreamed of being chased down an endless broad street in the dark by unseen pursuers. Teri with an *i* was there, too, standing on the corner by the railings in her little black hat and yet at the same time somehow keeping pace with him as he ran, chatting to him, the pennies in her handbag jingling.

It was Bunny the nurse who put a hand on his shoulder and woke him, telling him he had another visitor — "You're fierce popular, so you are." His arm had gone numb but the hand at the end of it was throbbing worse than ever. The curtain was no longer around the bed opposite, and the old man was no longer in it. How long had he been asleep? The nurse moved back and Phoebe Griffin stepped forward tentatively, with a pained and sympathetic smile. "Quirke told me what happened," she said. "You poor thing."

He was not glad to see her. He was tired and dazed and in pain and wished to be left alone, to deal with himself and sort out his thoughts. That fitful sleep had only served to bring home to him more sharply how dreamlike and implausible all this was — the abusive phone call, the attack in the street, his lost finger, this bed, that old man dying in the bed across the way, and now Phoebe Griffin with her jittery smile and her handbag clasped to her breast and her hat, which reminded him of the one the whore had worn. "I'm all right," he said gruffly, forcing a smile of his own and struggling to raise himself on his elbow.

"But your finger," Phoebe said, "— why?"

"I can only tell you what I told Quirke — I don't know." Oh, he was tired, very, very tired. "How are you?"

She shrugged that aside. "I'm all right, of course. But you — my God!"

He sank back against the pillows. He was thinking again of the infirmary at Newtown school, and of his mother at her lavish weeping and his father standing back looking bored. He had believed for a while that he was falling in love with Phoebe Griffin, and now the awful realisation that he must have been mistaken clanged in him like a cracked bell. At once, of course, he felt a rush of tender concern for her; had he been able he would have taken her in his arms and rocked her like a baby.

"You were good to come," he said weakly, trying for another smile.

She was still leaning over him, but now she stiffened and drew back an inch. She too was seeing the realisation that had come to him; he saw her seeing it, and he was sorry.

"Well, why wouldn't I come?" she exclaimed, with a breathily unsteady little laugh. She hesitated a moment, then sat down on the metal chair where Quirke had sat. "You needn't tell me about it, if you don't want to. It must have been dreadful."

"I can't remember much."

"That's good, I'm sure. The mind protects itself, by forgetting."

"Yes." Was she thinking, he wondered, of the things that she, for her part, needed to be protected against remembering? He knew so little about her — how could he have thought he loved her? Again he felt a hot rush of tenderness and pity. What was he to do with her? How was he to be rid of her? "I spoke to Dannie," she said.

This brought a cold stab of alarm that he could not quite account for. "Oh?" he said. The thought of Phoebe and Dannie in communication, without him present, was unsettling. How did Phoebe come to have Dannie's number, even?

"I hope it wasn't a mistake," Phoebe said. She had caught his look. "I thought she'd want to know."

"It's fine," he said, "fine." He looked away distractedly. "What did she say?"

"She was upset, of course. And of course she was baffled, as we all are."

"Yes. She gets . . . excited."

"I know."

There was a pause. The hubbub in the ward had been steadily growing as the morning advanced, and by now they might have been conversing on the corner of a busy city street. It always fascinated him, the noises that hospitals make — for it seemed as if the place itself were producing all this clamour, this ceaseless buzz of talk, these distant hortatory calls and unsourced crashes, as if whole drawersful of cutlery were being dropped on the tiles.

"You don't think," Phoebe said tentatively, "— you don't think this attack had something to do with Dannie's brother's death?"

He stared at her. That was exactly what he thought, although until this moment he had not known that he was thinking it. "How?" he said. "What connection could there be?"

"I don't know." Her hands were in her lap, the two sets of fingers plucking at each other, making him think of underwater creatures meeting and mating. "Only it seemed so odd, that day, on Howth Head . . ."

"What seemed odd?"

"I don't know — I don't know what I mean. I just felt there was something — something neither of us knew, you or me." She looked at him. "David, who was it that killed her brother? Do you know?"

He said nothing. He was struck less by the question than by the plangent way she spoke his name. He should never have let himself become even this much involved with her. It was bad enough to be burdened with Dannie Jewell and her problems. Now somehow in addition he had acquired this second troubled girl.

Bright-faced Bunny arrived then to take his temperature. Phoebe she pointedly ignored. "I hope you're not letting yourself get over-excited," she said to Sinclair, her bright look marred by a sour little smile.

When the nurse had gone the two of them were left at a loss, like a pair of strangers who had been thrust briefly into intimate contact and now did not quite know how to disengage and step back and reinstate a proper distance.

"I should go," Phoebe said. "The nurse is right, I'm sure you're tired. I'll come again, though, if you like."

He caught the faint plea in those last words, but ignored it. "I'll be out in a day or two," he said. "Maybe even tomorrow. There's bound to be someone genuinely sick and in need of a bed."

They smiled at each other, then Phoebe's eyes flicked to the side. "I'm sorry I phoned Dannie," she murmured. "I'm sure I shouldn't have."

"Why not? It's fine, I told you." For a moment the forced briskness of his manner filled him with disgust. She deserved better than this, at the end. "I'm sorry," he said falteringly. "You're right, I'm tired." He saw that she did not have to ask what he was apologising for. "Do come again, if you can."

She stood up. "Well," she said, with a valiant smile, "goodbye."

"Yes. Goodbye." He wanted to say her name, but could not. "And thank you for coming. I'm glad you did, really."

She nodded once, then turned and walked away quickly between the long rows of beds. He lay back against the pillows again. They wheeled in the old man opposite on a trolley. He was unconscious — they must have operated on him — but he had not died, after all.

Sergeant Jenkins kept glancing in the driving mirror, a little anxiously, trying to see what was going on in the back seat. It appeared that nothing was going on, and it was precisely this that he found unsettling. His boss and Doctor Quirke had been pals of a sort from way back, he knew that, and had worked together on more than one case, but this morning they were saying nothing to each other, sitting far apart and looking determinedly out of their separate windows, and the silence between them was tense, and even tinged with rancour, or so it seemed to Jenkins.

Jenkins, in his tentative way, revered his boss. Although he had only recently been assigned to the inspector he felt that he already knew his ways — which was not, of course, the same thing as knowing the man himself — and could empathise with him, at least on a professional level. And this morning the inspector was troubled, and annoyed, and Jenkins wished he knew why. The two men had been to the hospital, the hospital where Doctor Quirke worked, to visit Doctor Quirke's assistant, who had been attacked in the street and whose hand had been mutilated, and apparently this incident had something to do with the death of Richard Jewell, though no one could say, it seemed, what the connection might be.

Quirke too could sense in Hackett the stirrings of distrust and resentment, brought on, no doubt, by the suspicion that there was something that Quirke knew but was not telling him. And Hackett was right — Quirke had not mentioned the thing he had found attached to the doorknocker when he returned home the night before. Why he had kept silent, and was keeping silent still, he did not know. He had thought that all the pieces of the puzzle were gathered, and that he had only — only! — to assemble them and the mystery of Richard Jewell's death would be resolved. Now the attack on Sinclair had presented him with an extra piece, of a lurid hue but hopelessly vague in outline, a piece that seemed to be from another puzzle altogether. He could not account for his conviction that Sinclair had been beaten up as a warning not to Sinclair but to him, a violent version of the warning Costigan had delivered on the canal bench on Sunday morning. But why had they fixed on Sinclair, whoever they were? It had to be because Sinclair knew Dannie Jewell; that was the only possible connection there could be.

They were driving by the river, and the slanted morning sunlight flashing out of the gaps between the buildings gave him a dazed sensation. In his mind he kept moving the pieces of the puzzle about, trying for at least a reasonable fit, but finding none. He thought of Richard Jewell dead, sprawled across his desk, and of his wife and his sister in that sunny room across the yard, with their cut-glass tumblers of gin, and Françoise d'Aubigny's bright talk, and of Maguire the yard manager slumped in shock, and Maguire's mousily vehement wife. He thought of Carlton Sumner in his gold shirt, mounted on his mighty horse, and of Gloria Sumner whom he had kissed one forgotten night long ago; of St Christopher's, looming on its crag above the leaden waves, and of soft-voiced Father Ambrose who could see into the souls of men. And now there was poor Sinclair, battered and mutilated by a pair of faceless thugs. Costigan was right: there were two worlds, distinct and separate from each other, the one we think we live in, and the real one.

"Will he be able to work all right?" Hackett suddenly asked.

With an effort Quirke stirred himself. "What?"

"The young chap — will it affect his work? Is he righthanded?"

"He needs both hands. But he'll adapt."

Quirke was watching Jenkins in the front seat, and thinking how aptly it could be said of him that he was all ears. They turned right at O'Connell Bridge. Hackett was still gazing out of his side window. "A queer thing, all the same," he said. "Wouldn't you say?"

224

"Queer, yes."

"Did you tell me the young fellow knew Jewell's sister, the one we talked to that morning, when we went down there, to Brooklands?"

"Yes," Quirke said, maintaining a toneless voice, "he knows her."

"A queer coincidence, then, the two of them acquainted, and him getting waylaid like that."

Quirke watched the gulls wheeling above the Ballast Office, their broad wings shining so whitely in the sun. How high they flew, and how sedate they seemed, at that height. Perne in a gyre. What was the line of Yeats that Jimmy Minor had quoted? Something about human veins — *the blood and mire of human veins*, was that it?

"Do you remember that fellow Costigan?" he asked.

Hackett shifted his weight from one haunch to another, the shiny serge backside of his trousers squeaking on the leather seat. "Costigan," he said. "That's the fellow that knew old Judge Griffin?"

"Yes. The fellow that came to warn me to keep my nose out of the judge's affairs, three years ago. The Knights of St Patrick, one of that stalwart band. Whose warning I ignored and subsequently got the stuffing beaten out of me."

Hackett shifted again squeakily. "I remember him."

"You didn't go after him, that time."

Jenkins was doing a complicated piece of parking outside the barracks, involving a three-point turn. Undersized heads of helmeted policemen fashioned from mortar looked stolidly down from their niches above the doorway, bizarre yet homely gargoyles. They got out of the car. The air was dense with exhaust smoke and the hot dust of the streets churned up by the traffic. They stepped into the cool shadow of the porch. "That'll be all, young Jenkins," Hackett said, and the sergeant went off through the double swing-doors with an unwilling air. "He'd live in your ear, that fellow," Hackett said crossly.

Quirke was offering him a cigarette, and they leaned in turn over the lighter's flame.

"*Did* you go after him — Costigan?"

The detective was examining the tip of his cigarette. "Oh, I did," he said, "I went after him, all right. I went after a whole lot of them, that time. With the result that you recall. Which was no result."

Quirke nodded. "I saw him again the other day."

"Oh?"

"It was the same thing as before. I was sitting on a bench by the canal, minding my own business, and along he came, pretending it was by chance."

"And what did he say?"

"He was delivering another warning."

"Right — but what about?"

Two uniformed guards came in from the street, sweating in their navy uniforms and their caps with the shiny peaks. They saluted Hackett and shuffled past.

"Let's go across to Bewley's," Quirke said. "There are things we need to talk about."

"Aye," the detective said, "I thought there might be."

They crossed the road and walked up Fleet Street, past the back door of the *Irish Times*.

226

"Did you notice," Quirke said, "where they put Sinclair?" The detective looked at him enquiringly. "The Jewell Wing," he said. "Everywhere we turn, he's there, Diamond Dick."

As soon as she had heard Dannie Jewell's voice on the line Phoebe had regretted phoning her. It was not that Dannie had sounded as if she were in one of her states, the ones that David Sinclair had told her about, but the opposite, for she sounded a bright and eager note, the same note that Phoebe had envied in her at the start of that strange and magical afternoon in Howth. What she had to tell her, Phoebe only at this moment fully realised, was a terrible thing, and would probably have a terrible effect on this troubled young woman who was not her friend but who might be, one day. There was a moment, after Dannie spoke but before Phoebe responded and gave her own name, when there was still time to say nothing, and ring off, but she could not do it; somehow it would be a betrayal, of what, she could not say, exactly, but of something, perhaps of that promise of future friendship.

"There's been," she said hesitantly, "— there's been an accident." She stopped, grimacing into the black hole of the receiver. Why say it was an accident when it was not? — and anyway, why would an accident sound less ominous than something else? Yet there was no single, accurate word that she could think of for what had happened. "An attack" might be anything from a heart seizure to a murder. She forced herself on. "It's

227

David. He was knocked down and — and he's lost a finger, but otherwise he's all right, except for bruises."

She could hear Dannie gasp. She asked in a small, tense voice, "What happened?"

"Really, he's fine," Phoebe said, "just in — just in pain, and drugged, of course." Could the drugs account for that sense she got, standing beside his bed, of him rejecting her, of blanking against her suddenly? No. It would be a comfort to think it, but no.

"Tell me," Dannie said, still in that tightened yet strangely calm voice, "tell me what happened."

"Someone attacked him, in the street."

"You said it was an accident."

"I know, but it wasn't."

"Who attacked him?"

"I don't know."

"A thief?"

"No — nothing was taken, his wallet, his watch, nothing. Only they — they cut off his finger, the ring finger, on his left hand. I'm sorry, Dannie."

This weak attempt at an apology — an apology for what? — Dannie brushed aside. "Does he know who it was?"

"No."

"You said 'they'."

"There were two of them, it seems. One stopped him and asked him for a match and the other came up behind him and hit him on the head with something. That's all he remembers."

"Where did it happen?"

"A laneway, somewhere around Fitzwilliam Square. He told me the name of the lane but I've forgotten."

"And when was it — when did it happen?"

"Last night."

"He was here last night."

"Where?"

"Here, at the flat."

Phoebe decided to put off consideration of the possible implications of this. "Then it must have been after he left."

Silence.

"Are you there?" Phoebe asked.

"Yes. I'm here." Her voice had turned icy cold. "Thank you for calling."

She hung up. For some moments Phoebe stood there in the hall below her flat, with the receiver pressed to her ear, frowning into space. She was frightened suddenly. She imagined Dannie putting down the phone and turning aside and . . . and what? She pressed the two buttons on the cradle and broke the connection, then dialled the number of her father's office, the direct line. But there was no reply.

CHAPTER
ELEVEN

Quirke usually found it pleasant to be in Bewley's of a summer morning. The place had a cheerful bustle to it, and there were the girls in their summer frocks to admire — he was at an age, he suddenly realised, when female beauty provoked admiration in him more often than desire — and sitting in one of the side booths on a faded-crimson plush banquette reminded him of the days when he was a student, drinking coffee and eating sticky buns here with his fellow students, deep in hot discussion and practising to be grownup. It seemed so long ago, that time, a kind of sun-dappled antiquity, as if it were an Attic glade he was remembering and not a shabby and overcrowded café in a faded little city with a past that felt far more immediate than its present.

"So," Hackett said, "what are these 'things' we have to talk about?"

He was sitting in his accustomed frog-like pose, with his knees splayed and his braces on show, his paunch bulging out over the waistband of his trousers and his hat pushed to the back of his head. They had ordered a pot of tea and a plate of bread-and-butter, and each had set his cigarette packet and lighter on the table in front of him; they had the air of a pair of gamblers about to launch into a serious game of poker.

"I thought I had a handle on Dick Jewell's killing," Quirke said. "Now I have to rethink it all."

Hackett leaned forward and spooned three lumps of sugar into his tea and stirred it. "Before you start rethinking," he said mildly, "maybe you'd like to tell me the nature of the handle on it that you thought you had."

Quirke shook his head, with a distracted frown. "No," he said, "I can't do that."

" 'Can't'?"

"Won't, then."

The detective sighed. He had a high regard for Quirke, but found him trying, sometimes. "All right. But what has occurred to bring about this grand revision of your thinking, if I may ask?"

Quirke took a cigarette from the packet of Senior Service, tapped one end of it and then the other on his thumbnail, took up his lighter, paused, flipped open the lip and rolled the wheel against the flint. Hackett waited with equanimity; he was used to waiting while someone sitting opposite him played for time.

"You remember," Quirke said at last, leaning back against the plush and blowing a stream of smoke towards the ceiling, "that day we talked to Carlton Sumner — he mentioned an orphanage that the Jewell Foundation funds, or used to fund, when Dick Jewell was alive?"

Hackett pushed his hat farther back and scratched his scalp with an index finger. "I don't remember, no," he said, "but I'll take your word for it. So?"

"St Christopher's, out near Balbriggan. Run by the Redemptorists. Big grey place by the sea."

Hackett bent on him a half-closed eye. "You know it?"

"Yes, I know it," Quirke said. He was silent then, watching the smoke from his cigarette curl upwards, and the policeman judged it best not to continue along that particular line of inquiry; he knew something of Quirke's orphan past, and knew enough not to probe overmuch into Quirke's memories of it. "The thing is," Quirke went on at last, "someone else knows about it, too."

"And who's that?"

"Maguire, the yard manager. He was there, after his mother died."

"How did you find that out?"

"His wife told me." He lifted his tea-cup by the handle, then put it back in its saucer, the tea untasted. "She came to see me, as you'll recall, worried that someone was suspecting her husband of doing in his boss, the someone being *you*."

Hackett could not see the connection to St Christopher's, and said so.

"I don't see it either," Quirke said. He paused. "I went out there, talked to the head man, a Father Ambrose. Decent sort, I think, innocent, like so many of them."

"Innocent," Hackett said, and pursed his lips as if to whistle in doubt. "I'd have thought that running an orphanage in this country would be a thing that would put a few smears on the old rose-tinted specs, no?" He took a slurping drink of his tea.

"Like everybody else here, they know what goes on but also manage not to know. It's a knack they share with many of our German friends."

Hackett chuckled. "So what about Maguire?" he asked. "Is there a connection?"

"With Dick Jewell's killing, you mean? I don't know. Maybe. It's just another piece of the jigsaw puzzle that doesn't fit."

"Another piece?"

Quirke's cigarette was finished, he took a fresh one and lit it from the butt, a thing he did, Hackett had often noticed, when he was thinking hard. "This business with Sinclair," he said, "that's another conundrum."

"You think there's a connection *there?*"

"I don't see how there can't be," Quirke said. He looked at the ceiling far above. "His finger that they cut off, they sent it to me."

This time Hackett did whistle, very softly, making a sound like that of a draught sighing under a door. "They sent it to you," he said.

"I came home and it was in an envelope tied to the door-knocker in Mount Street."

"You knew whose it was?"

"No. I didn't know whose it was until I called you, last night. But I knew what it represented, after Costigan had his little chat with me."

"And what was it?"

"A warning. A pretty crude one, this time — not Costigan's style at all, I would have thought."

Hackett was stirring his tea again, though he seemed unaware of it. "Should I have a chat myself with Mr Costigan?"

"I don't see the point. When he accosted me he covered himself well, never used a threatening word, the smile never faltered throughout. As an enforcer he's very practised, and covers his tracks — you found that out, didn't you, last time? No" — he had finished his second cigarette and was reaching for a third — "Costigan is irrelevant. What matters is, who's behind him."

"Well? Who?"

The waitress came, a wizened personage with steely curls showing under her bonnet, and asked them if they wanted anything more, and Hackett requested a fresh pot of tea, and she tottered off, talking to herself under her breath.

"There was something the priest, Father Ambrose, said to me at St Christopher's," Quirke said. "It's been nagging at me ever since."

"What did he say?"

"He said that Dick Jewell wasn't the only benefactor they have, that Carlton Sumner, too, is involved."

"How, involved?"

"In funding the place, I suppose. Or helping to fund it — it's notionally a state institution, but by the look of the carpets on the floor and the sheen on the lawn there's a lot more money going into it than the government's annual seven-and-sixpence."

Hackett leaned back and massaged his belly thoughtfully with the palm of a large square hand. "Are we still talking," he enquired, "about the demise of Mr Richard Jewell?"

"I think we are," Quirke said. "That is, we're talking about it, but I'm not sure what we're saying."

"What *you're* saying, you mean," Hackett said. "— I'm only trotting along behind you in the dark." He took a sighting at his cup with one eye shut. "Why didn't you tell me about them sending you that poor young lad's finger?"

"I don't know," Quirke answered. "Really, I don't. We're both stumbling in the dark here."

"Are we?"

Quirke lifted his eyes and they looked at each other in stillness for a moment.

"What do you mean?" Quirke said.

The detective heaved a slow and ample sigh. "I have the impression, Doctor Quirke, that you know a thing or two more than I do about this business. I suspect, for instance, you've been talking to the widow — am I right?"

Quirke felt his forehead flushing pink. Had he imagined Hackett would not know by now that he had been doing far more than talking to Françoise d'Aubigny? "Conversing with Mrs Jewell," he said carefully, "is not necessarily an enlightening process. She tends to be somewhat opaque."

"*Opaque*, now, that's a grand word. And what about the other one — the sister?"

"To Miss Jewell," Quirke said with sardonic emphasis, "I do not talk. Sinclair knows her, as I've said, and so, I believe, does my daughter. I gather she's something of an enigma, and not without problems, even before her brother met his messy end. Trouble" — he touched a finger to his temple — "upstairs."

The elderly waitress came quakingly with their new pot of tea. Hackett asked for a clean cup, but either she did not hear or chose to ignore him, and wandered off. A woman laden with parcels entered and sat down at a nearby table, and Quirke stared at her, for she had something of the look of Isabel Galloway. Isabel was still much on his mind. He knew that he must telephone her, and would, one of these days.

Hackett poured the dregs from his cup into an empty water glass, refilled from the new pot, added milk and sugar, tasted, and winced at the unexpected hotness. "So," he said, gingerly smacking his scalded lips, "where are we?"

"Lost in the wilderness," Quirke promptly answered. "Lost in the bloody wilderness."

Dannie Jewell now saw what she had to do. She must make a true act of contrition. When she was little she was sent to school to the Presentation Convent where unknown to her mother — her father would not have cared — she pretended that she was a Catholic like all the other girls and took religious instruction and learned about confession, absolution and redemption. We are all sinners, she was assured, but even the blackest sins would be forgiven if the sinner showed to

236

God that she was truly sorry for having offended Him and made a firm resolve never to sin again. She was not sure that she believed in God any more — she did not give the matter much thought — but those profound early lessons had left a lasting impression on her. She had felt guilty all her life, or for as much of it as she could remember. Things that befell her, and even things that befell those around her and for which it did not seem she could be responsible, were, she knew, her fault, at the deepest level, for secretly she had been the cause of them, by a process so subtly wicked that it was not visible to the ordinary eye. If they had happened, she must have willed them to happen, for things did not happen unless someone wanted them to. That buried sense of being the cause of so much wickedness and the shame that followed on it were the twin roots of all her troubles. Because of all this she found herself, simply, disgusting, a soul besmirched.

How could she have thought that she could have David Sinclair for a friend? Had she not known that her mere presence in his life, the mere fact of her existence in relation to him, would inevitably cause him damage? Everyone she came in contact with was made to suffer in some way. When she heard the story of Typhoid Mary, who passed on the disease to others while she remained immune, she recognised herself in it at once. For she did not suffer, not really, or not enough, at any rate, as a result of the calamities for which she was responsible, as a result of the injuries of which she was guilty. Others suffered. Because of her silence, others were condemned to endure years of misery and abuse; because of her prattling, someone was knocked down in the street and had his finger hacked off, just as someone had to substitute for her and be tainted for life, because she had grown up and stopped being a child. Meanwhile she was pampered and protected, had money and freedom, nice places to live in, a financially secure future — she was even beautiful! And the others suffered. That would have to end; at least one of the many wrongs of which she was the cause would have to be set right.

She did not know why David had been attacked. She knew how it had come about, but not the reason for it. Not that the reason mattered. It was a part of the pattern, of course, she knew that, the pattern that had been in place for ever, so it seemed; she thought of it as a huge hidden thing propagating itself endlessly, throwing off millions and millions of spores, like a growth of mushrooms, unstoppably. All she could do was lop off one strand of it, the strand that had wrapped itself around the people who had the misfortune to be close to her.

Yes, a firm act of contrition, that was what was required of her now.

Carlton Sumner had offices in the top two floors of one of the big old Georgian houses on Leeson Street, not far from the corner of St Stephen's Green. "You'd think," he said savagely, "the goddamn air would be a little fresher up here, but it's worse than at ground level. And, of course, over here they've never heard of air-conditioning."

238

It was another sweltering day under a hot white sky. The traffic in the streets jostled and clamoured like a panicking crowd. There must have been a fire somewhere for there were sirens going in the distance and there was a faint acrid reek of smoke in the air. Quirke sat by one of two low windows in an uncomfortable chair made of steel and canvas, nursing a half-empty glass of orange juice that had been ice-cold but had now turned tepid. "I drink this stuff by the quart," Sumner had told him, holding aloft his frosted glass. "One of the girls buys the oranges on her way in and squeezes them with her own fair hands. Why is the concept of fresh juice another thing unknown to you people?" He wore a pair of white deck-trousers and slip-on shoes with tassels, and a white silk shirt that had a large damp patch where he had been leaning against the back of the black leather chair behind his desk. He had put his glass down on his desk, was pacing the carpet now, tossing a sweat-darkened baseball from one hand to the other. Quirke remembered the snow-globe that Françoise d'Aubigny had been holding in her hand that Sunday at Brooklands, and wondered idly where it was now.

"I didn't see an orange until I was in my twenties," Quirke said. "Then the war came and they disappeared."

"Yeah," Sumner said with heavy sarcasm, "you guys sure had it hard."

"It wasn't so bad. We were neutral, after all."

Sumner stopped at the window and looked down into the street, frowning. He pitched the ball with increased force and caught it in each cupped palm with a loud thwack. He had expressed no surprise when Quirke telephoned and asked if he might come and talk to him. It would take a lot, Quirke supposed, to surprise Carlton Sumner, and a lot more to make him show it. "That's right," he said now, darkly. "Neutral." He turned to Quirke. "You want a real drink? I've got Scotch, Irish, vodka, gin — you name it."

"Juice is fine," Quirke said.

Sumner left the window and crossed to his desk and sat back with one haunch perched against a corner of it. The desk was vast and old and made of dark oak, with brass fittings and many drawers, and the top was inlaid with green leather. There were three telephones, one of them white, a large square crystal ashtray, a mug of pens stencilled with the badge of the Vancouver Mounties — Sumner saw Quirke looking at this last and said, "The baseball team, not the cops on horses" — a roller blotter with a wooden handle, an antique silver cigarette box and a fancy Ronson lighter the size of a potato. "So," the owner of all this said, "what can I do for you, Doctor Quirke?" managing to put a faintly comical inflection on the word "Doctor".

It was a straightforward question but one that always left Quirke feeling in a quandary. All his life he had struggled with the unhandiness of concepts, ideas, formulations. Where to begin putting all that chaotic material into short strings of words? The task always baffled him.

"I went out to St Christopher's," he said.

Sumner looked blank. "St What's?"

"The orphanage that Dick Jewell funded —"

"Oh, yes, right."

"— and that you fund, too."

This, Sumner frowned over for a moment in silence. "Me, fund an orphanage? You've got the wrong rich man's son, Doc. Haven't you heard? — I don't give to others, I take from them. It's a grand old family tradition." He put the baseball on the desk, where it rolled a little way and stopped. He flipped open the lid of the cigarette box and selected a cigarette and took the lighter in his fist and made a flame. "Who told you I bankroll motherless boys?" he asked.

"The man who runs the place," Quirke said. "A priest. Father Ambrose." Who smoked the same cigarettes that Sumner did.

"Never met him, never heard the name. What's he like?"

"He said that you and Jewell had set up something called the Friends of St Christopher's."

Sumner suddenly pointed a finger. "St Christopher's, now I remember — that's the place where Marie Bergin used to work, right, before the Jewells took her on?"

"Yes."

"Right, right." A thoughtful look had come into Sumner's eyes, and he was frowning again. "St Christopher's. Dick Jewell's pet project. So — what about it?"

The white telephone rang, making Quirke start, and Sumner plucked up the receiver and listened a moment, said, "No," and hung up. He produced a large handkerchief from the breast pocket of his shirt and used it to wipe the back of his neck. "Jesus," he said, "isn't there supposed to be a temperate climate here? I can't take this heat — I grew up in a place of cool, pine-scented air and snow-capped peaks, you know?" He stood with his cigarette and walked to the window again. "Look at it," he said. "It could be summertime in downtown Detroit."

"So you're not a Friend of St Christopher's, then," Quirke said.

"Listen, pal, I'm not a 'friend' of anywhere. I'm a businessman. Businessmen can't afford to be friendly." He looked at Quirke over his shoulder. "You want to tell me why you're really here, Doc?"

Quirke straightened himself with an effort in the baggy canvas chair and put his glass down on a low table before him. "I'm really here, Mr Sumner, because I'm coming to believe that St Christopher's, not to mention the Friends of St Christopher's, is somehow connected with the death of Richard Jewell."

Sumner turned his gaze back to the window and the street below. He nodded slowly, drawing up his mouth at one corner and sucking thoughtfully on his side teeth. His lavishly pomaded dense dark hair glistened in many points, a miniature constellation. "Where's your sidekick today," he asked, "old Sherlock? Does he know you're here, or are you off on a frolic of your own?" He turned, a hand in a pocket and the cigarette lifted. "Listen, Quirke, I like you. You're a miserable sort of guy, I mean you specialise in misery, but all the same, I do like you. Since you came down to Roundwood I've been rummaging through my memories of those golden days full of gaiety and full of truth when we were young and fair and roamed like panthers around this poor excuse for a city. You were quite the boy then, as I remember. Many a young lady, even including, if I'm not mistaken, the present Mrs Sumner, had an eye for you. What happened to you in the meantime I don't know, and, frankly, don't care to hear about, but it sure knocked the fun out of you. This game of gumshoe that you're playing at, I don't mind it. We all have to find ways of passing the time and relieving the *taedium vitae*, as that old bastard who was supposed to teach us Latin at college — what was his name? — used to call it. Where's the harm in you and your cop friend flat-footing around and asking questions and searching after clues? None. But listen" — he pointed with the hand that held his cigarette — "if you think for a minute that I had anything to do with Diamond Dick Jewell getting popped, I've got to tell you, my friend, you're barking up the wrong suspect."

Sumner walked around his desk and threw himself down sprawlingly in the leather swivel chair, his linen-clad legs out to one side and widely splayed. "I'm a tolerant sort of chap, *Doctor* Quirke," he said, "despite what you hear to the contrary. Live and let live, that's my motto — not original, I grant you, but sound, all the same. So I don't mind how you choose to amuse yourself or what sort of games you like to play. That's your business, and I make it a rule not to interfere in other people's business, unless, of course, I

243

have to. But lay off the suspicion, right? Where I'm concerned, lay off."

The white telephone rang again, as if on cue, and Sumner snatched it up angrily this time and shoved it against his ear and without listening to whoever was calling said, "I *told* you, no!" and hung up, and smiled at Quirke with his perfectly even, perfectly white big teeth. "They never listen," he said in a tone of mock-distress, "never, never listen."

Quirke was lighting one of his own cigarettes. "A young man who works with me," he said, "was attacked in the street last night."

When Sumner frowned, his entire forehead crinkled horizontally, like a venetian blind being shut, and the line of his shiny brown hair lowered itself by a good half-inch. "So?" he said.

"Someone had already rung him up and called him names — Jewboy, that sort of thing. He's a friend of Dannie Jewell, as it happens."

Sumner sat forward and planted an elbow on the desk and rested his jaw on his hand. "You're losing me again, Doc," he said, and once more did his film star's toothily lopsided smile.

"Also," Quirke went on, "a fellow called Costigan came to me a few days ago, after I'd been to St Christopher's, and warned me to mind my own business. You wouldn't know him, I suppose, this Mr Costigan? He's one of the Knights of St Patrick, and probably a Friend of St Christopher's too, for good measure."

244

Sumner gazed at him for a long moment, then laughed. "The Knights of St Patrick?" he said. "Are you serious? — is there really an outfit called the Knights of St Patrick?"

Quirke looked to the window. Either Sumner was a masterly dissembler, or he was innocent — innocent, at least, of the things Quirke had thought he might be guilty of. "Tell me," he said, "why do you think Dick Jewell was shot?"

Sumner held out his hands with empty palms turned upwards. "I told you, I've no idea. Half the country hated him. Maybe he was playing mommies and daddies with somebody's wife — though from what I heard he wasn't much of a one for that particular kind of thing."

Now Quirke did look at him. "What does that mean?"

"What does what mean? The word is that where romance was concerned he had specialised tastes, that's all."

"What kind of specialised tastes?"

"Specialised!" Sumner shouted, laughing in exasperation. "Maybe he liked to screw sheep, or boxer dogs — how do I know? By all accounts he was pretty weird, but hey — who's to say what's normal? I told you my motto: live and let, et cetera."

Quirke rose abruptly, picking up his hat from the low table, and Sumner blinked in surprise. "You're not going, are you, Doc," he said, "not when we're having such a grand time here, surely?"

"Thank you for seeing me," Quirke said. "I know you're a busy man."

He turned to the door, and Sumner rose and came around the desk, running a hand through his hair. "Not at all," he said. "Drop in any time, always glad to see you. By the way" — he laid a large and not unfriendly hand on Quirke's shoulder — "I hear you're helping the widow to handle her grief. That's very large of you."

Quirke looked at him, and at the hand on his shoulder, and at its owner again. Sumner was not as tall as Quirke, but he was a big man, muscular and strong.

"You seem to hear a lot of things," Quirke said, "up here in your eyrie."

"Eyrie," Sumner repeated admiringly. "I've never been sure how to pronounce that word — thanks." He leaned forward and took the doorknob and drew open the door. "Say hello for me to dear Françoise," he said. His secretary, a shapely young woman in a tight skirt and an angora jumper, leaped up from her desk in the next room and came tripping forward hurriedly. "Belinda, my beauty," Sumner said to her, "please show Doctor Quirke the stairs, will you?" He turned to Quirke again. "So long, Doc, see you around."

At that moment, seemingly out of nowhere, Quirke had an inspiration. Or no, it was not out of nowhere: he was remembering, he realised, the parting shot that Hackett had fired off seemingly at random that day in Roundwood when he and Quirke were leaving Sumner's house, empty-handed then, too.

Sumner had been about to step back inside his office and shut the door when Quirke turned. "By the way,

Mr Sumner," he said, leaning back into the doorway, "— your son, did he know Dick Jewell? Or does he know Jewell's sister, maybe?"

Sumner's hand was still hovering somewhere near Quirke's shoulder, and now he fastened it in place again, more firmly and more menacingly than before, and drew him back into the room, and shut the door in his secretary's startled face.

"What do you mean?" he asked. His eyes were narrowed, and all the humour and the playfulness were gone.

"I don't mean anything," Quirke said easily. "It's just a question."

"What do you know about my son?"

"Very little," Quirke said, in the mildest and most disinterested tone that he could muster. "Inspector Hackett mentioned something about him, after we left you that day in Roundwood."

"Oh, he did, did he?" Sumner said evenly, though a vein was beating visibly in his left temple. Quirke could see him riffling in his mind through all the possibilities of what things Hackett might have mentioned about — what was the name? — Teddy, yes, that was it, Teddy Sumner. "Quirke, listen to me," Sumner said quietly. "I don't care that you come here and try to cross-examine me, I really don't, but you leave my son out of this — out of whatever this is you've got your busy nose stuck into. You got me?"

"I wasn't aware of bringing him into it," Quirke said. "I only asked —"

"I know what you asked, I heard you." Sumner's voice was very quiet now and the words came very fast. "Contrary to anything you might hear, Quirke, I'm a temperate man, like your climate is supposed to be. I don't want trouble, I don't look for trouble. I just try to live my life and conduct my business in an easy and an orderly fashion. But when it comes to my family, and my son especially, I find that I'm inclined to lose my temper, despite myself. There's all kind of things going on here that I don't understand, and that I don't care to understand, much less meddle in. I don't know anything about this man of yours that got jumped last night. I don't know who gunned down Dick Jewell, nor do I care much about that, either. Most of all, I don't know what business it is of yours who my son might or might not be acquainted with — in fact, I don't know what business you have asking anything about him."

Quirke looked again at that hand on his shoulder.

"The reason I ask," he said, "is that my assistant was attacked in the street last night by two hired thugs who sheared off one of his fingers and sent it to me wrapped in a chip bag and stuffed in an envelope. Another reason I ask is that I know your son's history of violence, as they say" — Sumner made to speak but Quirke held up a hand to quiet him — "and I wonder if there might be a connection between your Teddy and my man's missing finger, though I admit I can't say what it might be. But I ask too because I think your son did know Dick Jewell, and because I think he was a member of the Friends of St Christopher's, along with Jewell." Sumner was staring at him glassy-eyed and

248

breathing heavily through his nostrils, and it almost made Quirke smile to think of a bull pawing the dust of the arena and getting ready to charge. "Nor can I say," he went on, "that I know how all this might be connected, but I believe it is, and I believe I'll find out. And when I do, I'll come back to see you, Mr Sumner, and maybe we can have another chat, maybe a more enlightening one, this time."

Sumner had taken his hand from Quirke's shoulder but was watching him with his bull's brow lowered and his jaw moving back and forth and those teeth silently grinding. "You take chances, Quirke," he said.

On the way downstairs Belinda the secretary spoke in tones of cheerful dismay about the weather, and the continuing heat wave. "Isn't it awful?" she said.

"Yes, it is," Quirke said. "Awful."

It was the middle of the afternoon and Sinclair was dozing when Nurse Bunny came and shook him gently and told him there was a phone call for him. "I think I've never had a busier patient," she said. He looked at her groggily, hardly able to lift his head from the pillow.

"Who is it?" he asked.

She said it was his brother. He made her repeat it. "Your brother," she said, speaking slowly and directly into his face, as if he were a half-wit; she had given him another of her purple painkillers. "He says it's urgent," she said. "He says it's news about your mother." She helped him up, and walked him out of the ward and along the corridor, where the look of the chocolate-brown gleaming lino made him feel nauseous. The public phone was fastened to the wall beside the nurses' station, with a scratched celluloid shield on either side affording a rudimentary privacy. The nurse passed him the receiver. He took it gingerly, as if it might explode in his hand.

He had no brother, and his mother was dead.

"You took your time," the voice said. There was an awful insinuating warmth to it, a sense of awful cosiness, as if the speaker were curled up in a big armchair beside a blazing log fire.

"Who are you?" Sinclair asked slurredly.

There was a snicker. "I'm your worst nightmare, Jewboy. How's the hand, by the way?"

"*Who are you?*"

"Temper temper." There was another sharp little laugh. "How did your boss like the present we sent him? I had a cat once that used to leave things at the door, chewed-up mice, dead baby rats — but never a finger. I bet that gave him a start. Though I suppose, with his line of work, he'd be used to that kind of thing."

"Tell me who you are," Sinclair said.

The nurse, who had been watching him from her desk, came out now and touched him on the arm and mouthed the words, "*Are you all right?*" He nodded, and she went back, somewhat reluctantly, to her station.

"You there still, Jewboy? You haven't fainted or anything? I'll bet that hand of yours is sore. Did you manage to sleep, at all? Pain is always worse at night, they say. The nurses looking after you in there? This

250

time it was a finger, next time it'll be your you-know-what —"

Sinclair fumbled the receiver on to its cradle.

CHAPTER
TWELVE

Inspector Hackett missed the countryside. He had spent the most part of his childhood summers on his grandfather's farm, and remembered those times as nothing but happy. The city did not suit him, not really. He had been stationed in Dublin for — what? nearly twenty-five years now — but still he felt an outsider. City people, there was something about them, a hardness, a shallowness, a lack of curiosity about simple things, that he had never got used to and that even yet tripped him up on the social side of his job. Petty crooks he could deal with, the dregs of the slums, but when it came to the likes of Carlton Sumner and the Jewells he was on shaky ground, in unfamiliar territory. That was why he needed Quirke as a guide and a protector. Although Quirke had come from nothing — literally so, almost, since he had no parents and had passed his childhood in orphanages — he had been taken up into the world of money and position when he was adopted by the Griffin family. Quirke knew his way about in places where Hackett felt lost, and Hackett was not ashamed to turn to him for help.

But Quirke was not with him today.

The summer weather that was a torment in town made the countryside a pleasure. Sitting beside young Jenkins as they drove out of the city and along the upper reaches of the Liffey on the way to Kildare, Hackett admired the dense greenness of the trees lining the roads, and, behind them, the squared fields where wheat and barley moved slowly, constantly, in polished waves. And then there were the rich warm smells, of grass and hay and beasts; he even savoured the stink of slurry. He regretted when they had to leave this river landscape behind for the flat yellow plains of Kildare. This featureless land had its own austere charm, he supposed, but he had been brought up in hilly country, among woods and water, and always he preferred the closer view; out here on the Curragh the horizons were too distant, too flat, too ill-defined. He liked things that could be touched.

Maguire the yard man had tried to put him off, saying he was too busy with the horses, that there was a big race meeting coming up and he was run off his feet. Hackett had insisted, however, in his usual cheerfully dogged way, and now when they drove into the yard Maguire was there waiting for them, though in a sullen pose.

"I told you all I had to tell you," he said straight off, getting in first before the detective had said no more than a hello. "I was out on the gallops — I wasn't even here to hear the shot."

"Aye," Hackett said, "you told me that, you did."

They went into the stables and walked down the long central aisle between the boxes. The horses watched them, snorting softly and rolling their great glossy eyes.

253

The dust and the dry reek of hay gave Hackett the wobbly sensation of wanting to sneeze while not being able to. "In here," Maguire said, and led the way into the harness room, where the smells were of leather and oil and horse feed. There was a calendar tacked to the wall, open at the page for August the previous year. Jenkins had made to come in with them but Hackett had motioned to him to stay outside.

"So," Maguire said, "what do you want?"

He wore a sleeveless leather jerkin and corduroy trousers tied under the knee with binder twine and cracked working boots. His big head, Hackett noted, was somewhat the same shape as Carlton Sumner's.

"I was wondering," Hackett said, in his most diffident manner, "about that orphanage — St Christopher's, is it?"

Maguire frowned, taken by surprise. "What about it?" he asked darkly.

"How long were you there for?"

"How do you know I was?"

The detective smiled, his thin-lipped mouth seeming to stretch from ear to ear. "We have our methods, Mr Maguire," he said with happy satisfaction; he never missed an opportunity to play up his role as a flat-footed copper.

"My da put me in there, after my mother died," Maguire said.

"That must have been rough."

"I didn't mind. There were seven others at home, and my da was out of work. At least in the Cage they fed you."

"The . . .?"

"It's what we called it. That's what it was always called. If you'd been in there you'd know why."

Hackett brought out his cigarettes, but Maguire shook his head. "That's one habit I never got," he said. "And mind where you put that match — this place is a tinder-box."

The detective shook the match to extinguish it and put the spent stub back into the box.

"It must have been a hard enough time, right enough," he said. "What age were you when you went in?"

"Seven. I told you, I didn't mind it. There were harder stations."

Hackett walked to where a small square window looked out into the yard. The four panes were grimed, and wreathed all over with ancient cobwebs, and some that were newer; in the toils of one a bluebottle was feebly struggling. There was a Land Rover in the yard that had not been there when he and Jenkins arrived.

"Mr Jewell, your late boss, was a patron of the place, I believe?"

"A what?"

Hackett turned his head from the window. "He raised funds, and put in some of his own money — is that right?"

"Why are you asking me? You know already, don't you?"

"He must have talked to you about the place, consulted you about it, you being an old boy, so to speak?"

Maguire shook his head. "I never heard him mention it."

Hackett was still looking at him sidelong. "Did you know Marie Bergin?"

One of the horses along the corridor set up a high-pitched neighing, and immediately others joined in, stamping their hoofs and banging their muzzles against the bars of the boxes. Maguire's frown deepened, and Hackett could see him struggling to cope with this switch in the line of questioning.

"I knew her when she was here, yes."

"And at St Christopher's? She worked there."

"What age do you think I am, seventeen? I was long gone before her time."

"But you knew she worked there?"

Maguire gave a sort of laugh and cast about him in forced exasperation. "Look," he said, "I'm a busy man, I have work to do. Tell me what it is you want here, or let me get on, will you?"

Hackett remained unruffled. He finished his cigarette and dropped it on the ground and trod on it, then bent and picked up the crushed butt and pressed that, too, into the matchbox. "I'm just interested in Mr Jewell's connection with the — what did you call it? — the Cage."

"Why?" Maguire snapped. "And why do you want to know about my time there, and if I knew Marie Bergin, and all the rest of it? What are you after?"

Hackett had his hands in his trouser pockets and was contemplating the broad toecaps of his black boots. "A murder was committed here, Mr Maguire," he said. "What I'm after is the person that committed it."

"Then you're wasting your time," Maguire said, grinding the words out harshly. "You're certainly wasting it talking to me — I don't know who pulled that trigger, if it wasn't Mr Jewell himself. I wasn't here when it happened, and I've heard nothing since to —"

He stopped. He was looking past Hackett to the doorway, where Françoise d'Aubigny had silently appeared. She wore gleaming black riding boots and jodhpurs of cream-coloured worsted and a narrow-waisted black velvet riding jacket. In one hand she carried a slender braided-leather crop and in the other a bowler hat with a stiff veil attached to the brim in front. Her dark hair was pulled back severely from her face and held at the nape of her neck in a netted bun, which gave an Oriental tautness to the outer corners of her eyes. Her lipsticked mouth was a narrow straight scarlet line.

"Inspector," she said. "What a surprise."

She made him come into the house and sit down in the kitchen. "Are you hungry, Inspector?" she asked. "I am sure we could prepare a sandwich for you, or an omelette, perhaps." Hackett thanked her and said no, that he would have to be getting back to town shortly. But he would have a cup of tea, she said — an Irishman would not refuse a cup of tea, surely? She went to the door that led into the house and called Sarah Maguire. Jenkins was standing stiffly at a sort of attention by the dresser, holding his hat in his hands. Maguire's wife came in, her mouth set in a crooked line, and put a kettle on the stove and brought a cup and saucer and spoon to the table and set them down brusquely in front of the detective. She said to him, casting a glance in Jenkins's direction, "What about him, will he have a cup too?" Hackett turned to the young man. "What do you say, Sergeant? Are you thirsty?" Jenkins swallowed hard and his Adam's apple bobbed. "No thank you, Inspector — ma'am." Hackett nodded approvingly and turned back to the woman in the riding jacket. "I was asking Mr Maguire," he said, "about St Christopher's — the orphanage, that your husband was a patron of?"

Françoise d'Aubigny lifted an eyebrow. "Oh, yes?" she said.

Hackett was aware of Maguire's wife eyeing him from the stove with a startled and frowning look. "Yes," he said to Françoise d'Aubigny. "A few things have come up that got us interested in the place."

"Things?" the woman said. "What things?"

"Oh, nothing definite, nothing specific." He paused, smiling. "You know Mrs Maguire's husband was there when he was a child. And so, as it happens, was Doctor Quirke. Isn't that a coincidence, now?"

He watched to see what her response would be to this mention of Quirke. There was none. So, then, what he had suspected was the case: she and Quirke were — what was the way they would put it? — seeing each other. This amused and interested him in equal measure. It went some way to explaining the oddity of Quirke's attitude to the case of Richard Jewell's murder — some way, but not all.

"They were not there at the same time, surely?" Françoise d'Aubigny said.

"No, no. Doctor Quirke has a good few years on your yard manager."

"That is what I meant." She was gazing at him coolly. It was plain that she knew what he had just guessed about her and Quirke, and plain, too, that she did not care that he had. "He is not with you today, Doctor Quirke?"

He did not answer, only smiled again. Maguire's wife brought the teapot in a woollen cosy and set it down near him on a cork mat. Now she would not meet his eye, and went back to the stove, wiping her hands on her apron. She was a high-strung poor creature, Hackett thought. He did not wish to add to the burdens she was carrying. Being married to a man like Maguire could not be easy. Françoise d'Aubigny turned to her. "Sarah, you may go."

Mrs Maguire looked surprised, perhaps offended, too, nevertheless she took off her apron meekly and hung it on a hook by the stove and went out and closed the door softly behind her. "And now, Inspector," Françoise d'Aubigny said, "I think I must go for my ride. I can tell you that I know nothing about this orphanage, or why you are interested in it. I believe my husband was killed for business reasons, though I cannot say why, or by whom, exactly, although I have my suspicions. And I think it would be much more profitable for you to follow that line of investigation, yes?"

"Which line is that, ma'am?"

"I recommended to Doctor Quirke that you should both talk to Carlton Sumner."

"And that we did," Hackett said calmly, pouring tea into his cup. "But that line of investigation did not lead far, I'm afraid, Mrs Jewell."

She gave him a narrow stare. She was about to say something further about Sumner, he could see, but changed her mind. "I really must go, Inspector, my poor Hotspur will be growing impatient."

Hackett smiled at her, nodding. "I apologise for taking up your valuable time, ma'am — although, of course, as I said, it was Mr Maguire I came to talk to, in the first place."

She too smiled, but thinly, her lips twitching. "Thank you, Inspector," she said. "And now goodbye."

She gave him a curt nod, glanced briefly in Jenkins's direction, and went out by the back door, fitting on her hat and veil as she went. When she was gone there was silence but for the hum of the refrigerator and the ticking of the big wooden clock on the wall beside the sink.

Jenkins, who seemed to have been holding his breath since they came into the kitchen, now expelled it in a rush. "What was all that about, boss?" he asked eagerly.

Hackett sighed, a contented sound. "Sit down here," he said to the young man, "come on, sit down and have a cup of tea."

Quirke on the phone sounded annoyed. He had been calling all afternoon, he said. Hackett told him where he had been, and that he had just got back. That shut

260

Quirke up. Hackett was sitting behind his desk in his attic office, trying to get his boots off. He wedged the receiver between his shoulder and his jaw and reached down and got a finger in at the back of the right one and jimmied his foot free. An unpleasant odour came up. His missus had bought him a pair of shoes with crêpe soles and no laces but he could not wear them. Granted, hobnailed boots, not to mention grey woollen socks, were hardly the thing for a heat wave, but this had been his footwear since he was a boy and he was too long in the tooth to change now.

Quirke spoke at last. "Was Fra — was Mrs Jewell there?" Yes, Hackett said. He was working on the left boot, clawing at the back of it with the toes of his right foot and trying to get a finger down the side. His feet, he supposed, must be swollen from the heat.

Quirke was waiting for him to speak but he would not speak; Quirke was not alone in being able to keep his own counsel. The boot came off at last, and Hackett closed his eyes in a brief moment of bliss. Quirke was asking now what Maguire had said, when of course the person he really wanted to hear about, Hackett knew, was not Maguire at all.

"The same Maguire," Hackett said, "is not the most talkative." He was holding the receiver in his hand again — it had begun to stick unpleasantly to his jaw — and at the same time trying to waggle a cigarette out of the packet on the desk. "He was not forthcoming on the topic we're both interested in. The Cage, as he calls it."

"The what?"

"The Cage. St Christopher's — was that not the name they had for it in your day?"

"Yes," Quirke said quietly after a moment. "I'd forgotten."

"I'd say there'd be quite a few things you'd prefer to forget about that particular institution." He got the cigarette to his lips, and now to get it lit he had to wedge the phone under his jaw again. "— Though Maguire said it wasn't such a bad place."

"I don't remember much about it. But listen, anyway — I went to see Sumner again."

"Oh?"

"He wasn't forthcoming either, but I think it's that he really hasn't much to be forthcoming about. I think it's his son we should be concentrating on."

"The son?"

"Yes. Teddy."

Hackett swivelled in his chair and looked out of the window behind the desk at the rooftops and the jumble of chimneys baking in the sun. Half past five and still as hot as midday out there. Teddy, now, the bold Teddy, eh? This was interesting. "What did Sumner say about him?"

"Nothing. But I think it's this Teddy Sumner, and not his father, who was involved in St Christopher's with Dick Jewell."

"Involved, now, in what way?"

"The priest out there, Father Ambrose, said that 'Sumner' was one of the Friends of St Christopher's, along with Jewell and others he didn't identify. I

262

thought he meant the father, but now I think it was the son."

"I suppose that would make sense, all right. I can't see Mr Carlton Sumner as the orphan's saviour."

A pigeon came and perched on the window-sill and through the glass regarded Hackett with a beady and speculative eye. Not for the first time Hackett wondered at the iridescent plumage of these birds that were universally disregarded. Another age might prize them beside peacocks and parrots. This one was slate-blue with shimmers of pink and pale grey and an intense acid green. Could it see him behind the glass, or was the directed focus of its one-eyed gaze an illusion? The bird had probably alighted in hope of being fed, for sometimes, when he brought sandwiches to work, Hackett would put the crusts out on the sill.

He was curious about the note of eagerness in Quirke's voice. Obviously he wanted Teddy Sumner to be involved in all this, but why? Was Teddy perhaps to be a substitute for someone else?

"And you know what I think too?" Quirke was saying now. "I think it was Teddy Sumner who sent that pair of thugs to attack my assistant."

"Do you, indeed?" Hackett said, chuckling. "—Would this be in the nature of a hunch, now?"

Quirke did not laugh.

They strolled in Iveagh Gardens in the cool of late evening. Françoise wore the trousers that were becoming so popular, black, narrow, tapered to the ankle, with elastic straps that went under the foot to keep them taut. Her blouse was white silk, and a crimson silk scarf was knotted loosely at her throat. Her hair was pulled back and tied in a net — she asked Quirke if it looked awful, said she had been riding and had not had time to comb it out. Quirke said it looked fine, to him. "'Fine'," she said. "What a way you have with compliments." She smiled, and ducked her head in the manner he had come to know, and linked her arm in his and squeezed his elbow against her side. "I am teasing you."

The child Giselle walked ahead of them, with a brand-new bright-red bicycle that her mother had bought for her the day after her father's funeral. Giselle had refused even to try to ride it, and wheeled it solemnly along the gravel pathways, clutching both rubber handles and now and then touching the bell with her thumb to make it tinkle. Her mother was watching her as she always seemed to do, with a muted, speculative anxiousness.

"I knew you were at Brooklands," Quirke said. "I spoke to Hackett."

"Ah," Françoise said, "the good inspector. I do not know why he came there. He wished to talk to Maguire, about orphanages, I think."

"Yes. St Christopher's."

"Where is that?"

She lied with such ease, such delicacy, seeming hardly aware of the words as she spoke them.

"Outside the city, on the sea. Your husband had an involvement in it."

"An involvement?"

"Yes. He organised funding. I thought you would have known that."

He felt her shrug. "Perhaps I did. He had so many 'involvements', as you call them."

They entered a patch of purplish shadow under trees. Ahead of them the child in her pale dress became a ghostly glimmer.

"Teddy Sumner was involved too," Quirke said. "Your husband had set up a fund-raising group, the Friends of St Christopher's. Teddy was a member."

She was smiling to herself. "Teddy Sumner? — A philanthropist? That is a little difficult to believe."

"You know him, then."

"Of course. I told you, we knew the Sumners very well, for a time. Teddy and Denise — Dannie — were close friends."

"She doesn't see him any more?"

"I don't know. Probably not." She glanced at him sidelong. "Why?"

For the space of half a dozen paces he said nothing, then, "I was in St Christopher's, you know. When I was little, and not for long."

"Oh, yes? How strange to think. The world is very small."

"And getting smaller all the time."

They had come out into the raked sunlight again, and ahead of them the child had stopped and was holding the bike unsteadily with one hand and reaching down with the other to detach something that had worked its way under the strap of her sandal. It was a cigarette packet, bleached by the weather and trodden flat. Quirke took it from her. "Let me show you what I used to do," he said, "when I was your age and had my first bike."

He folded the wafer of cardboard in two and then in four, tightly, and squatted down and clipped it securely between two struts of the back wheel so that it poked through the spokes. "Now go on," he said to the child, "it will sound like a little motor."

She gazed at him for a moment, the pupils of her eyes seeming huge behind the twin moons of her spectacles. She wheeled the bicycle forward, and the cardboard flickered between the spokes and made a dry fast ticking sound. The two adults followed on, and Françoise again pressed his arm tight against her ribs. "She likes you, you know," she whispered.

"Does she?" Quirke said, raising his eyebrows. Ahead, the child stopped again and bent and detached the cardboard from between the struts and dropped it on the gravel and then went on again. Quirke laughed. "Well," he said, "she doesn't seem to think much of me as a gadget-maker."

Françoise wore a serious look. "You must not be hard on us," she said.

"'Us'?"

"On Giselle — on me. We are coming through a difficult time, you know. We are suffering, in our different ways."

They walked on, hearing the gravel crunching under their tread. There were courting couples on the grass, among the trees; in that slanted tawny light they might have been so many fauns with their nymphs.

266

"What will you do?" Quirke asked.

"What do you mean?"

"Will you stay here, or go back to France?"

"Ah." She smiled, somewhat wistfully. "The future, you mean."

"Yes."

She kept her gaze fixedly ahead. "The future will depend on many things, not all of them things that I have control over. There is, for example — forgive me for being frank — there is *you*."

He was suddenly aware of the heat under his collar, and of a cold dampness in the small of his back. "Am I a part of the future?" he asked.

She laughed, softly, as if she did not wish the child ahead of them to hear. "I do not think that is for me to say, do you?"

"Let's sit," Quirke said.

They had stopped by a wrought-iron bench and now Françoise called to the child, who pretended not to hear and walked on. Quirke said they should let her go, that she could not go far and that anyway they could keep her in view from here. They sat down side by side, and Quirke took out his cigarette case and his lighter.

"I do not think I can go back," Françoise said, and dipped the tip of her cigarette into the flame that he was offering. "Not for ever, certainly. Of course I miss France — it will be at some level always my home, my birthplace. And then" — she smiled — "there are grown-up people there, you know?"

"Unlike here?"

"Your — innocence is part of your charm."

"You mean everybody, or me in particular?"

With her shoulder she gave him a fond little shove. "You *know* what I mean."

He stretched an arm along the back of the bench. "What about Giselle? Does she think she's French, or Irish, or neither?"

Françoise frowned. "Who can say what Giselle thinks?" They watched her. She was quite a way off now, a tiny phantom figure moving along the pathway, between the vast dark trees, wheeling her vivid bicycle. "I think of myself there, when I was her age, long before the war came. I was happy."

"Perhaps she'd be happy, too."

She leaned forward and propped her chin on her hand. "I worry about her. I worry about her all the time. I do not want her to be — to be damaged, as I was." She stopped, and Quirke waited. "Do you know what it is I think that drew us together, you and I?" She turned up her face and looked at him, her glossy dark eyes large and serious. "Guilt," she said. She continued gazing at him. "Don't you agree? Think about it, *mon cher.*"

He did not have to. "Tell me," he said carefully, "about *your* guilt."

A long moment passed before she replied. She was watching her daughter again, off at the other side of the long-shadowed lawn. "I killed my brother," she said, so softly he hardly caught the words, and wondered if he had misheard. She leaned back abruptly and took an almost violent drag at her cigarette. "At least I aided him to die."

268

Again she was silent. He put a hand over one of hers. "Tell me," he said.

She cleared her throat, frowning, still following the far-off little girl.

"He was at Breendonk — you know, I told you, the camp in Belgium? They had the Gestapo there."

"What was your brother's name?"

"Hermann. My parents were great admirers of the Germans and all things Germanic. I am surprised they did not call me Franziska." She spoke the name as if to spit on it.

"What happened to him, to Hermann?"

"He was in the Resistance. I was, too, but not like him. He was very brave, very — very strong. He was high up, too — one of the leaders, in the early days."

"Your father and your mother, did they know?"

"That we were *résistants*? No — they would not have believed their children capable of such a thing, such a *trahison*. Even when the Germans captured Hermann and took him away, my father refused to believe it was not a mistake. He knew someone in the Boche army, one of their commanders — that was how I was able to visit Hermann in that terrible place where they were keeping him." She dropped her cigarette on to the gravel and ground it slowly under her heel. "He knew a great many things — not just names but secrets, secret plans, places where there would be attacks, targets that had been decided upon. They should not have let him know so much, it was too dangerous for him. And then, when he was captured, they did not believe he would not break under torture and betray everything. So they sent me to visit him." She paused. She was still looking at the foot that had crushed the cigarette, gazing at it unseeing. "At first I would not agree. They warned me of what would happen if Hermann betrayed us, that our cell would all be rounded up and shot, including me, that other leaders would be captured, that everything would be lost. So I took the German commandant's pass that my father had got for me and I went to Breendonk. It was the night train. I shall never forget that journey. They had given me, the leaders in our cell — they had given me a capsule to deliver to Hermann. I knew what it was, of course. I sewed it into the lapel of my coat. I was not thinking. I did not believe I would give it to him, I told myself that at the last minute, before I arrived at that place, I would take the capsule and throw it from the train window. But I did not." She shivered, and Quirke took off his jacket and draped it over her shoulders; she seemed not to notice him doing it. "Hermann knew, of course, when he saw me — somehow he knew why I had come, what I was bringing. He was so gay, you know, I mean pretending, for my sake, laughing and making jokes. Already they had begun torturing him. When I saw him first, in that empty room where they put us together, I hardly recognised him, he was so thin, so pale. I remember the darkness under his eyes" — with her fingertips she touched the places on her own face — "and the fear in them, you know, that he tried to hide but which I remembered, the same fear that was there when he was a little boy and had done something to anger our father, only so much more strong, now. That is what he

270

was like that day, like the little boy I remembered. I gave him the capsule and he put it in his mouth straight away, without hesitating a moment. I think the — what do you call it? — the casing, yes, I think the casing was made of glass, some very thin kind of glass. He pressed it down here" — again she lifted a finger and pointed, to her jaw this time — "and kept it there while we talked. What did we talk about? The time when we were children, I think, when we were happy. Then they took him away, and made me leave. By the time I got back to Paris my father had heard through his contacts that Hermann was dead. They did not suspect me, they thought someone else had given him the capsule, one of the other prisoners." She shivered again, and pulled the lapels of his jacket tight around her throat. "My poor beautiful brother," she said. "My poor Hermann, so brave."

They sat quietly for some moments. Quirke heard himself swallow, felt his throat expand and close again. He did not want to look at Françoise, did not want to see her suddenly gaunt and ashen features. The sun had fallen below the treetops and the lawn was in shadow. He felt chilly without his jacket. He looked for the child, and could not see her. He stood up. "What is it?" Françoise said. She too peered across the darkling grass. "My God," she whispered, "— where is she?"

"You go around the pathway," Quirke said, "I'll run direct across."

She stood up quickly and whipped the jacket from her shoulders and thrust it into his hands and turned and set off along the path, tottering a little even as she hurried. Quirke, struggling into his jacket, ran across the grass, feeling the dew wetting his ankles. He reached the far path only seconds before Françoise did, he saw her rounding the corner by the big oak and running towards him with her arms stretched out incongruously at either side, as if she were attempting to fly. "Where is she?" she cried. "— Where *is* she?"

Quirke could feel the panic rising in him, a hot heavy wave surging up through his chest. He must be calm. The gardens were empty by now. Was there a gate-keeper? — would the gates be locked? He cursed himself for his inattention; he cursed himself for many things.

They searched for a long time, running separately here and there, fleeting through the gathering shadows of night like a pair of frantic ghosts, calling the child's name. At a turn in the path they almost collided with each other, coming from opposite directions. Françoise was weeping in fear, great desolate sobs tearing themselves out of her like grotesque hiccups.

Quirke grabbed her arms above the elbows and shook her. "There must be somewhere that she went," he said. "Think, Françoise — where would she go?"

She shook her head, and flying strands of hair that had come loose from the net at the back of her neck turned her for a second into a Medusa. "I don't know — I don't *know*!"

Quirke looked about wildly. He was gasping — had he run so far, so fast? In the dark the now deserted garden was a looming presence, spiked with shadows and seemingly sourceless glints of phosphorescent

272

radiance. The trees above them had set up an excited vague whispering. A thought came to him. "Is there a way into the garden, into the garden of the house? Is there a door, or a gate?"

She made a gulping, choking sound. "No," she said, and then, "— yes! Yes there is — there is a gate, I think."

They ran along where they knew the boundary wall of the domestic gardens must be, and there it was, a little wooden gate, as quaint as on a postcard, with a wild rose bush on one side and a clump of woodbine on the other. In the darkness they could smell the perfume of the woodbine blossom, sweetly cloying. Françoise thrust open the gate and went sprinting through. Quirke followed along a narrow clay pathway, and then through another gate, this one metal, with a lock on it that was unlocked, into the Japanese garden. The child's bicycle was there, resting against the wall of the house beside the french windows, which were open. Once inside the windows Françoise stopped, and leaned forward with her hands braced on her knees, panting. Quirke thought she was going to be sick, and tried put a hand under her forehead to help her but she jerked her head away. She was muttering to herself in French, he could not make out the words. He went on, past the kitchen and along the corridor to the front of the house, and without hesitation veered into the big high-ceilinged drawing room to the left of the front door. A chandelier with electric bulbs was burning above the big mahogany table, its light reflected in the depths of the polished wood. The child was sitting in the chair where she had sat the first time he saw her here; she had her book open, and was sucking her thumb. She took her thumb out of her mouth and looked at him. He could not see her eyes behind those opaquely reflecting lenses.

"There is a leaf in your hair," she said.

Teddy Sumner arrived at the Pearse Street Garda barracks looking cocksure and disdainful. He parked his little shiny green motor at the pavement, where it made the surrounding staff cars seem like so many heaps of scrap metal, and announced himself at the desk in a loud, firm voice. While he waited for someone to come and fetch him he walked about the day-room with his hands in his pockets, ignoring the duty sergeant's minatory eye and idly scanning the notices — a rabies alert, warnings against unchecked ragweed, a couple of missing-persons posters with grainy photos that he made a show of examining closely, smirking. Then he lit a cigarette and dropped the spent match on the floor. "Pick that up," the sergeant said. He was a red-faced bruiser with a broken nose and hands the size of hams. Teddy looked at him, then shrugged and bent and retrieved the match and put it in a wastebin in the corner. He was wearing his navy-blue blazer with the Royal St George Yacht Club crest, dark trousers, white shirt and a cream-coloured cravat. He had taken off his sunglasses and hooked them casually by one earpiece over the top button of his shirt. He was wondering idly how it would feel to be put in handcuffs and given a beating by someone like the sergeant, in his blue uniform and his broad, shiny belt. He was not worried. Why would he be worried?

Detective Sergeant Jenkins, in a cheap suit and an awful tie, emerged at the swing-doors behind the desk and lifted the counter flap and motioned Teddy through. He did not say a word. They walked along a corridor painted a mucoid shade of green, went down a dim set of stairs to another, windowless, corridor, at the end of which they entered a cramped low-ceilinged room, also snot-coloured, also windowless. It was empty save for a deal table at which two straight-backed chairs were set facing each other. "Wait here," Jenkins said, and was gone. Teddy crushed the stub of his cigarette in the dented metal ashtray on the table embossed with an advert for Sweet Afton. Behind the silence he heard the faint hollow hum of a distant generator. He thought of sitting down, but instead put his hands in his pockets and slowly paced the floor. He wondered if there was a hidden spy-hole somewhere. Perhaps he was being watched, at this very moment, watched, studied, judged.

What could they have on him? Nothing. When he had got the summons to come here he had telephoned Costigan, and Costigan had checked with the two hard men — they were brothers, Richie and Something Duffy, from Sheriff Street, the most inaptly named street in the city — and they had heard nothing from the guards or anyone else. Sinclair would not have identified them — how could he? Then what, Teddy asked himself, was he doing here? Maybe it was not about Sinclair at all. Had he done something else lately that the police would want to quiz him about? For all his money and powerful connections Teddy lived in a state of constant vague unease. He had a recurring dream about a body that he had buried — the details of the dream changed but there was always a corpse and always he had hidden it — and sometimes the dream leaked into his waking mind where it seemed not a dream but a hazy and yet frightening memory. It was conscience, he supposed, suppressed or ignored during the day but insinuating itself into his sleeping mind. He liked to think he had a conscience . . .

He heard heavy footsteps outside in the corridor, then the door opened and a short pudgy man came waddling in. He had a clammily pale face and a neat fat belly like that of a pregnant girl. He wore a blue suit and red braces and what must be hobnailed boots. "Ah, Mr Sumner!" he said, and his thin lips stretched in a broad smile. "Thanks indeed for calling by. My name is Hackett, Detective Inspector Hackett." He crossed to the table, and Jenkins entered behind him and shut the door and took up position beside it, with his back to the wall and his hands clasped in front of him. "Sit down," Hackett said to Teddy, "and take the weight off your feet." He took a packet of Player's from his pocket, flipped up the lid and pushed the cigarettes into view with his thumb and offered them. "Smoke?"

They sat down, Hackett facing the door and Teddy opposite him. He did not like having Jenkins behind him, silent as a totem pole. Hackett struck a match and they lit up.

"I don't know why —" Teddy began, but Hackett, smiling, lifted a hand to stop him.

"In due course," he said lightly, "in due course, Mr Sumner, all will be revealed."

Teddy waited. Hackett, leaning on his elbows, gazed across the table at him with what appeared to be happy curiosity, a lively intent. The seconds passed — Teddy was convinced he could hear his watch ticking — and the hum in the air reasserted itself. He knew he should meet and hold Hackett's gaze and not waver or blink, for that was surely the rule of these things, but the fellow's cheerful scrutiny, and his big, greyish, comically froggy face, made him want to laugh. He was reminded of how when he was a child his father would tickle him mercilessly until he cried — once even he had peed himself — and it was this more than any present menace that had a sobering effect. He should have called his father before coming here; his father would want to know about this, the reasons for it. But what could Teddy have told him? The realisation nudged at him that he was, after all, in trouble.

"Do you ever go to Powerscourt, at all, these days?" Hackett asked in his pleasantest tone.

"Powerscourt?" Teddy said, and licked his lips. What was this, now? Had that old business come up again? The one he had given a few smacks to that night, after the hunt ball, was she whingeing again? He could not even remember the bitch's name. "No," he said, "I haven't been out there for ages."

"Is that so? Do you know a young man called Sinclair?"

Teddy blinked. So it *was* Sinclair — dear Jesus. How had they found out?

"Sinclair?"

"That's right. David Sinclair. He's a doctor, a pathologist, at the Hospital of the Holy Family. Do you know who I mean?"

Teddy heard behind him the squeak of Jenkins's shoes as he shifted his weight from one flat foot to the other.

"No, I don't know him. — Or wait, yes, I know the name. He's a friend of a friend of mine, I think."

"Oh, yes?"

"Yes. I think so. But I don't know him."

When Hackett smiled he leaned his head forward and lowered his eyelashes so that for a second he looked like a portly little Chinaman. "Would you be willing," he asked gently, "to divulge the name of this friend?"

Teddy suddenly had the sensation of teetering on his tiptoes at the head of a precipitous flight of stairs, above an unlighted hall; in a moment he would be flailing his arms and arching his back so as not to go pitching forward head over heels into the darkness. He would have to stay calm. His mind began rapidly calculating. If worse came to worst he could say the whole thing had been Costigan's idea and that his only involvement were the phone calls he had made to Sinclair. Why, oh why, had he not let his father know he had been summoned here? Summoned, or summonsed? Was he going to be arrested?

278

"Her name is Dannie — Denise. Dannie is her nickname."

"Would she be a class of a girlfriend of yours? Come on now, Mr Sumner" — this with an avuncular twinkle — "young men are allowed to have girlfriends. It's not a crime."

"No, she's just a friend."

"And she's a friend of David Sinclair's, too."

"Yes, that's what I said."

"Is she *his* girlfriend?"

"No."

For some reason this possibility had never occurred to Teddy. Or maybe it had, without his realising it; maybe he was jealous, and that was why he had got fixated on Sinclair. But why jealous? And if he was jealous, which one was he jealous of? He was getting confused, he could not think straight. The air in this room — it was more like a cell than a room — was hot and oppressive, and there was a slow sort of thudding in his ears, as if he had been swimming under water and had come to the surface too quickly. The policeman — what did he say his name was? Hackett, yes — seemed not to mind the stifling atmosphere, he was probably used to it, he probably spent most of his working days in rooms like this. He said now, "She seems a very abstemious sort of a girl, this friend of yours who is nobody's girlfriend. What's her second name, might I ask?"

He knew very well what her name was, that was clear.

"Jewell."

"Ah. She'd be one of *the* Jewells, would she?"

"She's Richard Jewell's sister."

Hackett pretended to be surprised by this. "Is she, now?" he said, throwing up his hands. "In that case, I've met her. Can you guess where?" Teddy said nothing, only gazed at the detective in a sort of trance of terror and loathing, loathing of his big face and thin-lipped smile, his twinkly eye, his insinuating good humour, loathing even of his boots and his braces and his greasy tie. He imagined lunging across the table and getting him by the throat and putting his two thumbs on his Adam's apple and squeezing until those frog's eyes of his popped out on their stalks and his tongue swelled up and turned blue. "It was a sad occasion," Hackett went on, as if they were playing a guessing game and he was giving a clue. "Down at Brooklands, in County Kildare, where poor Mr Jewell met his sad end. That was where I met his sister, the day Mr Jewell died. Did you know him, too?"

Teddy considered. He was still at the head of those steep stairs, still teetering there, ready to tumble at any second. How was he supposed to answer these questions? They sounded so mild yet he knew each one of them was stretched tight like an invisible piano wire that would trip him up. Maybe he should refuse to say anything more. Maybe he should demand a lawyer. That was what people in the pictures did when they were being given the third degree, although always in the end they turned out to be the guilty ones. Should he admit he knew Jewell? If he denied it, Hackett could easily find out that he was lying. Probably Hackett was well aware that he did know him; probably this was just another wire he was stringing across the top of that dark abyss.

"Yes," Teddy said, "I knew him slightly. He was a friend of my father — used to be a friend of my father."

"Oh? Was there a falling-out?"

"No, no. Or yes, yes there was. There was some business deal that Dick — that Mr Jewell wouldn't go along with."

"So there was a row?"

Teddy felt the beads of sweat forming on his upper lip. He took out his own cigarettes — Marigny, a French brand he had recently discovered — and lit one. The presence of Jug-ears behind him by the door was like an itch that he could not scratch. He dropped the match in the ashtray. "I don't know what happened," he said, keeping his voice steady. "Why don't you ask my father?"

"I could do that," Hackett said, "I could indeed. But for the moment let's turn back to you and your friend Miss Jewell, and her friend, Doctor Sinclair. By the way" — he leaned forward, cocking an eyebrow — "you do know why you're here, don't you?"

"No, I don't," Teddy snapped, and then wished he had bitten his tongue instead.

"Oh," Hackett said, "I assumed you did, since you didn't ask, at the start."

"I tried to tell you I didn't know why you had called me in like this. You said" — he curled his lip and mimicked Hackett's accent — "that all would be revealed."

"So I did — you're right." He signalled to the fellow at the door. "Sergeant, I think at this juncture what's called for is a cup of tea. Or" — turning his attention back to Teddy — "would you prefer coffee? Mind you, I don't believe we have the facilities for making coffee here at the station — have we, Sergeant?"

"No, Inspector," the Sergeant said, "I don't believe we have."

Oh, very droll, Teddy said to himself — they were like a music-hall turn, this pair, Mr Bones and whatever the other fellow was called.

The sergeant went out, and Hackett leaned back comfortably on his chair and laced his fingers together over his paunch. He was smiling. He seemed to have been smiling without interruption since coming into the room. "Are you enjoying the good weather?" he enquired. "There's some I've heard complaining about the heat wave, but they're the same ones that'll be complaining when it comes to an end. There's no pleasing some people."

Teddy was asking himself how he could have been such a fool as to think he would get away with the Sinclair business. Why *had* he done it, anyway? He did not even know Sinclair, had never met him, and had only seen him the one time, with Dannie in Searsons on Baggot Street during the Horse Show last year. He had not liked the look of him, with his swarthy face and his big Jew nose. He had started to go up to them, to say hello to Dannie, but something about Sinclair had put him off. He was, Teddy had recognised, the kind of fellow who would make smart jokes, jokes that did not seem jokes at all, jokes that Teddy would not get, and Dannie would see him not getting them, and the two of them, Sinclair and her, would stand there trying to keep a straight face while he floundered. He had been in that kind of situation with Dannie before — he knew what she could be like when she was with her clever friends, the ones she would not introduce him to. She was a Jew as well, of course. Imagine, a Jew called Jewell! He recalled the nickname they had for Dick at St Christopher's, it always made him laugh. He supposed Sinclair too would be circumcised. How would his thing look, with no skin, just the big purple helmet? No, no, it was gross — think of something else. Think of Cullen, the boy at St Christopher's, pale as an angel, with his straw-coloured hair like a halo and his skin so soft and cool —

"This room," Hackett said, looking about with a smile of happy nostalgia, his hands still clasped comfortably over his belly, "I wonder how many times I've sat in this room, in this very chair, and then, before that, how many times I stood there at the door, like young Jenkins, bored like him and dying for a fag, my poor feet aching and my innards rumbling for want of their dinner." He paused to light another cigarette. "Did you notice the duty sergeant when you came in, the big fellow with the broken nose? Lugs O'Dowd, he's called — isn't that a great name for a guard?" He chuckled, saying the name over again, to himself, and shaking his head. "Lugs was some man when he was on the beat. He used to bring fellows down here to question them — he'd shut the door and first thing off he'd give them a good whaling, just to get them in the right mood, as he'd say. 'The superintendent,' he'd tell them, 'has his office directly above us here,' and when they started to answer his questions he'd keep telling them to speak louder, that the superintendent couldn't hear them. 'Come on,' he'd shout, and give them another clatter across the jaw, 'come on, bucko, speak up, the super can't hear you!'" He laughed, wheezing. "Yes indeed," he said, "Lugs was some man, I can tell you." He paused, and his look turned sombre. "Then a young fellow died one night, and Lugs was taken off the beat and put on the desk up there, where he is not happy, no, he is not happy, at all."

Sergeant Jenkins came back with two big thick grey mugs of thick grey tea and set them down on the table and went back to his post by the door. Teddy swivelled in his chair to look at him but the sergeant stared ahead stonily, his hands behind his back now. Teddy turned to Hackett again. Hackett was stirring his tea pensively. "I believe," he said, "you and Mr Jewell used to do good works together." He looked up. "Is that right? Out at that place in Balbriggan, the orphanage — what do you call it?" Teddy only gazed at him, wide-eyed, as if in fascination. "St Christopher's, is that right? I think it is. The Friends of St Christopher's, isn't that what you called yourselves? And Mr Costigan, he's another one, isn't he another Friend of St Christopher's. Hmm?"

So he knew about Costigan, too. He must know everything, and all this, this cross-examination or whatever to call it, was just a charade. He was being played with; toyed with. He would have to protect himself, that much was clear.

It was Costigan who had put him in touch with the Duffys. He had not told Costigan what he wanted them for, and Costigan had not asked. Costigan was careful like that, not wanting to know things that might get him in trouble. Then, when he heard what had happened, what the Duffys had done to Sinclair, he went into one of his rants. Teddy did not know why he should be so angry — it was only a prank, after all, and a good one, too; he would tell Pooh Bear about it, some day. Sinclair was a smug bastard and deserved a lesson in what the world could do to you. Costigan did not understand what it was like to be Teddy, always being sneered at and made to feel small, and stupid. All the same, it was Costigan's idea, when he had cooled down, to send the envelope with Sinclair's finger in it to Phoebe's old man. "Quirke can do with a caution," Costigan had said, and had even laughed that laugh of his — Teddy had pictured him baring his crooked bottom teeth — despite being so annoyed with Teddy.

Should he say, now, that it was all Costigan's doing? He could claim Costigan had put him up to it, that it was Costigan's idea, cutting off Sinclair's finger and sending it to Quirke because Quirke had been asking questions about St Christopher's. And as for St Christopher's, he could blame Dick Jewell for all that.

"Will you share the joke, Teddy?" Hackett asked.

Teddy had not realised he was laughing. "*Baldy Dick*," he said. "That was Jewell's nickname at St

285

Christopher's. It's what all the boys called him, Baldy Dick."

"Why was that, Teddy?"

Teddy gave him a pitying look. "Because he was a Jew! — get it? Baldy Dick?"

"Ah. Right. And you used to go out there with him, to see the boys?"

All this, Teddy suddenly thought, was a waste of time. He wanted to be gone, wanted to get out of this room and into the Morgan and motor off somewhere pleasant, Wicklow or somewhere. "We all did," he said, "we all went along — Costigan, too." He laughed again. "He was a regular visitor." He might even drive out to Dun Laoghaire and book himself on to the mail boat and take a little jaunt down to London; that would be nice.

"Costigan, too?"

Hackett was staring at him.

"What?"

"You said Costigan was a regular at St Christopher's, along with you and Mr Jewell."

"Yes. Costigan, and the others" — he grinned — "all the good Friends of St Christopher's." He sat up straight on the chair and boldly returned the detective's look. "But Costigan is your man, Inspector," he said. "Costigan is your man."

Hackett leaned forward and rested his elbows on the table again, and smiled, almost tenderly. "Go on, Teddy," he said. "Tell me all about it. Speak up, now, so the super can hear you."

★ ★ ★

286

An hour later they telephoned Carlton Sumner and he came in shouting for his son and threatening to get everybody in the place fired. Hackett drew him to one side in the day-room and spoke to him for a little while, and Sumner stared at him, and grew quiet, turning pale under his yachtsman's tan.

Although he had not been away for much more than a couple of days, Sinclair felt almost a stranger in the flat. It was because of his hand that everything had a new and problematical aspect. Right-handed all his life, he felt now like a left-hander being forced clumsily to use his right. It was a strange sensation, very confusing. He could not get a grip on things, or no, it was not that he could not get a grip, but that he did not know quite how to come at things, what angle to approach them from. When he held the kettle under the tap in his right hand he had to turn on the tap with his left, in a series of minute calibrations, for even the tiniest effort caused the stump of his missing finger to flare and throb. He thought of his hand as an animal, a feral dog, say, slouched on its hunkers with its fangs bared, and himself frozen in front of it, fearful of giving the brute the slightest provocation. It was not so much the pain that hampered him as the fear of pain, the paralysed anticipation of it. And if such a simple action as filling a kettle was so awkward, how was he going to use a tin-opener, or a corkscrew, or a bread knife, or any of the ordinary things that life required the use of?

He would have to have help, it was as simple as that. He would have to get someone to come and assist him, or just to be there, at first, until he got the hang of things, until he got over being afraid all the time of starting up the pain again. He sat down at the kitchen table while the kettle boiled. How would he get the tea caddy open? He felt like a child, an infant. Yes: he would have to call someone.

He got her at last at the hat shop. It was where he should have called first, had he been able to think straight. It was the middle of a weekday afternoon, so of course she would be at work. Two days in hospital, a mere two days of being plied with cups of tea and having his pillows plumped for him, and he had forgotten the simplest facts about life outside the ward.

Even dialling the phone was a problem, he had to put the receiver on the table and dial with his right hand and then snatch it up again when the number started to ring.

She sounded surprised to hear his voice. "I'm sorry," he said, "I couldn't think who else to call. I mean, you were the first person I thought of calling, when I realised I had to call someone." He paused; the kettle was about to boil. "I feel a fool, I feel like a big baby. Can you come?"

She came, as he had known she would. "It's all right," she said, "I was due time off, and Mrs Cuffe-Wilkes was in a good mood." Mrs Cuffe-Wilkes was the owner of the hat shop. Phoebe smiled. "Though you're lucky — she's not in a good mood very often." She was wearing the black dress with the white collar that was her working outfit, and a black cardigan, and patent-leather pumps. Her hair was tied with a red ribbon, it went over the crown of her head and down past her ears and was tied somehow at the back of her neck. Her face with the dark hair drawn away from it seemed made of porcelain, delicate and fine and pale.

They were shy of each other, and tried not to touch at all yet only succeeded in bumping into each other at every turn. He had given up in his attempt to make tea and now she filled the kettle with fresh water and set it to boil, and put out cups, and found the sugar bowl and the butter dish, and sliced the bread.

"Does it pain you all the time?" she asked.

"No, no. It just makes me clumsy. I thought, since there's nothing wrong with my right hand, I wouldn't have any problem, or not much, but everything seems to be the wrong shape and the wrong way up. It's all in my mind, it'll fade."

"I could stay and make you some dinner," she said, not looking at him. "If you'd like."

"Yes, I'd like you to stay. Thank you."

They were sitting at the table, and when the kettle was boiled and she got up to make the tea the sleeve of her dress brushed against his cheek.

"Phoebe," he said. She was at the stove, busy with the teapot and the tea. She said nothing, and did not turn to meet his gaze. "Thank you for coming."

She brought the teapot to the table, and when she put it down he took her left hand in his right. She looked at their two hands, entwined. "I thought you hadn't —" she said. "I thought you didn't —"

"Yes," he said. "So did I. We were both wrong, it seems."

He smiled up at her but she did not smile in return. He still had hold of her hand. He gave off, she noted, a very faint hospital smell. He stood up then and kissed her. She did not close her eyes. A curling wisp of steam rose from the spout of the teapot, as if the genie, the genie who would grant all wishes, were about to materialise, with his turban, and his big moustache, and his stupid, his wonderfully stupid, grin.

David at last drew his face back from hers. "Phoebe —" he began, but she cut him off.

"No, David, wait," she said. "I have something to tell you. It's about Dannie."

Dannie could have gone to David Sinclair; even though he was in the hospital she could have gone to him. But instead it was to Phoebe, her new friend, that in the end she came. And it was a new version of Dannie, too, that Phoebe met. For Dannie was in a state, oh, a royal state, as she said herself, with almost a laugh. It was one of the refinements of her mysterious condition — the doctors, it seemed, were baffled by her — that even when she was in the deepest distress there was a part of her that was able to stand off to the side, observing, commenting, judging, mocking. She said, "Not bad enough to feel so bad, I have to see myself feeling it, too."

Phoebe had been returning from work, strolling thoughtfully along Baggot Street through the summer dusk, when she had spied Dannie sitting in a huddle on the steps in front of the house with her arms around her shins and her forehead resting on her knees. It was the evening of the day that she had made that painful visit to David Sinclair at the hospital. Dannie seemed in a daze, and Phoebe had to help her up, and when they were inside, in Phoebe's room, Dannie made at once for the bed and sat down on it, with her feet flat on the floor and her hands palm upwards in her lap and her head hanging. "Dannie, please, tell me what's the matter," Phoebe said, but Dannie only shook her head slowly, moving it from side to side like a jerky pendulum. Phoebe knelt beside her and tried to see into her face. "Dannie, what is it? Are you ill?"

Dannie muttered something but Phoebe could not make out the words. Phoebe stood up and went to the little stove in the corner and filled the coffee percolator and set it on the heat. She did not know what else to do. Her own hands were shaking now.

When the coffee was made Dannie drank a little of it, clutching the cup tightly with both hands, her head still bent and her hair hanging down. At last she cleared her throat and spoke. "You know I'm Jewish."

Phoebe frowned. Had she known? She could not remember, but thought it best to pretend. She went back and stood by the stove. "Yes," she said, "yes, I know."

"I went to a Catholic school, though. I suppose my parents wanted me to learn how to fit in." She lifted her head, and Phoebe was shocked by the look of her, the expression in her eyes and the deep mauve shadows under them, the slack and bloodless lips. "What about you, where did you go to school?"

"I went to the nuns, too," Phoebe said. "Loreto."

Dannie's features realigned themselves but it took Phoebe a moment to realise that she was smiling.

"We might have known each other. Maybe we even met at a hockey match, or some choir thing. Do you think that's possible?"

"Yes," Phoebe said, "it's possible, of course. But I'm sure I would have remembered you."

"Do you think so, really?" The look in Dannie's eyes turned vacant. "I'd like to have known you. We could have been friends. I would have confessed to you about being a Jew and you wouldn't have minded. Not that anyone was taken in, they all knew I was different — an outsider." She blinked. "Have you a cigarette?"

"Sorry, no. I gave up."

"It doesn't matter, I don't really smoke. Only I get so fidgety I try to find something to do with my hands."

"I could go out and buy some — the Q & L is probably open still."

But Dannie had lost interest in the subject of cigarettes. She moved her blurred gaze about the room. She seemed exhausted, exhausted and in desolation — the word came to Phoebe and seemed the only one that fitted. Desolation.

There was shouting outside in the street, a couple arguing, they sounded drunk, not only the man but the woman, too.

"Have you been to see David?" Dannie asked. She sounded vague, as if she were thinking of something

292

else, as if this were not quite the question she had meant to ask. The man in the street was cursing now, and calling the woman names.

"Yes," Phoebe said. "I went to see him this morning, at the hospital."

"How is he?"

"His hand is very painful, and they had given him some drug, but he's all right."

"I'm glad," Dannie said, more vague than ever. She was still clutching the coffee cup, though she had taken no more than a couple of sips of the coffee. "So this is where you live. I wondered."

"It's terribly small. Hardly room enough for one."

Dannie made a flinching movement and lifted up her face with its stricken look. "I'm sorry," she said. "Do you want me to go?"

Phoebe laughed and went and sat beside her on the bed. "Of course not — that's not what I meant. It's just that I don't realise how tiny the place is until there's someone else here. My father keeps trying to get me to move. He wants to buy a house for the two of us to share."

Dannie had turned her head and was gazing at her now in what seemed a kind of dreamy wonderment. "Your father is Doctor Quirke."

"That's right."

"But your name is Griffin."

Phoebe smiled and lowered her gaze awkwardly. "That's a long story."

"I hardly remember my father. He died when I was very young. I remember his funeral. They say he was a terrible man. I'm sure it's true. Everyone in our family is terrible. I'm terrible." More striking than the words was the mildly pensive way in which she spoke them, as if she were stating a truth known to all. She looked into the coffee cup. "You know that what happened to David was my fault."

"Your fault? How?"

"Everything has been my fault. That's why I've come here — do you mind?"

Phoebe shook her head. "I don't understand."

Dannie set the cup on the floor and lay back abruptly on the bed. She folded both her arms over her eyes. Phoebe had not switched on a light and the last of the dusk was dying in the room. Dannie looked so strange, lying there, with her feet on the floor and her head almost touching the wall behind the bed. When she spoke, her words seemed to be coming out of a covered hollow in the air. "Do you remember," she said, "at school when we were little, how they used to tell us to prepare ourselves mentally before going to confession? I used to go, you know, even though I wasn't supposed to. I always liked examining my conscience and making a mental list of my sins." She lifted her arms and squinted along the length of herself at Phoebe. "Did you invent sins?"

"I'm sure we all did."

"Do you think so? I thought I was the only one." She put her arms back over her face and her voice became muffled again. "I used to pretend to have stolen things. I'm sure now the priests knew I was lying, though they never said. Maybe they weren't interested — I often

294

thought they weren't even listening. I suppose it was boring, a string of little girls whispering in the dark about touching themselves and talking back to their parents."

She stopped. The couple in the street had gone, swearing and shrieking as they went.

Phoebe spoke: "What did you mean when you said that what happened to David was your fault?"

There was no reply for a long time; then Dannie dropped her arms away from her face and put her elbows behind her and pushed herself up until she was half lying, half sitting on the mattress. She coughed, and sat up fully, and with both hands pushed her hair away from her face.

"Phoebe," she said, "will you hear my confession?"

It was dark in the room when Dannie fell asleep. She had drawn up her legs and lain down on her side and joined her hands as if for prayer and placed them under her cheek, and within moments her breathing had become regular and shallow. All the tension had drained from her and she seemed at peace now. Phoebe sat by her, not daring to move for fear of waking her. She wondered what she should do. The things she had heard in the past hour seemed a sort of fairytale, a dark fantasy of injury, loss and revenge. Some parts of it, she supposed, must be true, but which parts? If even a little of it was the case, she must do something, tell someone. She was frightened, frightened for Dannie and what she would be like when she woke up, what she might attempt; she was frightened for herself, too, though she did not know what it was exactly that she feared might happen to her. Yes, it was like a fairytale, and she was in it, wandering lost by night in a dark enchanted forest, where strange night-birds whistled and shrieked, and beasts moved in the thickets, and the brambles with their terrible thorns reached out to twine themselves around her limbs and hold her fast.

At last, cautiously, anxious not to make a sound, she stood up from the bed. She made to switch on a lamp but changed her mind. At the window the light from the street-lamp outside had erected a tall box of faint grainy radiance into which she stepped, searching in her purse for change. On her way out she paused by the bed and lifted the hanging half of the coverlet and draped it over the sleeping young woman. Then she went down to the hall and on the telephone there called Jimmy Minor.

Jimmy was in the newsroom at the *Clarion*, writing up a report on a train crash out at Greystones. "No," he said, "no one killed, damn it."

She told him the gist of Dannie's story, hearing how unlikely it sounded, how crazy, and yet how persuasive too, in all its awfulness. By the time she was finished, her pennies had run out and Jimmy said he would call her back. She waited by the phone but five minutes or more passed before it rang. Jimmy's tone had changed now: he sounded distant, almost formal. Had he been speaking to someone in the office, had he sought someone's advice? He said he thought Dannie must be having a breakdown, and that Phoebe should call a doctor for her. Phoebe was puzzled. She had thought

Jimmy would leap at the story, that he would drop everything and grab his hat and coat, like a reporter in a film, and come rushing up to Baggot Street to hear it for himself, from Dannie's own lips. Was he afraid? Was he worried for his job? The Jewells still owned the *Clarion*, after all, and Richard Jewell's brother Ronnie was expected to arrive any day from Rhodesia and take over the running of the business. Phoebe was disappointed in Jimmy — more, she felt abandoned by him, for despite any reservations she might have about him she had always thought of Jimmy as a fearless friend.

"She's raving," he said coldly, "she must be. She's half mad most of the time, isn't she? Or so I hear."

"I don't think it's all a fantasy," Phoebe said. "You didn't hear her, the conviction in her voice."

"Loonies always sound convincing — it's what keeps the head-doctors in employment, trying to find the grain of truth in the sackloads of chaff."

How glib he is, she suddenly thought, glib and — yes — and cowardly. "All right," she said dully. "I'm sorry I called."

"Listen —" he began, with the whine that came into his voice when he felt called on to defend himself, but she hung up before he could say any more.

Why should she listen? He had not listened to her.

She had no more pennies, but she found a sixpence at the bottom of her purse, and pressed it into the slot, and dialled.

★　★　★

Rose Griffin, who was rich, had made her husband Malachy sell his house in Rathgar after he married her, and now the couple lived in glacial splendour in a square white mansion on Ailesbury Road not far from the French Embassy. It was almost midnight when the taxi carrying Dannie Jewell and Phoebe drew up at the high wrought-iron gates. Rose was standing in the lighted doorway, waiting for them. She wore a blue cocktail dress with a light shawl draped over her shoulders. She had been to dinner at the American ambassador's residence in the Phoenix Park. "Your phone call caught me just as I came in," she said, in her broadest Southern drawl. "What an evening — my dears, the tedium! Malachy, by the way, is off at some conference or other — all about babies, I'm sure — so I'm all alone here, rattling around like a dry old bean in a dry old pod." She turned to Dannie. "Miss Jewell, I don't believe we've met, but I've heard of you."

She led the way along the hall, over the gleaming parquet. They passed by large lofty rooms with chandeliers and crammed with big gleaming pieces of dark furniture. Rose wore high heels, and the seams of her stockings were as straight as plumb-lines. She prided herself, Phoebe knew, on never being caught unprepared. On the phone she had listened without comment or question while Phoebe told her about Dannie, and then had said at once that they must take a taxi, both of them, and come to Ailesbury Road. "I would send the car for you, but I told the driver to put it in the garage and go home."

Now she stopped and opened the door on to a small but splendid study, with leather-upholstered armchairs and a small exquisite Louis XIV writing desk. There was a Persian rug on the floor, and the curtains were of yellow silk, and the walls were hung with small dark-framed oil paintings, one of them a portrait by Patrick Tuohy of her first husband, Phoebe's grandfather, the rich and wicked late Josh Crawford. A small fire of pine logs was burning in the grate — "I know it's supposed to be summer here," Rose said, "but my American blood is awfully thin and needs constant warming in this climate. Sit down, my dears, do. Shall I have the maid bring us something — some tea, perhaps, a sandwich? I know she's still awake."

Dannie was dazed after her sleep, but she was calm; just coming here had calmed her, for Rose was the kind of person she was accustomed to, Phoebe supposed, rich and poised and in manner reassuringly remote. Phoebe said no, that she wanted nothing, and neither did Dannie, that they had been drinking coffee and she was still fizzing from the effects of it. And it was true, her nerves felt like a pit of snakes, not only because of the caffeine, of course. This night and the things that had happened and were happening still had taken on the dark lustre of a dream. Perhaps Jimmy Minor was right, perhaps Dannie was suffering from delusions, delusions that Phoebe had foolishly entertained, and now was asking Rose to entertain as well. But Rose at least was real, with her drawling voice and lazily accommodating smile, and that look she had, both tolerant and sceptical, made Phoebe trust her more than anyone else she knew.

Dannie sat down in one of the leather armchairs, and lay back between the out-thrust wings with her arms folded tightly across her breast as if she, too, were in need of warming. Rose remained standing, leaning against the writing desk, and lit a cigarette and peered at Dannie with interest. "I know your sister-in-law," she said to Dannie, "Mrs Jewell — Françoise. That is, I've spoken to her on occasion."

Dannie seemed not to be listening. She was gazing into the fire with a drowsy expression. Perhaps, Phoebe thought, she would not speak now. Perhaps she had said enough, sitting for that hour on Phoebe's bed, in the gathering dark; perhaps, now that she had made her confession, her mind was at peace and needed to lacerate itself no further. Phoebe glanced at Rose and Rose lifted an eyebrow.

Then Dannie did speak. At first it was no more than a sort of croaking sound that she made, deep in her throat.

"Pardon me, my dear?" Rose said, leaning forward where she stood. "I didn't catch that?"

Dannie looked at her, as if seeing her for the first time. She coughed, and gave herself a sort of shake, embracing herself more tightly still. "I killed him," she said, in a voice that was suddenly firm and clear. "I killed my brother. I'm the one. I took his gun and shot him." She laughed, a short, sharp, barking sound, nodding her head vigorously, as if someone had tried to contradict her. "I'm the one," she said again, adding as if proudly, this time, "I'm the one that did it."

Phoebe wandered through the grand rooms of Rose's house. They had the air of rooms that were meant not to be lived in but only looked at and admired. They were too brightly lit by those great ice-storms of crystal suspended under the ceiling with their countless blazing bulbs. She felt that she was being watched, not just by the portraits on the walls, with their moving eyes, but by the furniture, too, by the ornaments, by the very place itself, watched, and resented. Rose and Dannie were still in the study, talking. Rose had made a silent signal to Phoebe to leave the two of them alone, and now she was pacing here, listening to her footsteps as if they were not her own but those of someone following impossibly close behind her, on her heels.

She heard the door of the study open and softly close, and then the sound of Rose's high heels on the parquet. They met in the hallway. "My Lord," Rose said, "that is a strange young woman. Come, dear, I need a drink, even if you don't."

She led the way into a vast drawing room with parchment-coloured wallpaper. There was a *chaise-longue* and a scattering of many small gold chairs. A fire of logs was burning here, too. In one corner a harpsichord stood, spindle-legged and poised, like a stylised giant mosquito, while above it a vast gilt mirror leaned at a listening angle, expectantly.

301

"Look at this place," Rose said. "They must have imagined they were building Versailles."

At an enormous rosewood sideboard she poured herself half a tumbler of Scotch and added a sizzling splash or two from a bottle of Vichy water. She took a judicious sip and then another, and turned to Phoebe. "Well," she said, "tell me what you think."

Phoebe stood in the middle of the floor, feeling stranded in the midst of so much space, so many things.

"About Dannie?" she said.

"About everything. This business of shooting her brother — do you believe it?"

"I don't know. Someone shot him, apparently. I mean Quirke thinks it wasn't suicide, and so does his detective friend."

Rose took another sip from her glass. She kept frowning and shaking her head in wondering disbelief. Phoebe thought she had never seen her so shaken.

"And all this other stuff," Rose said, "about how her brother treated her. And these orphans — can it be true?" She looked at Phoebe searchingly. "Can it?"

"I don't know," Phoebe said. "But she thinks it is, she thinks it all happened."

Rose walked with her glass to one of the windows and draw back a side of the curtain and gazed out into the darkness. "You think you've seen the worst of the world," she said, "but the world and its wicked ways can always surprise you." She let fall the curtain and turned to Phoebe. "Have you spoken to Quirke?"

"No, not yet." She could not have brought Dannie to Quirke; it had to be a woman.

"Well," Rose said, and gave her mouth a grim little twist, "I think it's time to speak to him now."

CHAPTER
THIRTEEN

The plane skimmed down and bumped twice on the tarmac. It ran swiftly along beside a line of tall palm trees, then slewed in a tight arc across the apron, its propellers feathering, and came to a sighing stop. The heat outside made everything shimmer in the windows, as if a fine sheet of oil were running down over the Perspex. Far off to the right the sea was a thin strip of amethyst against an azure horizon. There were far hills, too, with a myriad tiny glitterings of glass and metal, and villas nestling among rock, and wheeling gulls, and even, beyond the roof of the terminal building, a glimpse of dazzling white seafront with turreted hotels, their bright pennants whipping in the breeze, and the neon signs of casinos working overtime in the glare of midday. The South of France looked so much like the South of France that it might all be a meticulously painted bright façade, put up to reassure visitors that everything they had hoped for was exactly what they would get. Even the Customs officials and the passport police scowled and elaborately shrugged, as they were supposed to.

Quirke's taxi rattled along the sweeping curve of the Promenade des Anglais. The driver, one elbow leaning out at the rolled-down window and his narrow dark moustache wriggling like a miniature eel, talked and talked, a disintegrating fat yellow cigarette wedged in the corner of his mouth. Bathers were breasting the surprisingly turbulent waves, and there were white-sailed yachts farther out, and in the sky a toy-like biplane chugged sedately along with a streamer trailing behind it advertising Cinzano.

Quirke was regretting his black suit. He already had a headache from the engine noise on the flight and the last gin and tonic he had gulped as the plane made its shuddering descent over the Alps, and now it was being made worse by the hot gusts blowing in at the taxi window and the driver's relentless jabbering. Quirke did not care much for foreign parts. Down here they seemed to have a different and far more vehement sun than the pallid one that shone so fitfully at home. Even the heat wave he had left behind seemed reassuringly overworked and earnest, with none of the heedless gaiety of this palmy paradise. He still had that sense of everything before him being a front, done in implausibly solid watercolours, as if it were all a set of giant billboards by Raoul Dufy that had been slapped up that morning and were not yet quite dry. All the same, it was lovely, too, even Quirke had to admit it; lovely, frivolous, assured, and none of it his.

Cap Ferrat was farther on past Nice than he had expected, and he watched in mesmerised dismay the clacking meter totting up the francs by the hundreds. The route down to Beaulieu led abruptly off the main road and wound its way athwart the steep hillside

305

between high stucco walls. Behind these walls more palm trees reared up their tousled heads as if they had been awakened rudely from a siesta. At intervals a dazzling glimpse of the bay of Villefranche was briefly shown and then whisked away again like a conjuror's playing card. Honey-hued girls in skimpy swimsuits and straw hats and white-rimmed sunglasses sauntered past, waggling their bottoms with what seemed a languorous disdain.

The house was on an undistinguished road. There were tall gates, and an intercom that the taxi driver spoke into, and the gates swept open by remote control. The driver got behind the wheel again and the taxi shot up a steep incline and shuddered to a stop under an outcrop of rock dotted with clumps of oleander and bougainvillaea. The house was set on top of the rock, long and low with a flat roof and a veranda and, on this side, a series of plate-glass sliding doors from floor to ceiling. Looking up at it, the taxi driver made a clicking sound in his jaw and said something that sounded appreciative.

A lift with a rickety metal grille for a gate was set into the rock and bore Quirke upwards swayingly and deposited him in a soundless lobby where he found himself facing two identical doors side by side. He knocked on the one to the right without result, then saw that the other one had a bell. He pressed it, and waited, quivering with something that was far more than travel fever.

She wore delicate gold sandals and a long loose robe of purple silk that gave her, with her sharp dark features and her black hair swept back, the look of the wife of a Roman patrician, an Agrippina, say, or a Livia. She stood with her arm raised along the edge of the door, with all the light of the south behind her, and something behind his breastbone clenched on itself like a fist.

"Ah," she said, "you came."

"I didn't know if you would see me."

"But of course. I'm happy you are here."

"Happy?"

"Glad, then — that is perhaps a better word, in the circumstances." She looked at his carpet bag. "You have no luggage?"

"I didn't plan for a long stay."

She let go of the door and stood back for him to enter. The room was enormous, with a floor of light wood and the wall of sliding glass doors on one side. Facing him as he stepped in was what at first he took for a big square painting of a palm tree, like a frozen green fountain, but then he realised that it was a wide-open window, and that the tree was real. In the background was the hillside above Villefranche, traversed by a thin white ribbon of road where he could make out tiny cars speeding along.

"Would you like something?" Françoise d'Aubigny asked. "A drink, surely. Have you eaten?"

"I came straight from the airport."

"Then you must eat. There is cheese, and salad, and this Picpoul" — she had gone to the big American-style fridge and was taking out a bottle — "is quite good, unless you would prefer red?"

"The white is fine."

He was angry, he realised; that was what he felt most strongly, a sullen anger, not directed solely at her but at so many other things as well, too numerous to try to trace and identify. He was tired of thinking of all this, this ghastly sordid mess. But it must have been anger, after all, that had brought him to her, that had propelled him into the sky and flown him over seas and land and dumped him here — at her feet, he caught himself about to think, at those shapely feet of hers in their exquisite gold sandals, her feet that he had clasped and kissed, while his conscience made a hum in his head, like the hum of travel that was at last, now, beginning to diminish.

She set two glasses on a white counter-top and poured the wine. "I should have called you before I left," she said. "It was wrong of me not to, I know. But after that night when I thought I had lost Giselle . . . It was impossible. You do see that, that it was impossible for me, yes?"

What was he to answer? He should not have come. She handed him the wine, and he tipped the glass against hers. "What does one say?" he asked. "— *Santé*?"

They drank, and then stood facing each other, in a sudden helplessness that was, Quirke thought, almost comic. Life's way of blundering into bathos never ceased to catch him out.

"Let me show you this place," Françoise said. "Richard was so proud of it."

Originally it had been a complex of four apartments that her husband had bought up and refashioned into one large living space. He had taken down the walls of the two apartments at this end to make the great room where they stood, and another room, not quite as large, separated off by pillars, where there were sofas and low armchairs and a big table of pale wood standing in the central well, strewn with books and magazines and record covers. The walls were white, and the paintings on them were originals, three or four Mediterranean landscapes by artists Quirke did not recognise, a garden scene that must be by Bonnard, and a small portrait by Matisse of a woman sitting by a window with a palm tree.

After he had inspected and admired these and numerous other things Françoise led him from the second room towards an open doorway giving on to a cool corridor where one wall was another set of tall glass panels. As they were crossing the threshold she paused. "Those rooms," she said, pointing back, "are for daytime living, and these others are for night — you see?" She indicated the lintel, on this side of which was stencilled in large black letters the legend *The Day Side*. They stepped through into the corridor, and above them here was written *The Night Side*. "Richard liked to label everything," Françoise said, with a faint grimace of amusement. "He had that kind of mind."

She showed him the bedrooms, the bathrooms, the linen cupboards. Everything down to the smallest detail had been finished, smoothed, polished with meticulous judgement and care. "Richard did all this," she said, "it was his project. He had good taste, yes? You look surprised."

She drew open a broad glass panel in the wall and they stepped out on to the silvery-smooth boards of the veranda. Out here it was suddenly hot. "There is a natural flow of cool air through all the rooms," Françoise said. "It might be sweltering outside but inside it's always comfortable. That was another of Richard's gifts, to know how to adapt things."

She led him to the edge of the balcony and they stood at the wooden rail and looked down to where below there was an outdoor swimming-pool cut into the rock. The jade-green water was veined in its depths with quivering white outlines, as if giant transparent amoebas were floating and flickering there. The child Giselle knelt at the pool's edge, playing with a tortoise. She wore a checked pink swimsuit with a scalloped hem and an enormous pair of sunglasses. Her hair was in pigtails and tied with checked pink bows. Feeling their eyes on her she turned and looked up at them, lifting a hand to shade her eyes. "She likes it here," Françoise said.

"And you? Do you like it? Do you feel at home here, among the grown-up people?"

Her hand was beside his on the rail. "I did hope you would come, you know," she said. "I could not ask you to come, but I hoped you would."

"Why couldn't you ask me?"

His hand wanted to close over hers but he held it back.

"Come," she said, "let's have our salad."

They ate sitting on high stools at the white counter. Through the window they could see down to the blue bay far below. The sea was roughly paved with flakes of shimmering white-gold light. "Villefranche is one of the deepest bays along the Côte d'Azur," Françoise said. "After the war it was crowded with American warships — I saw them. I remember thinking how heartless everything seemed, the sun and the light and the gay people, and so many millions dead."

Quirke refilled their glasses from the bottle of the sharp and almost colourless Picpoul. Françoise turned to him suddenly. "You saw her, yes — you saw Dannie?"

He set down the bottle and kept his gaze fixed on it. "I saw her," he said.

"How was she?"

He shrugged. "As you would imagine."

"I can't believe it."

"No," Quirke said, "I'm sure you can't."

She looked away.

Giselle came in, still in her swimsuit and carrying the tortoise under her arm. The creature had withdrawn into its shell, and in the shadows there its ancient eyes glinted.

"Say *bonjour* to Docteur Quirke," Françoise said.

The child gave him her accustomed sceptical glance. "Hello," she said.

"What's he called?" Quirke asked, indicating the tortoise.

"Achille." She pronounced it in the French way.

"Ah. Achilles. That's a good joke."

She gave him that glance again and set the tortoise on the counter. In the back of its shell, in the centre, a small white jewel was inset. Françoise spoke to the child in French, and the child shook her head and turned and walked off into the other room and threw herself down on one of the sofas and began to read a comic book. Françoise sighed. "She is on hunger strike," she murmured. "I cannot get her to eat."

"She must be very upset, still," Quirke said. "It's hardly more than two weeks since her father died."

Françoise went to the fridge and brought back a dish of small dark olives. "Try these," she said. "They are from the region, and very good." He dipped his fingers into the dish and brought up three or four of the oily beads. She was watching him again. "How is your friend, the detective —?"

"Hackett."

"He will take care of Dannie, yes?"

"Oh, yes," Quirke said, "he'll take care of her, all right."

"What will they do to her? — they will let her off, surely?"

He lifted a cold eye to hers. "They'll put her away for life," he said, "in the Dundrum Hospital for the Criminally Insane. That's what they'll do."

Her eyes once more skittered away from his. She picked up her glass, it trembled slightly in her hand. "Is it a terrible place?" she asked.

"Yes." He held his gaze steady on her. "Yes, it is."

She gathered up their plates; she had eaten almost nothing. "Come," she said softly, glancing over her shoulder in her daughter's direction, "let's go outside again. There are chairs, in the shade."

The chairs were low and wide, their wood weathered silver-grey like the flooring. Quirke set down his glass at the side of his chair and lit a cigarette. From the angle here they could see through a gap in the landscape all the way to the sea, a wedge of mirage-blue stillness in the distance. The breeze coming down from the hills was soft and carried the perfumes of lavender and wild sage.

"I met Richard here," Françoise said.

"Here, in Cap Ferrat?"

"Yes." With a hand over her eyes she was squinting off in the direction of the white road winding across the hillside. "He was a gambler — did you know? He came for the casinos. He would visit them all, along the coast here, in Nice, in Cannes, Monte Carlo, San Remo. He was very bad at it, he had no luck, and always lost a great deal of money, but that would not stop him."

"And you?" Quirke said. "What were you doing here?"

"When I met him first? Oh, I was with my father. He used to come every summer to a little hotel in Beaulieu. My mother had died that year. I believed my life, too, was coming to an end." She shifted in the chair, with an effortful sigh, as if she were indeed far older than she seemed. "I think I might have died, except that I still had my brother to mourn, and my father to hate. Richard I met at a tennis party one day, I cannot remember at whose house it was. He looked very handsome, very *fringant*. He *was* a handsome

313

man, you know, in a savage way — rough, I mean. He was what I thought I needed. I believed he would help me to hate, that together with him I would — how do you say? — I would nurture my hatred, as if it were a child, our child." She turned to him. "Is that not terrible?"

"Was your father so bad, to merit such hatred?"

"No, no, it was not just my father I hated — but everything, France herself, and those who had betrayed us, the collaborators, the Pétainist, the ones who made their fortune on the black market. Believe me, there was no shortage of people to hate."

On that triangle of distant blue a tinier triangle had appeared, the leaning white sail of a yacht.

"But Richard you loved," Quirke said.

To this she made a very French response, dipping her head from side to side and blowing out a ball of breath through pursed lips. "Love?" she said. "Love, no. I do not know what to call it. I married him for revenge, revenge on my father, on France, and on myself, too. I was like one of those saints, punishing myself, falling to my knees and whipping myself, whipping and whipping, until I bled. There was joy in that, a frightful joy." She turned to him, her eyes glittering and her lips drawn back some way from her teeth. "Do you understand?"

Oh, yes, he understood. It was guilt that had drawn them together, she had said, but guilt was a knout made of many strands, all of them stiff and sharp to cut good and deep into the flesh.

"My father at first was approving," Françoise said. "He liked Richard. I suppose he recognised one of his own type. He refused to believe he was Jewish — 'How can a man with the word "Jew" in his name be a Jew?' he used to ask, and he would laugh. It seemed to him too ridiculous. And of course it is true, Richard was not really Jewish except by blood — he was not religious, and cared nothing for the history of his people. But blood, of course, was what counted for my father."

The side of the hill that they were facing was becoming flat and shadowless as the sun angled full upon it, and they could feel faintly on their faces the heat reflecting back off the rocks and even the orange clay itself. A single-engined plane droned overhead, its wing-struts shining. There were dark birds, too, Quirke now saw, wheeling in slow arcs at an immense height.

"Why did he marry you?" Quirke asked.

"Why did — ? Oh, I see what you mean. Why did he marry any woman, since it was not women that he wanted." She paused. "Who knows? I suppose it was because I too, like him, was violent, cruel, wanting my revenge on the world. 'I like your *ferocity*,' Richard used to say. It was one of his favourite words. The way that I hated — hated my father, my country, everything — that amused him, gave him pleasure." Again she stopped, gazing out from the veranda's shade into the harsh light of afternoon, nodding to herself. "He was a very wicked man, you know? Very — *malicieux*."

"When did you find out about him? — about St Christopher's, what he did there, all that?"

She considered. "I do not know if I ever 'found out'. That kind of knowledge comes slowly, because it is resisted, so slowly that one almost does not notice it. But come it does, eating into the mind, into the conscience, like acid."

"But sooner or later you did know, even if you tried not to. And you tolerated it."

She scrambled up suddenly from the chair as if she had been pushed, and walked to the wooden rail again, where the sunlight fell full upon her in an almost violent splash. "I knew, yes," she said, facing sideways so that he would hear her, but not looking at him. "Of course I knew. He brought me there, once, you know — to the orphanage. He wanted me to see, he wanted me to be impressed by the place, by what he had made of it, how he had stamped his will on it, and on those poor children, those poor little boys."

"Did you see Father Ambrose?"

"Ambrose? I saw him, yes, Richard made sure of that, too."

"I met him. He seemed to me not a bad man."

She turned her head fully now and stared at him. "That priest?" she said. "He is a devil, a devil like Richard. They are all devils, there."

Quirke recalled Father Ambrose's wispily gentle voice, the way that he drew close, how his gaze seemed to reach out blind fingers to feel all over what was before him. He recalled too the boys sidling past in the corridors, their downcast eyes. How could he have missed what was plain to see, what his own experiences as a child in places like this should have taught him never to forget?

"And Dannie," he said. "— Did you know about Dannie, too, what Richard did to her?"

"No!" She slapped both her hands down hard on the rail. She was glaring at him with eyes ablaze, and then, as suddenly as it had flared up, the fire in her went out, and her shoulders slumped, her face grew slack. "I thought it was only little boys he cared for," she said, almost in a whisper. "I did not know it was little girls, too. He wanted the young, you see, always and only the young. *Fresh meat*, that is what he would say, *fresh meat*. And he would laugh."

"When did you find out?"

"About Dannie? Not until — not until that day, that Sunday, at Brooklands. The thing had broken in her, had snapped. She could not keep it secret any longer. Because of Giselle, you see." She glanced back in alarm towards the glass doors and the room where the child was, and her voice again became a whisper. "Because of Giselle."

Quirke heard voices faintly, and he too turned to the glass, behind which a shadowed form was approaching. The door slid open and a young woman stepped on to the veranda. She was dark as a gypsy, with hooded eyes and a shadowed upper lip. She wore a blue housecoat and white shoes like a nurse's. Seeing Quirke, she hesitated. "Ah, Maria," Françoise said. "*Cet homme est Docteur Quirke.*" The girl smiled uncertainly and put her hands behind her back. Françoise turned to Quirke. "Maria takes care of Giselle in the afternoons," she said. She went forward and took the young woman by the elbow and steered her back indoors.

Quirke extricated himself from the low chair and, lighting a cigarette, walked to the rail where Françoise had stood. Despite having removed his jacket and then his tie he was hot, and could feel himself sweating, the beads of moisture running down and stopping at the small of his back. Below in the valley the cicadas had started up, draping the air with their crepitant drone. He fancied he could hear too the noise of traffic on that distant white road, the blare of trucks, the insect whine of a motorcycle.

He should not have come.

After some minutes Françoise returned. "They have gone out," she said. "Will you come back inside?"

Quirke wanted a drink. The bottle of Picpoul was three-quarters empty. He offered it to Françoise but she shook her head, and he filled his own glass. The wine had warmed up; it did not matter.

The tortoise was gone, and in its place on the counter was a snow-globe; he recognised it, with the little town inside it, the miniature streets and the château and its pointed tower. They went into the other room and sat down on the sofa where the child had sat. Quirke offered his case and Françoise took a cigarette. It was so strange, Quirke thought, so strange to be here, in these rich surroundings, drinking wine and smoking, as if there were nothing except that, two people sitting in a white room in a sunny town, being themselves, being together.

Françoise said, "That Sunday she told me, Dannie told me, what had gone on between her and Richard for so many years. Richard must have been — I don't know." She leaned forward and dashed the tip of her cigarette at an ashtray standing on the low table. "Is it possible to be addicted to such things?"

"It's possible to be obsessed, yes," Quirke said.

"But with him, you know, I do not think — *obsession* does not seem the right word. He was like a man with a — a pastime, a hobby. It amused him, it entertained him, to use these children, the boys at the orphanage, young people at the newspaper, poor little Marie our maid, Dannie his sister — his *sister*. Yes, it amused him. Can you understand this? Him and those other devils, destroying lives, destroying souls, for their *amusement*."

They were silent for a time, then Quirke spoke. "Do you know a man called Costigan?"

She waved a hand in a dismissive gesture, as if pushing aside a cobweb. "I do not know names. There was a group of them."

"The Friends of St Christopher's."

She gave a bitter laugh. "Yes, that is what they called themselves." She turned herself sideways on the sofa to look at him. "You know they used that place as a brothel, yes? The priest, Ambrose, he was the — what is the word? — the *souteneur*."

"The pander?"

"Yes, the pander — the pimp."

Quirke stood up and went to the counter again and poured the last of the wine, and walked with his glass to the window with the palm in it and looked down towards the bay. The child was down there, with her nurse, walking along by the water. He heard Françoise approach and stop behind him.

"Why did you leave like that," he asked, not turning to her, "without even a telephone call?"

She was behind him now, he could feel the warmth of her and smell her perfume. "I told you," she said. "That night in the garden, when Giselle went back to the house and we had to search for her — I thought I had lost her. I thought they had got her."

" 'They'?"

"Richard's people. I was so frightened, in such a panic. You do not know what they are like, what they are capable of."

He saw himself again in Mount Street, staring into the gutter, at what was lying there. He had not told her about Sinclair.

He turned to face her. "Tell me what happened, that Sunday."

There was a silence. She was looking at him now as she had not looked at him before, as if for the first time, her head tilted to the side and her eyes narrowed. "You know," she said softly, "don't you?"

He nodded.

"When?" she whispered.

"The day we had lunch, that first time, at the Hibernian. You tried to get me to suspect that Carlton Sumner had killed your husband."

"But — how?"

"I don't know. But I knew it had to be you."

"And Dannie —?"

"Dannie couldn't have done it, I was certain of that. Maguire? No. Carlton Sumner? Possible, but very unlikely. His son, Teddy? No. So that left you."

"You knew, and yet you — we —"

"Yes."

Yes, he thought, I knew, and still I went with you, over to the side of night.

The shore was a pebbled slope running sharply down into a sluggish sea. Directly before them a huge yellow-gold moon sat fatly just above the horizon, its broadening track shimmering and swaying upon the inky water. Fishing boats were out there; they could see their bobbing lights, and more than once they thought they heard the fishermen calling to each other. The night air was soft and cool. They sat on a wooden bench at the edge of the pebbles. Quirke was smoking a cigarette, and Françoise lay against him with her head on his shoulder and her legs drawn up under her. Maria had put the child to bed, and they had come down the hill to walk by the sea. Now they sat listening to the waves at their ceaseless small turning.

"She told me that day, you see," Françoise said. "Dannie told me not only about what Richard had done to her for all those years when she was a child, but what Richard was doing now with Giselle. She had spoken to him that morning, had pleaded with him, but of course he only laughed in her face. *I had you when you were young*, he said to her. *Now I have a new one, all of my own.* When I arrived at Brooklands I found her lying on the floor — on the floor, yes — curled up, you know, like a little baby. At first she would say nothing, then she told me. She had his shotgun on the floor beside her. She said she had tried to make herself go up to the office again and confront him, threaten him — shoot him, even. But she was not strong enough."

"And you were."

"Yes, I was." She took the cigarette from his fingers and drew on it with a quick hissing sound and then gave it back to him. How eerie the smoke looked when she exhaled it, like ectoplasm dispersing into the darkness. "Will you believe me," she said, "if I tell you that I have no memory of doing it? Or no, no, I have one memory. It is of Richard's face when he heard me behind him and turned. He was sitting at his desk, going through papers. He was wearing his old tweed jacket with — what do you call them? — patches, yes, leather patches on the elbows. It was what he always wore when he was dealing with the horses, he thought it brought him luck. When he turned and saw me, with the gun, do you know what he did? He smiled. Such a strange smile. Did he think I was playing a joke? No — no, I think he knew very well what I was going to do. And he smiled. What did it mean — can you say?"

But Quirke said nothing.

"And then," Françoise said, "I must have fired the gun, straight into his face."

They walked up the hill slowly, laboriously, as if they had suddenly become old. By now the moon had

322

swung itself higher above the bay, and below them its gold track on the sea had narrowed. There were night-birds of some kind, pale things, swooping in silence furtively among the palms. Music was playing somewhere, dance-band music, tiny and gay in the distance. They could hear the faint swish of traffic, too, far off down on the Promenade. Quirke looked up and saw a strew of stars like a smear of mist down the centre of the sky.

As they came through the gates they could see the lights of the house up on the rock, burning behind the glass side wall.

"He used to taunt me, you know," Françoise said. "He never admitted anything, of course, but he knew I knew, and he would tease me. He brought Marie from the orphanage to work for us. She had been a child when she started there, and now she was too old for him, but still he wanted to keep her, as he wanted to keep them all, as if they were trophies, to display before his friends, before me." She leaned against Quirke as if she suddenly felt faint. "How could I have let him do such things? How could I? And how could I let him go on doing them?"

They went up in the little lift together, not speaking. The sense of her, the smell of her, so near to him. The gate of the lift clattered open.

"Why two doors?" Quirke asked, as they stepped out.

"What?"

"Why did he keep the two front doors, your husband, when he was putting the four apartments into one?"

323

She looked at him. "I don't know. He was like that, he had to keep everything."

"Even you."

She turned away, searching for her key.

Once inside, she went off to check on the child, and then came back. "I have told Maria that she can sleep in the guest room," she said. "Shall I get you a drink?"

"Whiskey," Quirke said. "Have you got whiskey?"

She found a bottle in a cupboard and poured a measure into a crystal goblet. She poured nothing for herself. Quirke felt a stabbing pain under his ribs on the right side, and was glad of it. He would be glad, now, of anything that was real.

Françoise handed him the goblet, and he drank.

"You did sleep with Sumner, didn't you," he said, "when he made that pass at you, here?"

She had been turning away from him and now turned back. She thought for a moment. "Yes," she said calmly, "yes, I did." She smiled. "I'm sorry, have I hurt you? You have that 'how could you?' look that men take on."

"And you didn't tell your husband," Quirke went on, "he found out. Is that why he threw Sumner out? Is that why they fought at that meeting in Roundwood?"

Her smile had turned pitying. "You think you know so much," she said, "but, really, you know so little. I asked them to go. It had become — inconvenient. Sumner, too, he is another little boy refusing to give up the toy he has stolen. You are all the same."

He nodded, gazing at her.

324

"You knew I knew, didn't you?" he said. "You knew I knew you had shot your husband."

She stared at him. "No," she said, her voice hardening, "of course not."

"But you were worried that I might guess. That's why you took me into your bed, in the hope that it would keep me from suspecting."

"How can you say such a thing?"

They were standing in the middle of the floor, facing each other, Quirke with the glass in his hand and Françoise d'Aubigny in her robe of Roman purple staring at him, her fists clenched in anger at her sides.

"I made a fool of myself for you," Quirke said. He felt calm; cold, and quite calm. The pain in his side had stopped; he wished it would come back. "I made a fool of myself for you," he said again. "I insulted my conscience."

The woman's face twitched, as if she might be about to laugh. "Your conscience," she said. "Please, do not lie. Lie to me if you like, but not to yourself."

He sighed, and walked away from her and sat down on a complicated little chair made of stainless steel and white leather. He sat there, looking at her.

"You shot him," he said, "but you didn't forget. You knew exactly what you were doing."

"I told you, it was because of Giselle —"

"I know that, I know. I don't even blame you. But what you said to me, I say back to you — don't lie. You shot him, and you took your handkerchief and you wiped the gun all over, and put it in his hands to make it look like suicide, and went back and told Dannie what you had done. Then you called the guards, and wouldn't give your name. And then you took the Land Rover and drove away, and stayed away, and then came back, as if you hadn't been there at all. Didn't you."

She was smiling, but still there was that faint twitch along her cheek.

"We could have been happy, you and I," she said. "You could have come to live with me, among the grown-ups. But you prefer your little life, don't you?"

He stood up from the chair — he felt so tired, so tired — and went to the counter and put the empty glass there. He picked up the snow-globe and cupped the cool weight of it in his hand. A few flakes of snow fluttered up, and one or two settled on the slanted roof of the château. A tiny world, perfect and changeless.

"Dundrum, that hospital," he said, "— it *is* a terrible place."

She gave him a quizzical look; it seemed to him she was almost smiling. "But you won't let them send her there," she said, "will you, Doctor Quirke?"

He put the glass globe into his pocket, and turned away.

In Dublin it was raining, and the air felt like steam. By the time Quirke got to the flat he was soaked through to the skin, and his shoes made a squelching sound. He shook as much water from his hat as he could and to keep its shape shoved it down on to the head of a life-sized plaster bust of Socrates that someone had given him once for a joke. The only room he had been able to find in Nice the night before was in a flea-pit up a lane run by an Arab with black teeth and a scar. He had not slept, only dozed fitfully, worried that someone would come in to rob him and slit his throat. At dawn he had walked on the front, looking at the sea that was already blue although the sun was hardly up, and had stopped at a café, and drunk three cups of bitter coffee, and had felt sick. And now he was home.

Home.

He did not phone, but went straight to Pearse Street. Hackett looked at him, and nodded, and said, "I can see you've been through the wars."

They went up to Hackett's office and Hackett summoned Sergeant Jenkins and told him to fetch a pot of tea. When the young man had gone he sat back on the chair and lifted his feet in their big boots and perched them on a corner of his desk. Behind him the grimed window wept. Quirke flexed his shoulders, and the bentwood chair on which he sat sent up a cry of protest. He had never in his life been so weary as he was now.

"So," Hackett said, "you're back from your travels. Did you see all you went to see?"

"Yes. Yes, I did."

"And?"

"I spoke to her."

"You spoke to her."

Quirke closed his eyes and gouged his fingers into them, pressing them until they pained. "What about Sumner?" he asked.

"Sumner the father or Sumner the son?"

"Whichever. Both."

The air in the room was blued from the smoke of Hackett's cigarette. He shifted his boots on the desk and wriggled his backside deeper into the sagging seat of his swivel chair.

"Young Sumner," he said, "will get a suspended sentence, and his daddy will ship him off to Canada, for good, this time."

Quirke was studying him, that big, pallid, smugly smiling face. "You did a deal," he said, "didn't you?"

"I did a deal. Teddy gave me Costigan and the Duffy brothers, who cut off your assistant's finger, and I gave him Canada. A fair exchange."

"And Costigan, what will he get?"

"Oh, that's for the court to decide," the detective said, putting on a pious look.

"What does that mean?"

"Every man is innocent until proved guilty."

"Are you telling me he'll get off?"

Hackett had his hands clasped behind his head and was considering the ceiling. "As you will remember from our previous dealings with Mr Costigan," he said, "the man has powerful friends in this town. But we'll do our best, Doctor Quirke, we'll do our best."

"And St Christopher's?"

"Father Ambrose is to be transferred, I believe."

"Transferred."

"That's right. Up north, somewhere. The archbishop himself gave the order."

"And of course there's no question of the place being closed down."

Hackett widened his eyes. "And what would become of all those unfortunate orphans, if that were to happen?"

"And the Friends of St Christopher's, what about them?"

Hackett took his feet off the desk and leaned forward, suddenly brisk, and scrabbled through the chaos of papers on his desk. Quirke knew this ploy of old. "Tell me," he said. "Tell me the worst."

"Oh, the worst may not be the worst. I'm in — how shall I say? I'm in delicate negotiations on that matter with the same Mr Costigan."

"You'll do a deal with *him*, in return for names?"

"Ah. Well. Now." Hackett found the document he had been pretending to look for and held it close up to his face, as if to read what was written on it, frowning and pouting, and running a hand blindly over the desk in search of his cigarettes. "I'd say," he said, "the question is rather whether *he*'ll do a deal with *me*. A stubborn sort of a fellow, is our Mr Costigan." He peeped at Quirke around the side of the document and winked. "Fear can do that to a man, you know, can make him awful stubborn and unco-operative." He found the packet of Player's and took one out and lit it. "As I say, I'll do my best —" He broke off. "But where, now, in the name of God, is that young clown with our tea?" He pressed an electric bell on his desk, and kept his thumb on it. "My alarm button," he said scornfully, "that no one pays one whit of attention to."

"How did Sumner take it?" Quirke asked. "— The father, I mean."

"Shocked, but not so surprised as you'd expect."

"He knew about Dick Jewell, about St Christopher's, all that?"

"He had a fair idea, I believe."

Quirke looked to the rain-streaked window, nodding. "So that's what they fought about that day in Roundwood — Sumner must have tackled Jewell for corrupting his son."

"I'd say that's a fair guess."

Quirke was glancing about for his raincoat; Hackett had hung it for him on the back of the door.

"You know," Quirke said, as if distractedly, "you know Jewell's sister is determined to confess that she was the one who shot him?"

"Is that so? But sure, we'd pay no attention to that, would we? Didn't you tell me she has trouble" — he touched a finger to his temple — "upstairs?"

"Then I can take it you won't be charging her — that you won't accept the confession she's so eager to make?"

"Ah, the poor young woman, she can't be held responsible for herself."

"And the one who can be held responsible?"

The detective, pretending again to be busy searching for something on his desk, gave no reply.

There was a tap at the door, and Jenkins manoeuvred his way in with a tray of tea things. "At last!" Hackett cried, looking up from his mock search. "We were about to succumb from the drought."

Jenkins, biting his lip and trying not to smile, set the tray on the desk, after Hackett had unceremoniously swept half the papers from it on to the floor.

330

Quirke stood up. "I must be going," he said.

The detective looked at him in exaggerated dismay. "Will you not stay and have a cup?"

Jenkins went out, edging sideways past Quirke. His ears were very pink today.

Quirke took his raincoat from the hook behind the door. "It isn't much, is it," he said, "— Costigan, and a couple of thugs, and a rotten priest transferred?"

"It's the times, Doctor Quirke, and the place. We haven't grown up yet, here on this tight little island. But we do what we can, you and I. That's all we can do."

Quirke returned to the desk. "I brought you something," he said, and reached into the pocket of his coat and brought out the snow-globe and stood it on the desk, beside the tea tray.

Hackett frowned at it.

"A present, from France," Quirke said. "You can use it for a paperweight."

He turned to the door. Behind him Hackett spoke. "Will she ever come back, do you think?"

Quirke did not reply. How could he? He did not know the answer.